Vivian, an adrenaline jur  about her life as a polyamorous lesbian. Her life in Sacramento, California, is going well until she is blindsided by unforeseen financial issues that lead her to consider a new career.

In an attempt to recharge and take a break, Vivian goes on a motorcycle trip with her best friend, Bear, but the adventure does not turn out to be the carefree break Vivian had hoped for. She returns to Sacramento where her partner, Ang, tries to push her down rather than help her pick up the pieces. Meanwhile, Vivian takes big steps with her other partner, Audre.

Vivian has an epiphany about what line of work she wants to pursue. As things start to stabilize, one of Vivian's partners commits an act of grave violence, resulting in life-changing consequences for all concerned.

Surrounded by friends, Vivian turns over a new leaf and finally finds the contentment she has sought for a lifetime.

CONCUSSION AND CONTENTMENT

Vivian Chastain, Book Three

Liz Faraim

A NineStar Press Publication

www.ninestarpress.com

Concussion and Contentment

Printed in the USA

ISBN: 978-1-64890-337-3

First Edition, August, 2021

Also available in eBook, ISBN: 978-1-64890-336-6

WARNING:
This book contains depictions of violence, attempted murder, homophobic slurs, alcohol/drug use, abuse of a child by a parent, abuse of a child by an adult, attempted suicide, references to suicide, and racism.

For "Bear" Garcia. I love you. I miss you. Fuck cancer.

Chapter One

SPRING 2006
Sacramento, CA

Sweat dripped and bass pulsed as hundreds of women writhed and bumped to the music. Tick, the club DJ, was killing it. The vibe was so good that I was high on it. There was a line at my station ten people deep, customers jostling for position while dancing and shuffling forward each time I finished a drink order. One of my regulars stepped up and waved a twenty-dollar bill at me. She was in her forties, sporting a bowler hat and forearm tats.

"Viv, show me them titties and tats!" she shouted over the thumping and chatter.

I had already stripped down to my sports bra, with my beater hanging from the back pocket of my Dickies. It was hot for April, and the press of sweating, dancing bodies had made the nightclub a sauna.

"Aw, Tig, you know I can't do that," I said with a smirk and turned my back to the crowd. Behind the bar was a wall-to-wall mirror. I gyrated my hips to Bubba Sparxxx's "Ms. New Booty," which had become a club favorite. I made eye contact with Tig in the mirror as she jumped to the beat, still waving the twenty-dollar bill at me. Shoving down the shyness that crept up, I slapped on the façade of the confident butch barkeep I wore to work. I pulled my sports bra up, just a bit.

She hollered to her friends, "She's doing it, she's doing it!"

Amidst the chaos, they leaned to the side to see my reflection in the mirror, their mouths agape, eyes laser focused on me. I kept the tease up for a minute, dancing to the song, pulling my bra up a bit and lowering it again. Each time I lowered it, there was a chorus of "Awwwww's" behind me. I finally relented and pulled my sports bra completely off. Their hoots and hollers made me grin, and I continued dancing for myself in the mirror.

Just as the song was ending, a bright light flashed in the mirror, reflecting straight into my eyes. I traced the light back along the mirror and saw it was coming from near the front door. Buck, our bouncer, stood on the rungs of her barstool by the door, flashing her Maglite at me. When we made eye contact, she tapped the top of her head three times, which was the sign that the cops were coming. I shimmied back into my sweaty sports bra, which was no easy feat, and turned back to my customers.

Tig pulled me into a hug across the bar. She tucked the bill into my waistband, her rough fingers lingering far too long on my skin. "Thanks, Viv. Looking good. Those tits and tats, you are so fucking hot. If I weren't married, things'd be different."

I patted her cheek and ended the hug, doing my best to keep my cool and stay in my role.

"Good to see you, Tig. The usual?"

She nodded and I poured her an Irish Car Bomb. She slapped some more cash on the bar, dropped the shot glass of whiskey and Bailey's into her pint of Guinness, and chugged the whole frothing mess while her crew cheered her on. She slammed the pint glass down, wiped her mouth on her bare arm, belched, and disappeared into the fray.

Jen, the barback, bounced up to me with her usual level of cheer, and began unloading glasses fresh from the washer. "Tig still trying to get into your pants?" Her voice dripped with disgust as she fingered the American Spirit cigarette tucked behind her ear.

"Always." I uncapped some beer bottles and rang up my next customer. "You know, I've been doing this job a few years now, and know that there's a certain level of shit we have to put up with if we want those tips. And I need those tips. But it's getting less amusing when people forget we are human and not a piece of meat."

Jen nodded knowingly. "How much did she give you this time?"

"Twenty bucks. More generous than usual. She must have just gotten paid."

"Well, don't include it when you tally up your tips tonight. When you tip me out, I don't want any of that. You earned it." There was a pitying turn to Jen's lips, and I nodded at her slowly.

We turned to watch as the police pushed their way past the line of women waiting to get into the club. Buck stopped them in the entryway at her lectern. She stood tall, her perfectly pressed uniform shirt tucked into her Wranglers. Jen slapped my ass and hustled back out to gather up empty glasses and beer bottles and likely drop her weed and pipe into one of the potted plants.

I spotted Sheila, our manager, mingling in the press of bodies and waved her down. I pointed toward the cops. She nodded and slithered her way through the crowd the way any seasoned bar or restaurant worker does. Sheila and Buck eventually convinced the officers to leave, which was a relief. Uniformed police in a queer nightclub were bad for business.

The frantic pace kept up until last call. Eventually Tick turned on the house lights and Buck worked her way around the place, breaking up lingering conversations with her usual: "You don't have to go home, but ya can't stay here." As she escorted out the last couple and locked the doors behind them, I posted up on a bar stool and counted out my tips and cash drawer.

My hip itched and I remembered the money Tig had put there. I pulled the sweaty bill out of my waistband and dropped it into my tip bucket with disgust. The rant I had been holding back burst forth to no one in particular.

"Who do the fuck do they think they are, putting their hands all over us like they own us? Like we're in a fucking petting zoo!"

"Pipe down, Viv." Sheila lit a cigarette and watched us like a hawk as we counted the club's money. I grumbled. "It's just part of the job. It's part of the atmosphere here. Remember what I told you way back on your first day?"

I turned and made eye contact with Sheila. Her brown eyes challenged me, a crinkle at the corners, her right eyebrow cocked just a hair. She took a long drag on her cigarette and blew it at me. She knew I was a runner and hated cigarette smoke, so I took it as a blatant sign of disrespect.

Speaking through clenched teeth I recalled, "On my first day you said: Know your place, stay in your role. Desirable. Flirty. Available but not attainable. Is that right?"

"Bingo." She pointed a nicotine-stained finger at me. "If you don't like it, you know there are a dozen other gals ready to take your spot. This is the only lesbian nightclub in Sac and it's hoppin'. Adjust your attitude or get out."

I went back to counting out my drawer. The bills were soggy with a combination of spilled beer and boob sweat. It was amusing how many women used their bras as a wallet, but at the end of the night the damp bills weren't so cute.

My relationship with Sheila had taken several hits because I had disappeared on her a few times. Once friendly and warm, my boss now barely tolerated my presence, and only because I brought in big money. The customers loved me. Sheila would be an idiot to fire me, and clearly, she resented the fact.

Over the last two years I had beat a thieving customer to a pulp, disappeared because I had to go into hiding after witnessing a heinous crime, and gotten myself hospitalized with sepsis. My attendance at work hadn't exactly been great because of all that, and Sheila didn't seem to trust me anymore. Since returning from my bout with sepsis the previous year I hadn't missed a single shift. That fact alone made me mad that Sheila hadn't warmed back up to me. Work used to be one of my favorite places to be, Jen and Buck were some of my favorite people, but

Sheila giving me the cold shoulder and my growing discontent with grabby customers were souring the pot.

Jen went about clearing the glasses, beer bottles, and trash that had been left all over the bar. Occasionally she would groan and announce whatever disgusting detritus she had found: used condoms and gloves tucked into the potted plants, puke in the corner, empty baggies, whippit canisters, and even someone's thong underwear.

I finished my count, my drawer balancing out perfectly, and shoved it across the bar to Sheila. I grabbed my gear and walked into the back bar to find Jen and give her a cut of my tips. Buck unlocked the door and followed me out. We walked down Twenty-First Street, which was mostly deserted at the early hour, aside from the occasional person sleeping in a doorway. We reached my truck and I fished out my keys. Buck wasn't much for small talk so when she cleared her throat, I was surprised.

"Things'll settle down. Stick around." Her gravelly voice tapered off as she gave my back a hearty thump, spun on her heel, and headed back to the bar.

"G'night, Buck." She looked over her shoulder at me and nodded, her mullet flapping in the breeze.

Chapter Two

Thankfully, I found a parking spot on Twenty-Fourth Street, close to my apartment building. Out of sheer habit, I looked up to the window over the front door awning to see if the lights were on. The window was dark. I expected to be disappointed, but I wasn't. I hustled down the steps into the chilly underground lobby and climbed the stairs to the first floor. At the top, I cast a glance at the door for apartment #101, the one with dark windows. I had experienced a wide range of emotions over the years because of the person who lived in #101. Her name was Ang. But all of that, the ups and downs, had leveled out into...nothing. Flatlined.

I clicked my tongue and took long strides down the dank corridor to my studio. I slid the key into the deadbolt and unlocked it slowly, careful not to make any sound. I double locked the door behind me and set down my tip bucket and gear in the carpeted, dark entryway. Once I'd stripped down to a beater and boxer briefs, I lined my boots up, mindful to tuck the laces in. I folded my work clothes and placed them in line with my boots. I walked silently into the main room of my studio, which was lit by the low blue glow of a little fish tank, and slid gently into the bed in my crappy old futon, careful not to shake the frame. I grinned at the warmth already within the sheets. Just as I closed my eyes to settle in, a smooth voice broke the silence.

"Babe, I didn't hear you come in. Hey." She rolled toward me and slid her soft hand under my beater, resting it on my hip.

I smiled in the dark and nuzzled my nose into her hair, placing a kiss on her throat. "Hey, Audre. Glad you chose to stay over. I was trying not to wake you up. And you know I love using the creep when I can. It's good practice."

"Vivian, you're a civilian now. I know you like to stay in prime soldiering condition, but all your sneaking in here is going to do is give me a damn heart attack."

Her hand on my hip gave a little tug and I slid my body up against hers. Hips to hips, breasts to breasts. Her lips found mine and I melted, returning her kiss with an urgency that surprised me. Drawing her bottom lip in, I gave it a playful nibble as I slid my thigh between her legs.

"Easy, cowboy. I have to be up for work in two hours," she said. I relented and shifted so her head was on my chest. She snuggled up to me, her breath slowing and evening out within minutes. I watched my fish float in their tank under the mellow blue light and listened to the sounds of my studio at 4:00 a.m.: the tank filter burbling, my upstairs neighbor walking around his apartment, and the light-rail bell clanging outside.

I tried to sink into the familiar sounds and allow the sensation of Audre sleeping on my chest to lull me into a slumber, but my thoughts spun. Frustration over my discontent at work and curiosity about my lack of reaction when I walked past Ang's apartment won out. Eyes closed,

I distracted myself by counting the footfalls as my upstairs neighbor continued his nightly pacing. At some point I drifted into intense, nonsensical dreams.

I was pulled out of the fray by the alarm on Audre's phone chiming. Her weight shifted and the alarm stopped. I rubbed my cheeks and cracked an eyelid. The gray light of dawn filtered in around the window blinds.

"Shit. Sorry I woke you, Viv. Go back to sleep," she whispered. The futon gave a small creak as Audre got up. The bathroom door shut with a gentle click, and I wondered if an hour and a half of sleep was going to be enough. A metal bar from the frame of the futon dug into my back through the thin foam mattress and I took that as my sign that I was not going to fall back to sleep.

I got up to feed the fish and registered my sore back. I sprinkled some flakes into the tank and stood for a moment, watching as the Tetras and Bettas came to life and darted about, gobbling up their breakfast. I had never liked the smell of fish food, oily and a bit like low tide, so I rinsed my fingertips in the kitchen sink. In a haze, I put on the kettle to make some tea, leaning against the kitchen counter until the water boiled.

Audre came out of the restroom and pulled me into a hug, her skin still warm from the sheets and sleep.

"Have a good day at work, babe," I said into her neck.

She nodded, her hair brushing my cheek. "Before I go, I wanted to check in with you on what we talked about yesterday." She ended the hug and scooped her purse up from the small kitchen table. Calling it a kitchen table was a stretch; it was actually a folding card table, but it fit the studio and worked for me.

I dug into my memory, searching for what she might be talking about.

Her mouth opened a bit, enough for me to catch a sliver of her teeth. The corners of her eyes tightened ever so slightly when I didn't respond right away.

"Viv. My family. Remember?"

"Shit. Yes. Yeah, I thought about it, and you're right. It's definitely time for me to meet your family. Just tell me when, and I'll be there."

Audre gave me a flippant grin, kissed my cheek, and headed toward the door.

"Nice save, Viv. Nice save. See you later." With that, the door closed, and the water for tea came to a boil. I pulled the pot off the burner and poured hot water over a tea bag, the peppermint aroma immediately filling my tiny kitchen. I stared into the cobalt-blue mug and watched the tea bag sink, leaving behind brown swirls, coloring the water as it went.

Audre was right; we had been dating well over a year, and I hadn't met her family yet. To be fair, she hadn't broached the subject until the previous day. I couldn't remember the last time I had been brought home to meet any of my partner's families. While past connections had been intense, the whole relationship escalator was not for me. All of which was complicated by my being polyamorous. So many people weren't out to their families about their own polyamory. I wasn't interested in putting on a monogamous front for their sake. Audre wasn't closeted; meeting her family just hadn't come up. Though it made me curious if any of her other partners had met her family. I flipped open my phone and sent her a text.

I know this probably isn't a great topic to discuss by text, and should have asked you yesterday, but I wonder if any of your other partners have met your family?

I folded the futon bed back into a couch, grabbed a banana, and sat down. Blowing into the mug, I took small sips as I awkwardly opened the book one handed, finding my page. The paperback, *Norwegian Wood* by Haruki Murakami, fell open mercifully just as I was about to spill my tea. I settled onto the couch and gladly ran away into the world of Watanabe, Midori, and Naoko.

"I want you always to remember me. Will you remember that I existed, and that I stood next to you here like this?"

"Always," I said. "I'll always remember."

The book was well loved, the spine cracked, the pages smudged and dog eared. Of all the times I had read it, those lines always stuck with me. A familiar sensation in my chest writhed as I studied the words, so I put the book down on my lap for a moment. The sensation was akin to a gap that had been there my whole life, yet to be resolved.

I had been working with my therapist, Alexia, on it for a couple of years. Long enough to know that the gap wasn't a gap, but more like a younger part of me, a part that hadn't been fulfilled in childhood and still sought to be seen and nurtured. A part that I had spent most of my adult life shoving down because it didn't feel good. In the past I would have suppressed it by going out for a run or gliding an X-Acto blade across my skin, but I was working to not do that anymore. So I sat, my eyes closed, and recited the lines in my head again, telling myself *I want you always to remember me. Will you remember that I existed, and that I stood next to you here like this?...Always. I'll always remember.*

The same writhing sensation rose. I focused on it and greeted it. Acknowledged it. Told it I loved it. Held it. All the loving things I hadn't experienced as a kid, I gave to myself in that moment. And only when the writhing slowed and eventually stopped did I pick the book back up and read on.

*

Soccer practice had ended, and the sun was well on its way to setting. The coach had finished packing up his gear. The other kids were gone, already picked up by their parents or had ridden off on their bicycles. I sat on an old railroad tie at the edge of the parking lot. Between my cleats, a dandelion grew up in the gravel. My legs were deeply tan from summertime play and lack of sunscreen. Heat from the day radiated up from the ground, though a breeze of cool air blew in from the nearby tomato fields, carrying with it the unique scent of the cannery across town. A scent I couldn't quite describe, other than to say it was sharp, earthy, and had a tinge of garlic to it.

Gravel crunched as Coach Jeff lowered himself to sit on the railroad tie next to me. His muscular, hairy legs looked like tree trunks next to my wiry kid legs.

"No sign of your mom yet, eh?"

"No," I said quietly, not wanting to talk about it.

"Hmph." He rubbed his mustache, which made a sandpapery noise.

Coach Jeff and I sat there, not speaking. He picked at his cuticles and periodically scrubbed at his face. I watched water birds fly toward the manmade lake and listened to traffic pass by on the nearby road. As dusk fell, a car turned into the parking lot, kicking up dust, going a bit too fast for the gravel. The headlights cut a path through the darkness. The car, a Nissan sedan, made its way toward us and finally pulled up in front of where we sat. I stood, grabbing my backpack, and climbed into the passenger seat. I put my backpack between my feet on the floorboard and looked at my mother. She sat in the driver's seat, hands gripping the wheel, her posture tight. Her brown hair fell just below her shoulders. She didn't say a word or even bother to look at me. Her resentment for my existence hung heavy in the hot air of the car.

Coach Jeff walked around to the driver's side and motioned that he wanted my mom to roll down her window. Without even looking at him, Mom pressed the accelerator, and drove out of the parking lot in a spray of grit.

*

Audre sent me a text in response.

> *Sorry for the delay, I was in a meeting. Yes, Darren and Shae have both met my family.*

My chest zinged painfully as I read her reply. I wondered why her other two partners, who were much more casual connections, had met her family first. I knew that thought missed the entire point of poly, but I'd always been a competitive person, and found myself hoping that her family liked me better than Darren and Shae.

Shaking my head at my own insecurities, I drew in a breath and scrubbed at my face, much as Coach Jeff had done so long ago. I took a deep pull of tea and flipped around *Norwegian Wood* until I found another favorite section. One that also made my chest writhe, but I wanted to contemplate it anyway.

> *"Do you think you weren't loved enough?"*
>
> *She tilted her head and looked at me. Then gave a sharp, little nod.*
>
> *"Somewhere between 'not enough' and 'not at all.' I was always hungry for love. Just once, I wanted to know what it was like to get my fill of it—to be fed so much love I couldn't take any more. Just once."*

I rolled the lines around in my head and chest and allowed myself to feel what came up. It was an exercise that forced me to work through whatever appeared, which were the same things I had been running from for years. Life in the army had been perfect for stuffing feelings down, but I was not a soldier any longer, and it was time to let go.

Tea and banana gone, it was time to get moving. I was confident that rush hour was over, and I could safely get on the road without much traffic. I peed, brushed my teeth and hair, slipped into some running clothes, shoved protein bars, almonds, bananas, apples, and a water bottle into my day pack, and headed for the door.

I chose to ride my motorcycle, rather than drive. In the underground parking garage, I pulled out riding gear from the bike's hard bags and put the jacket and pants on over my running clothes. I shoved my day pack into the hard bags. The bike's engine purred in the underground garage. It was a 2003 Honda ST1300, and I adored it. As I backed the bike out of my parking space I glanced toward Ang's reserved spot. Sure enough, there was her Subaru. Her road bike was loaded up on the roof rack, which meant she would be returning to the garage. Her bike was worth thousands, and I knew she never left it unattended long. I pulled up to the sensor which opened the gate, and rode up the steep, narrow driveway until I popped out on Twenty-Fourth Street.

Once on the freeway I moderated my speed until I reached the west side of Davis. The natural flow of traffic, when there wasn't a jam, always picked up around that point. My bike was warmed up and running smoothly. I accelerated and checked the speedometer, which read 90 mph, though the bike didn't give any hint of the speed. Not a single wobble or strain. The tires and shocks absorbed the bumps and cracks of Interstate 80. My black riding pants flapped a bit. Cool air found its way up the sleeves, and down the back of my riding jacket. My head snug inside the helmet pads, my face behind the full-face visor, I sliced through the wind.

Between Dixon and Vacaville were a few miles of farmland. Green foothills began to rise on the horizon. I knew they would be golden-brown and dry within a month. When the grasses died and the hills turned from green to gold, I struggled to enjoy the vistas. The heat and dusty dry dirt brought to mind memories of childhood and my time in the military. Hot, dusty, dry places had never been good to me. I focused back on the road and realized I had just passed a car in a blur. My eyes flicked to the speedometer—110mph. I turned the throttle a bit more, hitting 120mph. The bike didn't bog down or whine, though even the slightest shifting in my seat made the bike wobble. I hunched down until my chest was resting on the gas tank. I approached the weigh station at the west side of Fairfield, knowing it was usually teeming with Highway Patrol. I didn't care, and blew past the weigh station, registering the blur of a Highway Patrol motorcycle officer on his Harley at the side of the road, radar gun in hand and pointed right at me. In a blink I had passed him and saw him fumbling to stow his radar gun. My exit was next, and I had to slow for the bend in the connector ramp, leaning into the turn so hard that my pegs scraped the road. I hit the throttle as soon as the road straightened and took off down the freeway as fast as my bike could go.

I recognized how reckless my reaction was. There was no reason for me to run. I was licensed, insured, and had a clean record. No warrants. Yet, there I was, smiling into my helmet, my thighs clenched tight to the bike, chest on the tank. Electricity coursed through me, heart racing, sweat forming under my jacket despite the wind. The freeway was only two lanes for that stretch, so I had to weave around cars and trucks. Traffic had built up a bit but was still moving so I split lanes between vehicles, so close I could have reached out and touched them on either side of me.

I clenched my jaw, forcing myself to focus. The blue and red police lights flashed in the side mirror. The cop was so far back, I was confident he wouldn't catch up to me. He was on a Harley, and I was on a bike built for speed and agility. By the time I reached the Benicia-Martinez bridge there was no sign of the officer in my mirrors, so I slowed to 80 mph, to enjoy the view of the water below and the huge form of Mount Diablo ahead.

On the far side of Martinez, I cut over to another highway, and then made my way through the back roads to Briones Regional Park. Briones was the place I went to when I was happy, and when I was suicidal, and everything in between. The park filled me up, no matter how empty I was, especially when the hills were still green.

I found a rare shady parking spot in the gravel lot and shut the bike down. The engine pinged as it cooled, while I stripped off my riding gear and put on running shoes. I locked up my riding gear in the hard bags of the bike and slipped into my day pack, snapping the hip and chest straps. My heart was still racing from the exhilaration of the ride. I jogged over to the cattle gate and let myself into the park, then jogged to the picnic area to use the outhouse.

The pit toilet was as disgusting as it always was. The park staff did a great job of keeping the outhouse stocked with toilet tissue and keeping the floors clean, but nobody seemed brave enough to clean the chute that led from the toilet seat to the pit below. The inside of the chute was without fail always covered in sprays of diarrhea. As if dozens of people, over time, had had explosive diarrhea in that park outhouse. It confounded me, and if a day ever came that I found it clean, I would be shocked. I exited the outhouse and used some hand sanitizer from my pack since the bathroom didn't have a sink or running water. I took a swig from my water bottle, put on my sunglasses, and jogged toward the gate.

Between me and the gate was a man with a huge stick. I slowed, scanning him. He gestured to me to stop. I halted about twenty feet away from him. He said something to me that I couldn't make out at first, his accent thick. He repeated himself and motioned to the ground with his stick.

"Rattlesnake," he said. And sure enough, there was a rattlesnake in the middle of the path, stretched out sunning itself. Its belly bulged, as if it had just eaten. The man kept nudging at it with the stick, trying to steer the snake toward a nearby creek bed. It slowly complied, not interested in biting anybody. Eventually the snake was a safe distance off the trail. I gave the guy a nod and said thanks. He nodded back and walked back toward his children, who were playing in the meadow.

The gate clanged shut behind me. That was a sound one could hear throughout the park, as there were similar cattle gates on most of the extensive trails. I adjusted to a jog and started the incline on Alhambra Creek trail. It wasn't ideal for trail running, with its narrow footpath and abundance of tree roots, but I pushed on. Up, up, up I went, winding my way through various trails until I crested the peak, my lungs and quads ready to explode.

I stopped for a much-needed water break at sign marker 22. As the water hit my guts they clenched up and I had a moment where I thought I might spew. Sitting heavily in the grass off the trail, I focused on slowing my breathing. My cheeks blazed from the exertion of the run. I forced myself to sit up straight to take pressure off my cramping guts.

The view was worth the discomfort. A panorama of squat trees and green hills interrupted only by the blue sky and wispy clouds. I drew in a deep breath through my nose, counting as I went. *One...two...three...four...five...* It was an exercise I had learned from a therapist long ago to help with anxiety, that was also helpful for other forms of discomfort. A gentle breeze rustled the grasses and bay trees. I blew out my breath slowly and opened my eyes when I heard footfalls coming up the trail from the opposite direction.

A hearty soul plodded by sporting heavy hiking boots, a floppy sun hat, and hairy, chiseled legs. We exchanged nods as he wiped a bead of sweat from the tip of his nose. He didn't stop to chat. Nobody ever did. The trails deep in the park, which were far less traveled, tended to draw hikers and runners who sought the solitude the inner reaches of the park offered.

As my body settled down, the cramping and nausea subsided. I stretched and got back on the trail, trying to do a better job of monitoring my body. I went down to the far side of the park, eventually reaching a nice flat trail that led to Bear Creek staging area. I flopped down onto a picnic bench, my legs and feet numb. Unbuckling my day pack with swollen fingers, I wiggled out of it and placed it on the weathered table. I dug out a water bottle, protein bar, banana, apple, and almonds. I sat and contemplated them for a beat and then scanned the area.

I was sitting on the outskirts of a large field, bordered by a parking lot. I had often started hikes and runs from this staging area and wasn't at all surprised to see an orange Subaru with bike racks on the roof parked there. Almost every time I had visited the Bear Creek side of the park, that Subaru, and the man who owned it, were there. Though there was no sign of him or his mountain bike. Just his car. Another breeze blew through the trees along the creek making a sound not unlike the sandpapery scrape of Coach Jeff's mustache under his calloused hand.

I ate, mindful to chew well and to not eat too quickly despite a ravenous hunger. The slow influx of water and calories helped, making the shakes begin to fade. Fatigue crept in, and I knew I had a choice to make before it got too bad: Take a nap or get back on the trail. I chose a short nap and set an alarm on my old Timex Ironman watch that I had worn forever. The fabric strap smelled like years of sweat and had salt stains on it. I lay down on the bench, placing the day pack under my head, and drifted off as the warm breeze stroked my skin and made the trees shiver.

Chapter Three

A skill I had learned out of necessity during my time in the military was how to fall asleep just about anywhere. Lying on the narrow wooden plank of the picnic bench seat, a pack under my head and a pleasant breeze blowing across my skin, was all I needed. Sleep overtook me swiftly and I spent some time navigating shallow dreams about waking up with no shoes and having to run back over the mountain in my socks.

I was pulled from my slumber by the sound of bicycle tires on gravel and cracked my eye open in time to see a man shoot by on an orange mountain bike. I sat up, smoothing my hair, and watched as he rode into the parking lot and pulled up to the orange Subaru. I gave a small shake of my head as I considered how amazing it would be to live so close to the park that I could visit it daily like he clearly did.

He began what I knew was his lengthy post-ride routine. If my previous observations of him were accurate, he would spend nearly an hour stretching, changing shoes, eating, hydrating, and checking every square inch of his bike before placing it back on the roof rack, like a daily meditation for him.

The short nap had revitalized me. I packed up, used the outhouse, and got on the trail. I opted not to return on the same trail that I took on the way in, and instead hoofed it over to Seaborg trail. I knew very well that I would not be able to run the entire route, because of how steep some of the inclines were. The challenge was what excited me, so as Seaborg eventually switched from a hard-packed flat surface to ass-kicking, lung-busting incline, I leaned into the pain and kept pushing until I had to relent and slow to a jog, and eventually walk.

My quads, glutes, and lungs were on fire with the exertion. Sweat and snot dripped, even in the cool afternoon air. My body insisted on stopping for a break, but I refused and continued to push, putting one foot in front of the other. Bay and oak trees covered the trail, intermittently blocking out the sun.

*

My entire body ached and throbbed. From the balls of my feet to the top of my head. My scalp had hot spots from the nylon webbing inside my Kevlar helmet. The helmet served as part of my PPE, but it was also three and a half pounds of weight digging into my scalp and compressing my neck. My entire Basic Training platoon was kitted out in BDU's, full rucks, LCE's, and carrying M16s.

We were taking the long way back to the barracks from the range. Why the long way? That was our prize for being the best scoring platoon in the company on the M16 range. So, after a long day in the field, we were rewarded with a couple of extra klicks of marching on the way back.

Fort Jackson had its share of hills, and we were in the middle of marching up one of them. I was new to soldiering, my body not fully transformed yet. Somewhere between soft civilian and hard soldier. The rucksack straps dug into the flesh of my shoulders. My tender feet were rubbed raw inside of my boots and my arms were numb from holding my M16 at port arms while marching endlessly.

Our drill sergeant had jogged on ahead, so I took the opportunity to take some of the weight of the rifle, at 7.76 pounds, off my arms by resting the grip on the buckle of my LCE.

I was in a sea of camouflaged, exhausted soldiers, all too tired to even try to sneak in a chat while the cadre was out of earshot. The only sounds were the shuffling of our boots in the dirt, a far-off woodpecker, and a chorus of cicadas.

I had not had an easy childhood, but nothing up to that point in my life had prepared me for the level of discomfort that Basic Training brought. And all I could do was just. Keep. Moving. I watched the bouncing rucksack ahead of me and did my best to focus on that rather than the pain throughout my body. Up and down, the ruck bobbed and swayed. Our boots crunched onward as the late day humidity reached its crescendo. The skies had been clear all day, the sun beating down on us relentlessly at the firing range. But dark-gray thunderheads had rolled in, blocking the sun and muting all the various shades of green I was normally surrounded with. I couldn't see any sign of the top of the hill because I was buried in the platoon, and the soldiers in front of me shielded my view of the road ahead.

A massive crack of thunder broke the silence, startling us out of our individual stupors. A murmur rolled through the platoon.

I had learned that while we were all training to be soldiers, some were scared to death of things like spiders, mice, and thunder.

Up ahead I heard the baritone of Drill Sergeant Rodriguez. He was a tiny man. Petite, with small features around a dagger-sharp mustache. He was an impossibly fast runner and had quick reflexes. He was rock steady.

While small in stature, he had a big, deep voice, and he was using it to motivate us. Before I could make out what Sergeant Rodriguez was calling out to us, another crack of thunder exploded overhead, so loud that it rattled around in my bones and my ears began to ring. Someone behind me let out a yelp.

Sergeant Rodriguez started over, and the platoon picked up his cadence immediately. It was one we had done before. He called the line, and we called it back to him, our voices echoing mightily through the forest.

Take the hill!

Take the hill!

Take the hill!

Take the hill!

Over and over, we shouted the refrain back to him, as we continued to climb. I was getting punchy from exhaustion and the pressing humidity. The storm clouds finally blotted out the last of the color. Everything a muted grayish green. Feeding off the crazy energy that my body had pulled from the dregs of my reserves, I doubled the volume of my cadence and was shouting as loudly as I could. The inside of my throat hurt as I hollered it raw. Snot and sweat flowed.

When we reached the top of the hill, our cadence faded out. Sergeant Rodriguez called a halt and water break. I stood in the middle of the trail, swaying on my feet when an explosion of lightning lit up the sky, much too close for comfort, followed in rapid succession by more bone-rattling thunder. And then...the clouds opened up. Sheets of rain dumped down on us. The humidity broke immediately, and the air cooled. The dusty dirt trail we were on turned to mud in an instant. Rivulets of water ran down the hill.

Soldiers in various stages of exhaustion all turned their heads to the sky, allowing the fierce rain to wash their faces. The drops were heavier and faster than a showerhead, splattering in my eyes and cooling my feverish skin. The punchy energy began to leave me, drawing out uncontrollable laughter.

I had been reserved and quiet my entire life. But in that moment, on top of a hill in South Carolina, surrounded by strangers who I would put my life on the line for, all I could do was laugh wildly. Huge waves of it worked their way out of me, and I let it out, breaking the rules of decorum and self-discipline. Much to my surprise, Sergeant Rodriguez joined in. His deep laughter was joyous and carefree. I caught a rare glimpse of the human behind the buttoned-up drill sergeant exterior.

Eventually calm was restored, and I was left with a hollow, hungry sensation. Shaky and extremely sad.

Completely soaked, I breathed in deep as the rain continued to wash the sweat and remnants of camouflage paint from my face. As I looked at my platoon, each soldier appeared to be lost in their own thoughts, water dripping from the rims of helmets and the tips of noses. Even Sergeant Rodriguez was having a moment of reflection as he leaned against a boulder, unfazed by the rain.

I made eye contact with the one soldier who wasn't drifting. I recognized him as being in my platoon, but he was not in my squad, so I hadn't interacted with him much. He squatted under a low pine tree, unbothered by the rain. He was solidly built, his BDU's strained around his quads and across his barrel chest. Veins popped on his huge hands and his neck was thick with muscle. He wore the uniform and bore the weight of the gear with ease. I couldn't make out much more beyond two piercing hazel eyes, and a finger that subtly crooked, beckoning me over to him.

Male and female soldiers weren't supposed to talk to each other without a battle buddy present. But I took advantage of Sergeant Rodriguez's lost focus and glided through lines of other lethargic recruits to the soldier who had invited me. I squatted under the tree with him, the weight of my ruck dragging me down. I snuck a quick peek at the name tape on his uniform. Ramirez. I looked at him and his eyes snapped up from my name tape. He extended a large hand to me.

"Ramirez," he said.

"Chastain," I replied.

"Jared, actually. But I guess it's supposed to be Ramirez when I am in uniform." His hazel eyes danced

as the corners of his mouth curled up in a shy smile. The sadness that had enveloped me recoiled into the deep recesses of my chest as his eyes and his smile connected with me.

"Nice to meet you, Jared. I'm Vivian," I whispered back, conspiratorially.

He paused, deep in thought, running a calloused thumb along his bottom lip.

"You're...you're going to be okay, Chastain. I feel it. I know it." He tapped a thick, yet graceful index finger square in the center of his chest, indicating that was where he felt it.

I stared at him, my brain skittering, unclear on how to respond. The first eighteen years of my life had been devoid of support, leaving behind an emotional vacuum. Internally I grasped for purchase, seeking the right way to respond to him. But I didn't know how.

A fat drop of water slid down the perfectly straight bridge of his nose. He grinned again warmly.

"It's okay, Chastain. You don't have to say anything. Just remember what I said. I know it's true. You're gonna be okay."

I nodded at him numbly, wondering how people knew how to receive care and concern. I could give it, but I couldn't receive it.

We remained under the creaking pine tree, no more conversation needed, listening to the sloshing of the storm.

*

I had a hard reentry from the stormy South Carolina afternoon back to a spring day on Briones Crest trail in California.

"Take the hill," I repeated to myself as I trudged the last few meters to the ridgeline. The sadness from the memory stuck with me, and anxiety reared its head to pile on with the sadness. There I was, jogging the ridgeline at Briones, one of my favorite places. My self-avowed Happy Place, but the head-clearing happiness was bogged down in anxiety.

I stopped in the middle of the narrow trail, panting, and turned to take in the view. Down below was the valley that held the cities of Pleasant Hill and Concord. On the other side of the narrow valley rose Mount Diablo. I spent some time taking the mountain in, starting on the north side, then along the ridgeline to the west side, which was scarred by mining, then over the peaks, and down the south side. That process slowed down the anxiety, and all I wanted in that moment was to have Jared on the trail with me. He had been my best friend since that day in Basic Training, throughout both of our enlistments, and then on to being roommates in Morro Bay after our discharges. He had had my back, literally saving my life amidst rapid gunfire and RPG's. He had been my rock for years, only faltering a few times. And in that moment, on that mountain top, I needed him more than ever.

I took a long pull on my water bottle and fished my cell phone from my day pack. On the ridgeline I had cell service, which was rare in the park. I dialed Jared's number, knowing he was probably at work at the hardware store.

He answered on the second ring.

"*Bueno. Bueno.* Hey, Vivi!" His deep voice was full of cheer.

"Hey, Jared. Is this an okay time?"

"Yup, if you can hear me okay. I am using a headset cuz I am driving."

"Yes. I can hear you. Thanks."

I listened to the road noise coming through the phone.

"Hey. Viv. Is something wrong?"

"No. I don't think so. I...you know how when we go running, I tend to, um, drift?"

He chuckled. "Yes. Where'd you drift to today?"

I kicked at a pebble on the trail with the toe of my running shoe. "So, I'm trail running today. You remember that route I took you on at Briones when you visited last year?"

"Oh damn, that's brutal. Are you by yourself?"

"Yes."

"That trail is probably one you shouldn't run alone. It is so desolate. No phone signal in the hills. Just...be careful."

"I'm careful." I patted the hard plastic case of the stun gun that was always clipped to the waist of my running shorts.

"Okay. So, where'd your mind wander off to?"

"Do you remember the day we met? The thunderstorm?" My eyes looked up at the blue sky as I said it, reassuring myself that I was in fact in California, years later.

He chuckled again. "Yeah. I remember."

I started walking along the trail, phone pressed to my ear.

"You know what stood out to me this time? Your nose." I let out a bark of laughter.

"My nose?"

"Yeah. Your nose was perfectly straight back then. And now...it's busted and crooked. Honestly, I like it better now. It gives you more of an...edge."

Our conversation flowed smoothly from there. We talked until my mood was lifted. I started to lose signal and he had reached his delivery stop. We said our goodbyes and I slid the phone shut before putting it back in my pack.

I had reached the start of the steep decline on the trail. It was time to pick up the pace again. Downhill trail running, especially on loose dirt and gravel, was insanely dangerous and incredibly fun. A balance of control while also letting go. I tightened the chest strap of my day pack and went for it.

It was the time of the afternoon when locals started their daily walks on the trails. Diablo View trail was close to the parking lot, so I encountered plenty of people and dogs climbing up the hill while I bombed down it, trying to not bowl anyone over or eat shit on the gravel.

My heart pounded, not from exertion, but from exhilaration. I was laser focused, hopping over the deep rivulets that cut through the path, my eyes watering from the wind.

"On your left," I shouted as I came up fast behind a pair of hikers working their way slowly down the wide trail. The hikers startled at the sound of my voice and pounding feet. One—who appeared from the back to be a middle-aged man, sporting one of those shirts that Jeff Probst wore on *Survivor*, cargo pants, and a floppy sun hat—seemed confused by my trail instruction and... stepped to his left, directly into my path. The heavily eroded trail was close to a 50 percent gradient, so he was below me in elevation. I had no choice but to jump; otherwise, we would collide at a high rate of speed, and he was built like a brick wall. My sneakers skittering in the gravel, I leaped, launching myself up and over, the back of my hamstring grazing his shoulder as I cleared him.

"Ack, *what the heck!*" he shouted and was no doubt shaking a fist at me, but I didn't look back. My focus had to remain on the trail and my movement. I landed in loose gravel as slick as ice, throwing my arms out to keep balance. I kept my feet moving, not losing a beat, and continued down the trail, laughing out loud. Laughter for how free I felt in that moment. Letting go of the anxiety and self-imposed rules I lived within. Just like when I was riding my motorcycle, the faster I moved, the better I felt.

Rolling green hills surrounded the trail and I fought the urge to take in the view, for fear of losing focus and losing my footing. I had lost my balance on a downhill trail run in Guerneville just a couple of years before, leading to a giant gash on my leg. I did not want to risk a similar injury, or worse.

Eventually I made it down to the trailhead at the base of the hill, where my motorcycle was parked. The day had warmed up and I found a shady spot to cool down, catch my breath, and hydrate before leaving.

A gentle breeze blew across the dirt parking lot. I watched a ground squirrel methodically pull strand after strand of dry grass from the ground. It had quite a large bundle of grass in its mouth before darting into its burrow, a blur of brown fur, spotted with black.

Another gust of warm breeze blew, drying the sweat on my brow, the salt causing the skin to stiffen and itch ever so slightly. Knowing it was time to go, I drew in a deep breath, smelling eucalyptus and bay, and dusted off my haunches as I stood up.

I pulled my riding gear back on, stowed my running gear, and rolled out. The ride back to Sacramento was serene and much less manic. After the white-knuckle ride to Martinez and the adrenaline dump from the downhill portion of the trail run, I was calm, centered, and not interested in rushing. I knew my therapist wouldn't approve of how I achieved that level of calm, but it worked, so I didn't much care if she approved or not.

I passed through Benicia, Suisun, and Fairfield, my eyes on the road, my mind adrift in a neutral place. On the stretch of Interstate 80 between Fairfield and Vacaville, I came up behind a cream-colored Toyota Corolla in the fast lane that was cruising at a steady ten miles per hour below the speed limit.

While not in a rush, I didn't want to be part of the log jam that was bound to pile up behind her. I looked through the back window of the Toyota to the rear-view mirror. The woman driving appeared to be focused on the road. I turned on my right blinker and got into the second lane to pass her. I was an experienced rider and knew not to linger in her blind spot.

As I overtook her, in the blink of an eye, the Toyota was in my lane. I had no time to think. My reflexes kicked in and I dumped my bike over as far as I could just as the

Toyota grazed my left knee and my side mirror. I ended up in the third lane. Stars sparked in my eyes and my heart was in my throat as I righted my bike, grateful that no one had been in the third lane.

I looked over to the Toyota and the driver was oblivious. Completely unaware that she had nearly killed me. She tapped her hand on the steering wheel to the beat of whatever song she was listening to. Hot rage dumped into my blood and I shrieked at her, the sound exploding inside my helmet.

I could have been reduced to a smear on the highway. My heart pounded, so hard that my vision thumped with it. I had been holding my breath, so I forced a few breaths and returned my focus to the road.

The old rage that I had been working so hard to leave behind was there again, riding pillion, breathing down my neck, and it wanted to get her back. I was riding in the lane next to the Toyota still, aligned with the passenger side door, so that lady would have to see me. I shot another glance at her and she was still rolling along, tapping her hand to the music, oblivious. My teeth ground so hard that I tasted blood.

I wondered what my friend Bear would do in this situation. Bear was normally very calm and cool, except when it came to cars driving like assholes around motorcycles. She kept nuts and bolts in the pocket of her riding vest that she would toss over her shoulder at cars who tailgated her, the perfect way to chip someone's windshield and paint. I knew exactly what Bear would have done because I had seen her almost get broadsided. Bear would boot the shit out of the car.

I nodded to myself and stretched my leg back precariously, kicking my license plate so the hinged flip plate engaged. My license plate folded up so it was no longer visible. Then I rode to the far left side of my lane till I was so close to the Toyota I could have reached out and touched it. I ducked down so I could stare at the woman driving. She finally became aware of my presence, her brunette hair swaying as she gave me several nervous sidelong glances. I flicked glances to the road ahead to be sure I was still safe and not about to rear end anyone. I waited until the woman looked at me again, and I flipped her off. Her lips parted slightly in astonishment and she turned her head back to the road. I took all the fury roiling inside my chest and guts, drew my left leg up and pistoned it out, slamming my boot into her passenger door, leaving a huge dent and a big black smudge. The impact rocked my bike, causing a dangerous wobble. I gripped my thighs to the gas tank, steadying it.

The woman slammed her brakes, trying to get away from me. There were cars behind her, so a series of screeching tires followed. I cut over into the fast lane and took off.

It took the remainder of the ride back to Sacramento to calm the anger that had poisoned my blood. One thing sure to set off my hair-trigger temper was someone taking something from me or doing something that could harm me. I knew deep down it was lucky the woman was safe inside a moving car. Had she not been, I likely would have pummeled her. I had broken plenty of noses and bloodied plenty of lips in fits of rage when someone tried to impose themselves on me. It was a problem I thought I had finally worked through and had control over. I had a therapy appointment the following day and dreaded having to confess what I had done.

I had finally made it to my apartment and rode down the steep driveway to the underground parking garage. I keyed in the gate code with a shaky hand, parked, and cut the engine of my bike. I stripped off my helmet in time to hear the gate open again. I watched as Ang gave me a little smile and wave as she parked her Subaru in her assigned spot.

As the rage and adrenaline receded, it left behind a shaky hollowness. A hug would have been amazing, but my relationship with Ang was no longer a relationship in that sense. We had transitioned from a "primary" relationship to a sexual friendship, so I didn't rely on her for support the way I used to. I drew in a deep breath and dug my trail running gear out of my hard bags. As I locked up, Ang approached, her hands full of grocery bags.

"Hey, Viv," she said, a warm smile on her lips.

"Hey, Ang." I gave her a tired smile back.

She tilted her head slightly, a small crease of concern forming between her eyebrows.

"You okay?"

"Yeah. Just pushed myself too hard on the trail and then had a really close call on my bike. I'll be fine."

"You'll be fine," she echoed, sounding unsure. "I'd offer to help carry your gear up, but..." She gestured with her grocery bags.

"No worries." I straightened up from the bike. I casually flipped the license plate on my bike back out so it was visible, and Ang, a deputy sheriff, raised an eyebrow at me.

I followed her to the lobby door, appreciating the lithe, athletic way that her body moved. Her chiseled calves supported all six foot three inches of her as she took long strides and then held the heavy security door open for me. I lifted my chin up and thanked her. We both eyed the rickety elevator and then took the stairs up to the first floor. Her apartment was right at the top of the stairs. We paused in front of her place as she dug out her key and unlocked the deadbolt.

"Why don't you come in, Viv?" She pushed the door open with her knee and crossed the threshold.

"I..." I looked down the hall at my own studio door. I wanted to make an excuse about having to get ready for work, but I had the night off. "Yeah. Okay." I closed the door behind me and dropped my armload of gear in her entryway.

I leaned against her dining room table and watched as she put away her groceries. The same dining room table I almost upended the night she had blindsided me, telling me she was solo poly and didn't want me as her primary partner anymore.

She brushed a loose strand of her brown hair, hooking it behind her ear, poured two huge glasses of water, and handed one to me. We both emptied our glasses in big gulps. The cool water hit my belly, which seized briefly but settled. We put our glasses down on the counter. I turned to thank her when she scooped me up into a massive hug. She was so much taller than me, and had a large, strong frame. Her arms wrapped me up and I froze for a moment, unsure if the hug was the right thing to do.

"I...I probably am filthy and smell like a goat after my run," I said into her shoulder.

She shook her head and held me tighter.

"Is this okay? I mean...since we reframed our relationship. I just...I want to be clear—"

"It's just a hug, Viv. I care about you, and you clearly need some comfort."

I relaxed into her and wrapped my arms around her waist. She rested her chin on the top of my head the way she had done so many times before our breakup and "reframing." My chest bloomed as tears rushed up. I clenched my mouth and eyes shut, focusing on forcing the tears back down. I knew damn well my therapist would have told me to just let it out, but I didn't want to come off as needy to Ang. She was so flighty about people having needs and emotions around her. I let out a shuddering breath and ended the hug.

"Thanks, Ang. I gotta get going."

"Are you sure? Join me for a shower?" She stripped off her T-shirt and headed for the bathroom. I stood in her kitchen and listened as the shower turned on.

"Fuck it," I said to the ceiling and began stripping as I followed her into the bathroom. I could go to my studio and wallow in the mess that was left behind by my rage on the freeway, or I could enjoy a nice hot shower with Ang.

I kicked off my boots and stripped out of my riding clothes in the hallway since there wasn't room for both of us to strip in her narrow bathroom. I climbed into the shower after her. She positioned me in the stream of water and lathered me up with a body wash that smelled of leather and cedar. She took her time, massaging my sore muscles as she worked her way over my entire body, taking extra time to outline the eight pack of my abs. She used the handheld showerhead to wash me off. We repeated the ritual in reverse as I then cleaned her. She had to duck down so that I could massage shampoo into her hair. I made my way down her body, taking my time working her solid frame and olive skin. Steam filled the bathroom as I finished rinsing the soap off her.

She placed the shower nozzle back in its holder on the wall and pulled me in. Our skin slippery with the flow of water, she leaned down and kissed me deeply. I returned her kiss and drew her bottom lip into my mouth, giving it a measured and solid bite. Ang let out a groan that echoed off the walls. I released her lip and kissed down her throat, nibbled along her collarbone, and then paused at her nipples, which were truly her on switch. I took my time sucking and biting her nipples, rolling my tongue around them firmly. With each roll of my tongue, she groaned and rocked her hips, digging her hands in my hair. I released her nipple from my mouth after one last sharp suck and got down on my knees. Ang gasped and then moved the showerhead over so the water wasn't flowing between us. I grabbed her ass and pulled her hips to me as I ran my tongue along her swollen labia. I had gone down on her so many times I knew exactly what she liked. I sucked her clit into my mouth, tightened my grip on her ass, and went to work.

As her breathing escalated, she grabbed the top of the shower door with one hand and the back of my head with the other, then bucked her hips so hard that my teeth cut into the backs of my lips, but I didn't care. I wanted her to climax so badly, and she did, in loud shuddering groans. Loud enough that the whole floor probably heard her.

She released my head, and I drew in a satisfied breath before straightening up. My knees popped in protest. Ang chuckled and pulled me in for another deep kiss.

"I love tasting myself on you," she said before cleaning my lips with her tongue. I shuddered with pleasure and gave her a wink. I rinsed my face off quickly in the shower stream before she shut it off.

We dried off with her oversized, super plush towels. I took a moment to ponder why I was still using my old threadbare army issue towels and made a mental note to buy myself some nicer ones.

I didn't want to put my grimy clothes back on so Ang said I could borrow her towel, and suggested I make a run for it down the corridor to my studio. I gave her a mischievous grin, wrapped myself up in her towel, gathered up my stuff, and poked my head out of the door. The corridor was clear. I had my door key at the ready and made a mad dash down the hallway, my bare feet barely making a sound on the thin, heavily worn carpet. Ang laughed heartily as she watched from her door, also wrapped in a towel.

I reached my door and unlocked it in a flash.

Just as I stepped through the door, I heard the familiar voice of our landlord, followed by Ang saying, "Oh shit," and the sound of her door slamming.

"Hey, uh, Viv." His voice carried down the corridor as I closed my door and stifled a laugh. I bolted it and shuffled into my studio, juggling my motorcycle helmet, riding jacket, boots, and running gear. I dropped it all in the bathroom and allowed the towel to drop too. I began sorting out items, putting away my running shoes and riding boots, tossing sweaty clothes and Ang's towel in the laundry basket, and hanging up my jacket. I stood in the bathroom, naked, and considered getting dressed. Wearing clothes seemed liked the last thing I wanted to do, so I opted for a pair of loose boxer shorts and a beater. I lotioned up and put on some fresh deodorant.

I considered calling Jared to tell him what happened on my ride home. He was normally the first person I talked to after I let the rage take over. But my mood had improved drastically, and the hollowness left was no longer an emotional void, but a physical one. I was ravenous and it was time for dinner. I threw together a quick vegetable and tofu stir fry with brown rice and plowed through it while I read the rest of *Norwegian Wood*.

By the time I finished the book, night had fallen, and the fatigue of the day had taken over. I pulled a blanket up to my chin, not even bothering to fold out the futon, and fell asleep immediately. My sleep tended to be light and fraught with bad dreams, but that night I was so deeply under no dreams came.

Chapter Four

I woke the next morning in the same position that I had fallen asleep. My body ached from the previous day's trail run, and not moving all night. I rose slowly, my joints popping in protest, and fed my fish before opening the blinds to let in the early morning light. Sliding the window open a crack, I was greeted by the sounds of Midtown waking up. Dogs barked, light-rail trains rushed by, car doors slammed, and the occasional bird sang.

I went through my usual stretching routine, followed by abs, pushups, burpees, lunges, and squats. My studio was over the garage, so I didn't have to worry about annoying any downstairs neighbors with my exertions. By the time I was through, sweat dripped and my body was nice and loose. The pain and stiffness had mostly receded.

Leaning against the kitchen counter, I sipped tea and checked my cell phone. I was not great about paying attention to it. Cell phones were still a fairly recent technology, and having grown up without one, I resented the importance people had suddenly put on having immediate access to me.

I had missed several text messages and a call from Audre, and I was slightly ashamed, knowing I should have checked in with her at some point during the previous day, especially after she had brought up meeting her family.

Audre was fairly unflappable. Her cool, calm demeanor a near constant. The text messages and voicemail turned out to be her expressing concern over my well-being, rather than the anger I had expected. I reminded myself that Audre was her own unique person, and what I had been trained to tolerate from others were not behaviors that Audre demonstrated. I smiled at my cell phone as I recognized and appreciated Audre for who she was. I sent her a text in return, confirming that I was alive and well, and asking for a phone date during her lunch break. She replied with *Yes!* :-)

With that, I went about getting showered, dressed, and fed before heading out to my therapy appointment. There was a small safe hidden under my bathroom sink where I kept my tip money...my life savings, really. Alexia got paid out of that pot of money, so I pulled out some cash and tucked it into my pocket.

I was in the habit of jogging to Alexia's office since it was in Midtown and parking in her neighborhood was difficult. It was a cool spring morning, and the jog was invigorating. I climbed the stairs to the second-floor lobby and took a seat. I leaned back on the bench feeling good.

It hadn't been too long ago when each time I arrived at Alexia's office I was in crisis, so to be sitting there at peace was a big deal. I looked down at the green carpet between my sneakers and pondered what I wanted to talk about, then I remembered the near miss on the freeway the day before and losing my temper. I groaned, running a hand through my short hair and resting my head against the wall to look up at the art deco design on the ceiling.

I heard the telltale delicate click of heels upstairs, followed by Alexia's face popping over the third-floor bannister, looking down at me.

"Come on up, Vivian." She smiled, and then her face disappeared. We had a routine where she met me at the door, invited me in, and I handed her $100 in cash as I entered her office.

"Have a seat," she said, her voice calm and mellow.

I sat in my usual spot, at the end of the leather couch, directly across from her chair. She closed the door and sat, crossing her legs and resting a yellow legal pad on her lap, pen in hand. Her usual pose.

"So, what would you like to talk about today, Vivian?"

I paused, not wanting to say it. Alexia tilted her head to the side ever so slightly. I broke eye contact with her and stared out of the massive picture window over her left shoulder. That was where I spent most of my time looking when I was in her office, because it was easier to talk to her if I wasn't looking right at her.

The building across the street was eternally under construction, and the tree outside her window was filling out with new spring leaves that shuddered in the breeze. Alexia waited patiently for me to speak.

I crossed my legs. "I...I lost my temper yesterday."

Alexia nodded, unfazed, and waited for me to go on.

I walked her through nearly being broadsided on the freeway by a careless driver, and how I lost it and booted the car. I went on to share how I had allowed myself to become fully engulfed in the rage and that I was disappointed in myself for going down that path after working so hard to garner some sort of control over my temper.

When I finally ran out of steam, Alexia jotted a quick note and looked back up to me. I made eye contact with her, ready to hear what she had to say. She didn't speak immediately. Her face remained calm and nonjudgmental, which was a relief. Though she had never had a negative reaction to anything I had said to her, I had been raised by a mother with a hair-trigger temper, which primed me to expect negative responses. But none came.

"Let me start by saying that I am glad you made it home safely. Your response is not unexpected, we've talked through similar reactions in the past, though it is clear you are disappointed by how you responded yesterday. And that's important."

She paused, and I pondered that last bit. *My disappointment in myself is important?* I had a moment where I thought Alexia was perhaps no longer a good fit but decided to hear her out.

"Because you're aware, Vivian. You are now aware that your aggression and rage are not always the correct response. That in itself is a big deal. Would you apologize to the woman now, the one whose car you kicked, if you could?"

"Of course!"

"Now think back to yourself five years ago, or even two years ago. I want you to really consider a time when the rage took over back then and how you felt about it afterward. Would you have been disappointed in yourself and would you have wanted to apologize?"

I thought back and cringed at a foggy memory of slamming a woman's hand in a door after I caught her stealing from my locker in the barracks. How I had felt nothing afterward aside from continued anger that she had tried to steal from me. No guilt over breaking her fingers and no disappointment in myself.

I looked back at Alexia, my eyes wide. She gave me a small smile in return, along with a slow nod.

"You've come a long way, Vivian."

I gave her a lopsided, uncomfortable grin. I wasn't good at accepting compliments.

"So, I'd like to talk more about where this comes from. We have already established that what triggers your anger, your rage, is when someone tries to take something from you or harm you. Do you agree?"

I nodded and looked out of the window again, picking at a cuticle.

"And we had previously discovered that it may be tied to your relationship with your brother, Joey, when you were children."

I snorted derisively. "I wouldn't use the word *relationship* to describe it. I was stuck with that sadistic bastard. He tormented me well beyond what would be considered normal sibling stuff. And our mom didn't do a damn thing to protect me. I survived my childhood, yes, but that's about it."

Alexia nodded, jotting down a quick note. She paused and appeared to reconsider her approach.

"Okay, so let's talk about that. When you were a child and still living with your mom and brother, how did you respond when your brother did something hurtful or harmful?"

I fixed Alexia with a glare. We had already been through that conversation and I didn't want to dredge it up again. She met my glare and didn't back down. I sighed.

"Fine. As far back as I can remember I would respond to his bullshit by losing my temper. I would try to dish out whatever he had done to me. But he was bigger and stronger and would strike back twice as hard. Many times, I would end up with a nasty deep-purple bruise, split lip, or black eye if I tried to stand up for myself. But I never stopped. Never surrendered. I'd stand up for myself and get beaten twice as hard. That's just how it was." I had picked my cuticle so badly that it was bleeding. I grabbed a tissue from the side table and wrapped it around my finger. "And you know what? My mom, fucking Bernadette, never questioned my injuries. Not once. Never offered an ice pack or to take me to the doctor. She'd always just say, 'Stop badgering your brother.'"

I gritted my teeth and squeezed my finger through the tissue. The pressure on my throbbing fingertip made it hurt more, which gave a bit of relief.

"And as a teenager and adult, when someone tries to take something from you or harm you. You've responded in the same way?"

"You know I have, at least, until I started coming here a couple years ago. I've put the brakes on myself so many times. Times when I normally would have lashed out. So, that's something. But yesterday, I backslid." I paused, listening to the street noise coming through the open window. I uncrossed and recrossed my legs. Alexia waited. "Look, I see where you're trying to steer me. Yes, I had a fucked-up childhood. My self-defense mechanism has carried into adulthood and has never actually helped me. I get it. And I'm doing better, but I backslid yesterday. So, I shouldn't be so hard on myself. Right? I get it."

"So, let's talk about what you can do differently next time, okay?"

I nodded at her and we talked through options for how I would handle it the next time I found myself reacting with anger. Options other than pummeling someone.

After our session ended, I was exhausted. I wanted a big hug and some good food. I texted Audre to see if she was available to meet up during her lunch break, and she was.

Chapter Five

I walked a few blocks over and caught the light-rail train, hopping off at *N* Street and walking the last couple of blocks to Audre's office building. She worked for the state as an analyst, inside an imposing stone building across from the state capitol. I spotted her standing out front, a big smile on her face as she watched me walk up. Her lips were a perfect deep shade of purple that coordinated with her eye shadow and blouse. Audre had a way with her makeup and outfits. She was always so well put together; her clothes were high quality and selected with care.

I took the hand she held out to me, her ring and bracelet shimmering in the sunlight, and pulled her in for a much-needed hug. Audre was not one to shy away from public affection, even in front of her office, and gave me a long, gentle hug in return. I nuzzled into the crook of her neck, inhaling the comforting scent of her lotion mixed with her perfume. I kissed her cheek and we walked hand in hand to a nearby restaurant frequented by politicians, lobbyists, and the press corps.

I was exceptionally underdressed in my jeans, running shoes, and a polo. Thankfully, they let me in because my shirt was collared. I had a moment of feeling out of place, but Audre sent a loving smile across the table at me and everything else fell to the wayside.

I indulged in the charcuterie plate, an Arnold Palmer, and green salad to round it out. Audre ordered a dish with risotto, prawns, and veggies plus a glass of white wine. I was surprised by that, since she had to return to work after lunch. As she took dainty sips of her wine I chuckled when I saw that her lip stain left a mark on the fine crystal.

She raised an eyebrow at me. "Yes?"

Stifling the chuckle, I spoke in a low tone, so as not to be overheard. "Do you recall the first time you came over to my studio and we made out?"

"Of course, how could I forget?" She gave a low chuckle of her own.

"Well, after you left, I saw in the mirror that I had your lipstick smeared all around my mouth. I tried wiping it off with a tissue. That didn't work. I tried washing it off and using a real towel. That didn't work. I don't wear lipstick, obviously, and hadn't dated anyone who wore it. It was that long wear stuff and man was it hard to remove. Jared got a good laugh at me over that."

Audre let out a delighted giggle that drew curious smiles from neighboring tables. I was self-conscious that people were judging us, but as I scanned the faces, they all appeared friendly, which helped me relax back into our lunch.

We took a break from the conversation to enjoy our meal. I savored the rich cheeses, meats, and olives on my plate, a rarity for me, as I mainly ate yogurt, bananas, quinoa, chicken, and vegetables. Audre took her time with her meal, exhibiting some of the absolute best table manners I had ever seen. She handled her utensils with grace, took tiny bites, and chewed delicately, occasionally dabbing at her lips with the deep-burgundy cloth napkin. My mother would have been impressed. The thought of my mother reminded me that we still needed to talk about her family.

I took a sip from the sweating wine glass in front of me that held a particularly good Arnold Palmer and then cleared my throat.

"You mentioned the other day that you're ready to introduce me to your family. Can we talk about that?"

"Of course. I would like to invite you over to my place this Sunday—if you're available. We always do a big family lunch after church, so that would be a great time for you to meet everyone and share a meal with them."

"I am available and that sounds really great. It's funny, we've been seeing each other for over a year and I haven't been to your house yet... I look forward to spending time with you in your own space, is what I'm trying to say."

"I'm looking forward to that too," she said, taking my hand briefly before returning hers to her lap.

"Is there anything I need to know?"

"Like what?"

"Like, are there any relatives I need to be given a heads-up about?"

"Even if there were, I wouldn't tell you. I want you going in without any preconceived notions. I want you to go in with a fresh slate and develop your own impressions of people."

"That's fair." I thought for a moment. "Is this going to be a problem?" I asked, motioning to my short hair and self as a whole.

"What are you getting at, Vivian?"

"Well, I look like a big old dyke, and I'm white."

Audre nodded, sipping her wine as she considered what I had said.

She set her glass down gently and gave me an appraising look. "Have you ever been the only white person in the room?"

"Sure, plenty of times when I was in the military in the south. I lived and trained in units where I was the only white person."

She nodded.

"I was asking more about your family. Will there be an issue that you're dating a) a white person, and b) a butch woman?"

Audre's expression lingered somewhere between amused and weary, and I got the hint.

"Like I said, Viv. You'll be fine."

I nodded and dropped it. We finished our meal in peace, and I walked her back to her office, her arm looped through mine. She gave me a gentle kiss on the cheek before we parted ways. I watched her walk through the tall, stately doors to her office building, her hips swaying and heels clicking on the stone entryway.

I caught the light-rail train and hopped off at the Twenty-Fourth Street station, right across from the back of my apartment building, thankful for an uneventful ride. I had plenty of time before I had to get ready for work, but

I didn't feel much like running after such a decadent lunch.

I changed into some shorts and a beater, grabbed a book, pen, and notepad, and headed down to the pool. I dragged a deck chair into the sun and sat back, pen in hand, and cracked open my well-worn copy of Clement Salvadori's *Motorcycle Journeys Through California*. It was time to plan another big ride before the summer weather arrived.

I had previously folded page corners for two rides I had wanted to do. The first being the Pozo Loop around Morro Bay and San Luis Obispo. At 244 miles, it would give me a great tour of my old stomping grounds and an excuse to visit Jared in Morro Bay.

Then I flipped to the back of the book to the other folded page. Ride #16. A lap of California. Coming in at a whopping 2,500 miles. To be attempted only between April and November, for good reason. I read through Clement's commentary about the ride and waffled between excitement and disappointment. I knew damn well I couldn't take that much time off work, especially with Pride season right around the corner. But damn I really wanted to do the full route. I huffed and turned back to the Pozo Loop section, rereading the chapter and wondering if I could actually pull it off and keep an enjoyable pace rather than rushing to get back to work.

I jotted some notes down on the pad. My script was bold, legible, all caps, as I had been conditioned to do in the military. There was the sound of someone opening a window overhead, but I didn't bother looking up. I knew I had no privacy on the pool deck and continued jotting notes, but noted the smell of cigarette smoke blow by, which annoyed me. I looked up and saw my upstairs neighbor leaning out of his window, smoking a cigarette. I was surprised to see him awake, as my observation of him was that he was nocturnal. His long, scraggly brown hair rippled in the slight breeze. I watched as his pasty-white skin turned pink from the sunlight in the short amount of time it took him to smoke his cigarette. He flicked the end of the cigarette, sending the burning cherry onto the concrete, and threw the butt into the bushes. I shouted at him as he began to slide his window closed.

"Hey! Hey!"

He paused and leaned back out of his window, looking down at me, a timid, slightly astonished look on his face.

"Yeah?"

I adjusted my tone to be less confrontational. "Dude. You need to come down here and pick up your cigarette butt."

He looked at me blankly, and then recognition registered. "Don't you live downstairs from me?"

"Yes. And you need to come down here and pick up your cigarette butt."

"Thanks for the cookies," he said as he slid the window closed and shut his blinds.

"What?" I recalled that the previous year I had lost my temper when he'd overflowed his bathtub, flooding my bathroom. I had gotten so mad that I went upstairs and pounded on his door, soaking wet and wearing nothing but a towel. I had screamed at him like a madwoman and stormed off. Later, I had baked him some cookies as a peace offering and left them at his door.

He had been somewhat of a nuisance the whole time I had lived there. Repeatedly overflowing his bathtub. Pacing all night long. And no doubt I got plenty of secondhand smoke from him. He was a hermit, and from what I had heard he was an author. An author of what, I had no idea. Either way, I had let him get under my skin. I had a choice to make...get angry or handle it like an adult.

I gathered up my stuff and went inside, passing through the underground garage to get from the pool to the main building. The garage was extra dark as my eyes adjusted from being out in the sun. I headed to the building manager's apartment, which was at the end of the corridor on the first floor. After I knocked, I heard a bunch of shuffling around and the sound of doors closing before the manager's door opened a crack. He pushed his face out and the smell of overflowing ashtrays, trash, and something chemical hit me. He looked like shit, his eyes rimmed red, skin greasy and blotched, his hair and goatee in need of a wash and brush.

"Hiya, Viv. What can I do for ya?" He spoke in a quick, clipped manner. I groaned internally. He had a bit of a meth problem and was clearly in the middle of a binge.

I did my best to keep my voice even and calm. "Hey, Paul. I wanted to let you know that the dude who lives upstairs from me—"

"Binks."

"Binks?"

Paul nodded in the affirmative and scratched at his scalp with dirty fingernails.

"Uh, okay, so I wanted to let you know that... Binks...just threw a cigarette butt out his window. I asked him to pick it up, but he didn't. I know the building owner is a stickler for us keeping the grounds clean, so...just giving you a heads-up."

Paul nodded again and continued scraping at his scalp frantically, the way a dog with a bad itch does. "Okay. Yeah. Thanks for letting me know. I'll handle it." I knew he would not do a damn thing about it.

"Thanks," I said and turned on my heel, heading down the dingy corridor back to my studio.

He called after me. "Oh, hey, Viv. I tried to catch you the other day, but you must not have heard me. I have something for you."

I walked back to his door. He slipped an envelope out through the crack and then closed the door before I could say anything more. I slit the envelope open and pulled out a single sheet of paper that looked semiprofessional. It notified me that the building owner was raising my rent by $100, which was bloody murder for my 418 square foot studio. I heard the deadbolt on Paul's door engage. The creep had probably been watching me through the peephole.

With an eyeroll so hard it hurt, I headed back to my studio, the letter clutched tightly in my hand.

Chapter Six

My heart pounded as I set up my station for work. I needed to make more money to cover rent, and I was nervous about asking Sheila for extra shifts. I heard her chatting with the bartender at the back station as she handed out tills. Their banter elicited lots of loud laughter from Sheila, which was a relief. Perhaps if she was in a good mood, she would go easier on me than she had been since I had returned from medical leave.

Sheila came up front and roughly put a till down on the spotless bar. As was customary, she stood by while I counted out the money and signed for it. My pen barely left the paper before she had snatched it up and stepped away.

"Uh, Sheila?" I asked hesitantly, hating the hint of desperation in my voice.

Sheila stopped but didn't turn to face me. "Yeah."

"I wonder if I can pick up an extra shift each week. They raised my rent."

Without a hitch she shot a glance at me over her shoulder and said, "Sounds like a personal problem. Get a roommate." She lit a cigarette and walked away, smoke trailing over her shoulder. I watched as she turned the corner, heading for the door to the smoking alley.

"Damnnn," Jen said as she walked up behind me.

I rubbed the freshly shorn hair on the back of my head and looked to Jen. She set down a tray of clean glasses and started stacking them, looking at me in the mirror behind the bar.

"What're you gonna do, Viv?"

"Fuck." *Cut back on therapy, I guess. That's my biggest expense aside from rent.* One thing I knew about Sheila was that she could hold a grudge for years. So, if she didn't trust me anymore, I was forever on her shit list. I gave it another moment of consideration. "Don't worry, Jen, I'll still tip you out like I always have."

I met her eyes in the mirror and the set of her jaw showed that she was offended. "This isn't about me, Viv. Just worried about you, friend."

"Thanks." I patted her lower back as I headed to the back to load up the ice bucket. My worries dissipated once the night got rolling and the club filled up. I was too busy to do anything but play my role as fun loving bartender. Thoughts of my life outside the bar doors were put on pause.

*

Sunday morning blew by in a flash. I slept for a few hours after work, went for a run around McKinley Park, showered, and dressed, choosing my clothes and styling my hair with care since I was meeting Audre's family for the first time.

I was ready a bit early, so I sat down with a protein bar and book to pass the last bit of time before I had to leave. Since finishing *Norwegian Wood,* I had picked up a well-worn copy of Tom Robbins' *Jitterbug Perfume* at the used bookstore across the street from work. I had read it many years before, blowing through it while riding in the back of a cramped C-130 on my way to a hot, dusty place that would test my mettle. I couldn't help but chuckle at the first few lines of the second chapter:

> *Real artists almost never live in studio apartments. There isn't enough space and the lighting is all wrong. Clerks live in studio apartments. File clerks, shop clerks, law clerks, community college students, elderly widows, and unmarried waitresses...*

I was no longer a student, but I was an unmarried barkeep. I enjoyed living in my studio. I liked having my own space. Space that was utilitarian and easy to manage. But faced with increased rent, the love for my home was tinged with anxiety. My phone pinged. Checking it, I saw I had a text message from Audre letting me know they were leaving church, and to head on over to her house.

We'd been dating for over a year and had always either gone out or spent time at my studio, though I knew she owned a home in the Colonial Village neighborhood. Her aunt, sister, and her sister's baby all lived with her. I had respected her choice not to introduce me over the first year, but it had bothered me a bit.

I set down the book, checked myself in the bathroom mirror, and headed out with butterflies in my stomach. It wasn't a long drive, and I arrived before she did. Parked,

I watched as her gleaming, glossy black 1970s Mercedes M Coupe pulled into the driveway. She stepped out, closing the door with a solid *thunk* that only well-made luxury vehicles produced. She stood in the driveway, smiling at me as I locked up my truck. She was dressed a bit more conservatively than I was used to seeing. Her skirt a bit longer, not as form fitting, her blouse not showing any cleavage, though she still wore impossibly high heels. Her outfit was as well thought out as always, highlighted with just the right necklace, bracelets, and earrings.

I strode across the street and took the hand she held out to me. She gave me a quick peck on the cheek, and we waited as her parents pulled into the driveway of their own home next door. I drew in my breath and configured my face with a confident smile. Audre squeezed my hand as her parents approached.

"Mom, Dad. This is Vivian. Vivian, this is my mother, Catherine. And my father, Frederick."

"Hello, Vivian," her mother said, extending a hand to me. We shook hands, her grip surprisingly firm given how petite she was. Her father also gave me a solid shake.

"Mr. and Mrs. Williams, it's a pleasure to meet you both."

Audre motioned for her parents to go on inside. We followed closely behind them, Audre giving me a hopeful smile and wink that helped me relax a tiny bit.

Inside I was greeted warmly by her aunt Dot, sister Josephine, and a little girl who jabbered at me in toddler speak. I stooped down to greet the little one, shaking her sticky hand, which she found hilarious and toddled off with a fit of the giggles.

"That's my baby, Ruby."

Before I could respond, Josephine cut across the room to stop Ruby from pulling all the coasters off the coffee table. I drew in a deep breath and found that the house was full of the savory smells of roasting chicken, lemon, and garlic, and a sweet note of some sort of cake. Audre put me to work, getting drinks for everyone, which I appreciated. The best thing for me when in a new social situation was to be given a job to do.

Once I had finished passing out drinks, Audre patted the empty spot between her and her mother on the couch, so I sat between them. Her father and aunt sat across from me on a love seat, and her sister was on the floor playing blocks with Ruby.

Everyone sipped on their drinks, not saying anything at first.

"It smells great in here," I said, clearing my throat. That seemed to break the ice because her aunt went into a description of what she had prepared for lunch, and the conversation flowed from there. We chatted for a while, everyone contributing except for Audre's dad, who sat listening.

All the women eventually got up to go set the table and finish up the meal prep.

"Is there anything I can do to help?" I asked but was told I should stay and keep her dad company. I raised my eyebrows at Audre, and she gave me a smirk.

Once we were alone, I tried to think of something to talk to him about as we sat awkwardly across from each other. I spotted the large military signet ring on his right hand and nodded toward it.

"Audre tells me you are retired from the air force, Mr. Williams."

"Yes. That's what brought us to Sacramento. Back before McClellan and Mather closed." He gave me an appraising glance, though it wasn't done in a threatening manner.

"You a veteran, Vivian?"

"Yes, sir. US army."

He grunted in approval. "What did you do there?"

"PsyOps, sir."

He cracked a huge smile, slapped his knee, and let out a loud bark of laughter. "A spook! Well, that tells me all I need to know about you."

I gave him a lopsided, unsure smile. "And you? What did you do in the air force?"

"Logistics. I was a loadmaster."

"Much appreciated. Thank you for your service." He nodded and clinked his signet ring on his glass, his face losing the smile, returning to quiet contemplation.

I took the opportunity to get up and look at the framed photos on the mantel and hung about the room. Pictures of Audre with her sorority sisters, photos of big groups of her family, a black-and-white picture of a younger version of her dad in uniform, looking sharp. As expected, Audre's house was tastefully decorated and immaculately clean. Accent pieces here and there that matched her furniture and paint scheme. Everything below three feet was methodically baby proofed for her niece.

As I stood peering at a picture of Audre as a little girl, front teeth missing and her hair tightly pulled into pigtails, a hand touched my lower back. I nearly jumped out of my skin. Audre's dad chuckled from across the room. I turned and found myself face to face with Audre.

"Ooh, sorry, Viv. Just wanted to let you know that lunch is ready."

"I love all of these pictures. Spending time in your space is really helping me get to know you even better. Thanks for inviting me."

She nodded and led the way to the kitchen table, which was down two low steps in what was clearly an addition to the small house. Once we were all seated, the family joined hands. I had Audre on my left and her Aunt Dot on my right. Mr. Williams led the family in a prayer, and I bowed my head like I knew was expected. Despite being an atheist, I listened and found his prayer incredibly thoughtful and full of love, which choked me up. We all said "Amen" when he finished. I dabbed at a tear, trying to be sly about it, but Mrs. Williams, who was sitting across from me, saw and gave me a warm smile.

We dove into the hearty meal of roasted chicken, rice, rolls, green salad with citrus, and finished up with Josephine's lemon cake. I enjoyed listening to the friendly banter around the table and joined in a bit. By the end I was stuffed and satisfied in more ways than one. I had been nourished by food and by Audre's family.

I helped clear the table and immediately took up the task of washing dishes. Audre and her Aunt Dot both scolded me, but I insisted, since they had done all the cooking. Audre's house was a bit older and didn't have a dishwasher, which was fine with me. I hand-washed the dishes, enjoying the view of her flower garden out of the kitchen window. Zinnias and marigolds swayed in the faint breeze.

Audre dried the dishes and put them away. Her parents and aunt filed through the kitchen to say goodbye and said a host of kind words to me. Her mother and aunt both gave me a peck on the check as I looked over my shoulder at them from the sink. Josephine waved at me from the threshold with a passed-out Ruby in her arms.

Not long after, we finished the dishes and moved into the empty living room. Audre snuggled up to me on the couch, my arm wrapped about her shoulder, her head on my chest.

"Is this okay?" I asked, a bit leery of someone walking in.

"Yes. Mom and Dad went to their house next door to nap. Dot, Josephine, and Ruby are all napping in their rooms down the hall. And even if someone did walk through, it'd be okay. Not to worry, they all approve of you," she said with a contented chuckle.

Her bracelets clinked gently as she took my hand in hers. I rested my chin on top of her head and we sat like that for a good long time, adrift in our own thoughts.

I had to chase off thoughts of Ang several times. My mind kept making comparisons about how spending time with Ang always left me feeling empty and lonely, whereas Audre always made me feel full and loved. Eventually those thoughts passed, and I went to that place where no thoughts came and I was able to just sit there in my happiness as Audre's breathing slowed and she fell asleep. I didn't want to be anywhere else. Right there, in that moment, I was at peace.

Chapter Seven

Spring and summer passed in a flash. I continued my sexual relationship with Ang, though in between dates I thought of her less and less. Thankfully work ramped up for the summer season and I was pulling in enough tips to absorb the higher rent without having to cut back on therapy. I was invited back to lunches with Audre's family every Sunday. My cold sesame bowtie pasta salad became a favorite of the Williamses and I was happy to bring it to share each week. I had a visit from Jared and went on several hikes and runs with my metamour, Kate. She and Ang were still going strong, which no longer stung like it used to.

Before I knew it, it was Labor Day weekend and the Rainbow Festival. The streets of Lavender Heights were closed off, where vendor booths and a big stage were set up. The summer season at the gay bars kicked off in June with the Gay Pride Festival and closed with the Rainbow Festival in September. I had a fourteen-hour day of slinging drinks ahead of me. The bar was crammed and stifling. The floor to ceiling windows on the front side of the bar were propped open, letting in a hot breeze that didn't help matters.

There was a ton of extra security inside the bar and out front. Buck had a line out of the door and around the corner. She did her best to check IDs, take cover charges, and keep count so we didn't go over the occupancy rate. Tick, the DJ, was killing it, and Jen was running nonstop to keep us stocked up with clean glasses, ice, and garnishes.

At one point in the afternoon, I realized I was out of cans of Red Bull, which was a problem since Red Bull mixed drinks were all the rage that year. Jen swished by, arms full of bottled water, headed for the cooler under the counter.

"Hey Jen. I'm out of Red Bull. And rum. Can you grab me some?"

She looked up at me as she crouched on the floor, lining up waters in the cooler.

"Shit. You're out too? So's everybody else and our order was short this week. We'll have to run over to Blue Sky and grab some from the boys. I'll go call them and grab Sheila to cover your station really quick."

I kept pouring beers and mixing what drinks I could until Jen returned with an agitated Sheila in tow. Sheila took over my station, throwing me a scowl and then turning around, all smiles to the line of women waiting to order drinks.

Jen and I grabbed an empty milk crate each and snuck out of the side door, ran across the street and through the alley. Cheer SF was doing a routine at the main stage at the intersection of K Street and Twentieth, but we didn't have time to watch. We slid our way past the long line to get into Blue Sky, waving to the bouncer as we squeezed through the door, much to the chagrin of the customers waiting to get in. Blue Sky was wall to wall bodies, so we had to weave our way through. I held the empty milk crate over my head so I didn't have to make room for it between bodies. As we passed down the main hallway, I heard hip-hop coming from one room, electronic dance music from another, and as we reached the back bar, there was country blaring. Under the DJ booth was a storage area. We met the bar manager there and he loaded up our milk crates with Red Bulls and bottles of rum. I signed for it all so our bar could be charged back for them. Both clubs had the same owner, so we often swapped supplies.

Once our crates were full, the manager snuck us out of the emergency exit that spit us out into the alley. We hustled back to our club in the 100-degree heat, sweating from our exertions. One of the bouncers out front of our place saw us coming and waved us through the side door, so we wouldn't have to navigate the front door and crowded lobby with our payload. Once we were back behind the bar Jen went about distributing the rum and Red Bulls between the bartenders.

Sheila finished up a transaction and turned my station back over to me.

"I've got the bar credit card. I'm heading to the store to get more Red Bull," she said as she dug her hand into my tip jar, took a wad of cash, and walked away. I stifled my immediate rage and desire to punch her in the back of the head.

"Asshole," I said under my breath before getting back to work.

As the afternoon blazed on and the crowd got more and more drunk and rowdy, I took solace in being behind the bar. I had control, even amid the chaos. In the early part of the evening, the crowd thinned out a bit as people left to get food. A new surge of people came in after dark, many sunburned, drunk, and dazed. Others looked like they had gone home for a disco nap and to freshen up.

After nine Ang and Kate came in, all smiles, giving me hugs across the bar. I was relieved to see that Ang appeared to be mostly sober. Later Audre and her crew showed up. Audre was dressed to the nines in a tight cocktail dress and heels, her hair in finger curls, and makeup on point. I couldn't help but ogle her a little bit between customers.

I was happy to see Ang, Audre, and Kate sharing conversation and laughs in the front room, and even all dancing together in the back room at one point. I made it through the rest of my shift in a blur, relieved when Buck finally said it was last call and Tick slowed down and stopped the music. The bouncers cleared the place out and locked up. I hurried through cleaning up my station while Jen went about picking up all the glasses, beer bottles, and discarded napkins and squashed lemon rinds throughout the bar. At last, I was able to count out my tips and till. My feet screamed with relief as I sat down. I took a moment to chug an entire glass of water before getting back to work. The other two bartenders joined me, spreading out their tills, calculators, and tip jars on the bar top.

We all got to down to business counting out our tills, under the watchful eyes of Sheila. My drawer was short. Really short. I was usually right on point, rarely short more than a few cents. I started over, counting my drawer out more slowly, but had the same result. I counted it out a third time and was still exactly twenty dollars short.

"Sheila, I'm short," I said, mystified. The other two bartenders looked at me curiously, knowing I was never off.

"Oh. How much?"

"Twenty."

"You know that won't do. Take it out of your tips." Her voice was syrupy and slimy, and I didn't like it.

I huffed and counted twenty dollars out of my tips, placed the money on top of my till, and handed the whole thing to her, my temper starting a low boil. We both signed off on it and she walked away, smiling smugly. I exchanged a look with Buck, who knew me and my temper well, and shook her head at me. I drew in a deep breath, counted out what was left of my tips, and slid a cut across the bar to Jen.

"Thanks for hustling today, Jen. You did good."

Jen tipped an imaginary hat to me, slid the cash into her deep shorts pocket, and went back to stacking glasses.

I slid into the narrow hallway where the timeclock was and punched out. It was a Sunday so the schedule for the next week was posted. I checked it to see if Sheila had been able to give me any extra shifts but found that I was not on the schedule at all. Someone named Amy was in my place. I stood there, staring with blurry eyes at the schedule thumbtacked to the cork board, for far too long, trying to comprehend what I was looking at. But the longer I looked at it, the more it sunk in that I was off the schedule.

I walked back out to the front bar where Sheila was signing off on the other two tills.

"Hey, Sheila?"

"Yup," she said, not even looking at me.

"I'm not on the schedule next week."

Everybody stopped what they were doing, looking at me in shock. Sheila finally turned to me, cigarette in hand, pen behind her ear, disdain on her face.

"You're right, you're not."

"I...why?"

"Slow season starts next week; we need to cut back."

"Cut back? There's literally someone else on the schedule in my place. I don't see how that's cutting back. And it's not like you are replacing me with someone cheaper. We all make seven dollars an hour and survive on customer tips."

"Take it up with Danny." She ashed her cigarette on the floor and walked out of the room with the cash tills under her arm. I stood in the middle of the bar, mouth agape, hands limp at my side. Everyone stared at me, frozen. I drew in a breath, shut my mouth, and looked to Buck who was leaning against the wall, arms crossed. She scuffed the toe of one of her boots on the floor and met my gaze with sad eyes.

The rage boiled up fast. Chest tight and heart pounding, I clenched my jaw so hard that my teeth ground loudly. My vision grew fuzzy and then became crystal clear. In that moment I wanted to hurt Sheila. It occurred to me that she intentionally shorted my drawer when I had run to Blue Sky to grab supplies. Then she blatantly stole from my tip jar. And last of all, took my job from me. My hands burned with my desire to pummel her, though she had no doubt locked herself in the office upstairs.

I grabbed my tip bucket off the bar and took long, angry strides out of the bar to the front hall. I pistoned back my leg and push-kicked the crash bar with all my night, flinging the massive front door open. It hit the stucco wall with a fierce crash as I strode through it. I wanted to put my fist through the front window, but knew it wasn't worth it. I had walked to work since parking was impossible during Rainbow Fest. But instead of catching a cab I recognized I needed to burn off the anger so opted to walk home. I headed up Twenty-First Street taking huge angry strides, jaw still clenched, metal tip bucket swinging at my side in a death grip. As I approached Twenty-First and *P*, no longer in queer friendly Lavender Heights, I spotted a crowd of guys taking up the entire sidewalk out front of another closed bar, smoking and screwing around.

One spotted me and elbowed his friend.

"Hey, dyke! What's the hurry?"

I kept walking toward them, not replying. He squared up in front of my path.

"Hey, I asked you a question, you fucking fag. Don't ignore me."

He was built like a refrigerator and had tattoos on his neck and knuckles. His friends looked to have similar backgrounds and were smirking at me, waiting to see what I'd do. Clearly the guy was hoping for me to cower in fear of him, perhaps beg to be allowed to pass. He was mistaken. I didn't slow down at all, in fact I sped up, wound back the arm holding my tip bucket, and using all the force behind my anger at Sheila, I brought the metal tip bucket down on the top of his shaved head. I drew back and swung it down again, this time landing a solid blow to his face as he crumpled.

I expected his friends to attack me, but they all just laughed at him heartily. "Damn, dude, you just got clocked by a chick!" I didn't stop, but hurried along until I had crossed *P* Street, and skirted down a few alleys until I popped out at my apartment building on Twenty-fourth and *Q*.

Hands shaking, I unlocked the lobby door, took the stairs two at a time to the first floor, and locked myself in my studio. In the kitchen I chucked my bloody tip bucket in the sink and sat down heavily on the folding chair. I sat there for a while, willing myself to calm down. By then it was 4:00 a.m. and the whole building was asleep aside from me and my upstairs neighbor, who took up his usual pacing.

Eventually the throbbing of my feet and legs got to be too much. I bent over and began untying my boots. I pulled them off slowly, followed by my disgusting socks. Bartending on particularly busy nights like tonight tended to leave one with sore feet and socks full of sweat and a variety of smells including vodka, Red Bull, beer, and mixers. I pulled out the wad of tip money from my sock, stripped down until I was naked, gathered up the pile of nasty clothes, and headed for the bathroom. I didn't bother turning on the light, preferring to shower in the dark.

After showering I put myself to bed in a beater and boxer shorts, legs still throbbing, and a man's blood drying on the bottom rim of my tip bucket.

Chapter Eight

I slept far into the afternoon, and woke with a foggy brain, stiff legs, aching muscles, and a fever. I hadn't had a fever since the time I had sepsis the previous year. A wave of panic rippled through me as I stared at the popcorn ceiling with burning eyes. I didn't need a thermometer to tell me I had a very high temperature; my aching muscles and joints, sensitive skin, and throbbing head told me all I needed to know. I didn't have any wounds, so I told myself it couldn't be sepsis again. Probably just picked up some crud at work.

All was quiet in the building. Given that it was a holiday, most people were probably at Lake Tahoe. Not much sound on the street, either, aside from occasional car doors slamming and the clang of the light-rail train.

I kicked off the blanket and huffed, annoyed at being sick. I had planned to go talk to Danny about being taken off the schedule. He could usually be found in his office during the day on Mondays, counting piles of cash that had rolled in over the weekend. He owned my club as well as Blue Sky and had an office on the top floor of Blue Sky.

I decided to try to force the fever to break by sweating it out, the way we had been made to do in the army. I sat up and swung my legs over the side of the futon. As my feet touched the thin carpet my head spun and my whole body began to shiver so hard that my teeth clacked together.

"Not good, Chastain. Not good," I said aloud, my voice hoarse and small.

Rather than standing up, I lowered myself to the floor and started doing pushups. I went slowly, as my muscles quivered and threatened to give out. I paused in a plank and held it through the shivers and muscles twitches. Winded almost immediately, I gasped shallowly for air.

I mumbled between gasps, "Fuck." When I thought I couldn't hold the plank any longer, I forced myself to double down and stay in that position. Sweat began to bead up on my forehead, armpits, and my lower back. The muscles in my core finally gave out and I collapsed onto the itchy carpet. I rolled onto my back and began alternating between flutter kicks and crunches. Every move hurt and I wanted so badly to take a cool shower and get back into bed. But as the sweat continued to flow, I kept going. Echoes of past sergeants ranted in the background, pushing me through until I simply couldn't go on. I had more willpower in the tank, but my body had had enough.

I lay on the floor panting, sweat running off me and pooling in the hollow of my neck and belly button. I waited until the room had stopped spinning and my heart had slowed down, then rolled onto my hands and knees and slowly stood up. My vision went black, and stars exploded as the throbbing in my head renewed. I put my hands out to keep my balance and squeezed my eyes closed until I felt steady enough to walk. I shuffled into the bathroom and turned the handle on the shower. As the water flowed, the sound of it hitting the bottom of the bathtub seemed far louder than my ears could handle. I stripped down and carefully stepped into the shower.

The water hitting my skin was like being pricked by a thousand needles. I reached up to adjust the flow and found some relief. The cool water flowed over me and I tried to relax, though the shivering continued. I took my time washing my hair and body, pausing often to rest against the wall and catch my breath. Once I had finished, I toweled off, applied deodorant, and dressed in loose jeans, a black T-shirt, and sneakers. I combed back my hair and put on a gray baseball hat, not wanting to deal with trying to style it. I popped a few Tylenol and sipped water straight from the sink faucet.

I shuffled into the kitchen, downed a big glass of cool water, and ate a banana as I leaned my hip against the counter for support. I didn't sit because I knew if I did, I wouldn't get up again. I waited until the Tylenol started to kick in. My headache and muscle soreness backed off just as bit, and so did the shivers. I knew I was contagious but couldn't be without a job and knew I needed to catch Danny before the bar opened.

I grabbed my keys and headed out of the door. Ang's door was opening as I walked feebly down the long corridor. I hit the button for the elevator. The elevator that I never took because it was a death trap. But I didn't think I could manage the stairs down to the lobby. Ang spotted me swaying near the elevator door, just across from her apartment. She finished locking up and approached.

"Jesus, Viv. You look like shit."

I nodded.

"The elevator?"

I nodded again, focusing so much on staying upright that I couldn't do much talking. The sound of the rickety elevator clanking down from an upper floor was disconcerting.

"Viv, you shouldn't be going anywhere. I'm sure whatever it is can wait."

I shook my head at her. The elevator dinged. I opened the door, pulled aside the gate, and stepped inside. The small compartment smelled like hot garbage and mechanical grease. I lifted my chin at Ang, my way of asking if she wanted to join me in the elevator. She shook her head. I closed the door and the gate, pressing the *L* button for Lobby. The elevator shook and rumbled as it lowered me down to the lobby at a snail's pace. It reached the lobby with a bone rattling *thunk*. I pulled aside the gate and pushed open the door. Ang was waiting for me in the lobby. I rolled my eyes at her and she frowned.

I stepped into the lobby, shutting the gate and door behind me. The subterranean lobby was surprisingly cold. The muscles in my lower back tensed up and the full-body shivers started up again.

"Viv, go back to your studio and lay down. You look like death. Whatever it is can wait."

"It can't."

"Cut the machismo army shit. You need to listen to your body. It is screaming at you to rest. I can see it from here. Go rest. You're going to land yourself in the hospital again, pulling this crap."

Talking was hard, and I knew I needed to reserve my energy for Danny.

"Thank you for your concern, Ang, but I need to go take care of something. I will rest as soon as I am done. I promise."

Concern furrowed her brow and the corners of her eyes as she growled in frustration. But as I stepped past her, she walked with me and held the lobby door open before she headed back in to take the back door to the parking garage.

I got into my truck and drove gingerly to Blue Sky. I snagged a parking spot in the alley and made my way around to the side of the building. I knew the place would be locked up tight, but that staff would already be inside getting ready to open for Happy Hour. I spotted one of the bartenders in back dumping a five-gallon bucket of ice into the bin at his station. On the weekends he bartended dressed in full drag, but right then he was bald headed and dressed in baggy khakis and an aloha shirt. I knocked on the window of the emergency exit and waved to him. He frowned and walked to the door.

"We're closed," he said roughly before turning to get back to work.

I knocked again and he turned. "Hey, I need to talk to Danny. I work around the corner." I was annoyed that he didn't recognize me, since I had seen him at plenty of all-staff meetings. Annoyed, he pushed open the door and let me in.

"Jesus. Looks like you had one too many at the Rainbow Fest, honey," he said before heading back to his station. I wished a hangover were my only problem. I wound my way through the dark, cavernous bar to the back stairs, which I took slowly, pausing often to catch my breath and allow my aching legs to rest. At the top I turned and made my way down the dark hallway to Danny's office. I could hear low voices and the distinct flipping sound of a money counter. I found the door was open.

I knocked on the doorframe, not wanting to barge in. Danny looked up. He was seated behind his desk, and the manager of the Blue Sky, Maggie, sat perched on the corner of the desk as she slid a band around a stack of cash. When she recognized me, she stood up and planted herself at Danny's side.

"What?" Danny asked gruffly. He took a drag of his cigar and his pinky ring glinted from the overhead light.

"Hi, Danny. May I come in? I wanted to talk to you."

"Depends. Who are you?"

Immediately pissed but too sick to care, I did my best to control my tone. "I'm Vivian. I've bartended for you at the women's club for the last six years."

"Oh, hmm." He looked to Maggie and she nodded at him, confirming what I had said. "Okay, Vivian. What do you want?"

I stepped in and stood in front of his desk, exactly three paces away and centered, as if I were reporting to my first sergeant.

"Well, I checked the schedule for next week, and I am not on it. Someone named Amy is in my place. I asked Sheila about it, and she told me to take it up with you."

Danny groaned and I heard him say "Fucking Sheila" under his breath. He took another drag from his cigar and blew the smoke straight up, where it clouded around the light fixture. He had the window closed and the glass was covered with aluminum foil. The room was cluttered with boxes of supplies, files, and in the corner was a table covered in stacks of cash next to a money counter. It was dark and dusty in there, and I began to feel ill between the stagnant, smoky air and the stress from the tension in the room.

Maggie bent down and whispered into Danny's ear. The pounding and ringing in my ears made it so I couldn't hear what she said. As she finished Danny scowled and looked at me.

"It's the slow season, Vivian. We have to cut back. I'm sure you understand."

"With all due respect, sir, I don't understand. I don't understand because there is somebody else scheduled in my place. Cutting back for the slow season doesn't make sense to me when you're adding another person in my place."

"*I'm* not doing *anything*," he said tersely.

"Yes, sorry, I misspoke. Sheila is adding someone in my place."

Danny nodded, appeased. "So, Vivian, just pick up more hours at your other job."

"I-I don't have a second job."

Danny chuckled. "Well, that's just irresponsible. All of the other bartenders have a second job. You can't expect us to pay your way in life." His tone was so heavily condescending I had to pause to make sure I had heard him correctly.

"I'm busy. Will that be all?"

I nodded dumbly, at a loss for words and struggling to remain upright.

"All right then. Buh-bye," he said and shooed me away with his hand, pinky ring glinting again.

I turned and, on my way out, I coughed into my hand and placed it on the door handle. As an excuse I looked over my shoulder and asked, "Do you want this open or closed?"

"Open," he said, not even looking at me. Maggie had returned to her task and Danny had turned to watch her.

I slid my hand off the door handle, hoping he picked up some of whatever the germs were that I had.

Taking the stairs one at a time, my legs threatening to give out on me, I heard the money counter flipping through piles of cash again. I let myself out through the emergency exit and climbed back into my truck. I leaned my head back on the head rest as the thudding increased from my exertions and elevated stress level. I drew in several deep breaths, fending off nausea and trying to slow down the throbbing.

I wondered what the fuck I was going to do. I had cash saved up in the safe under my bathroom sink, but it wouldn't last long. My eyes lost focus as I stared at some graffiti on the cinderblock wall. I was startled by a loud chiming and vibration from the glovebox. Apparently, I had forgotten my cell phone in my truck the day before. Groaning with exertion, I leaned over and flipped open the glovebox and pulled out my cellphone. I didn't recognize the number and really didn't want to talk to anyone but opened my phone and pressed it to my ear.

"Hullo," I croaked.

"Uh, hello. Vivian Chastain?"

"Speaking."

"Hey, Vivian, this is Sergeant Brickhouse."

I straightened up in my seat and my eyes snapped back into focus. "Hi, Sergeant. What can I do for you?"

"How've you been?"

"I, uh, things have been good."

"You sound terrible. Allergies?"

"Probably. How are you, Sergeant? Catch any good cases lately?"

"Actually, I'm not assigned to investigations at the moment. I oversee the Sheriff's Training Academy now."

"Oh, hey, that's great. I can totally see that being a good fit for you. Congrats." I paused, wondering what he wanted from me. "Normally when you call me it's to talk about Crystal Wylie. But, as far as I know she is still locked up at Chowchilla. Unless...did she get early release or something?"

"No, no. Ms. Wylie is still serving out her sentence. I realized the anniversary of your run-in with her had passed, and I wanted to check in on you to see how you're doing. I know that what she did really created upheaval in your life, and if you need support, there are a lot of resources out there. Tell me how you've been faring lately?"

"I, uh. Well, I think you may recall that I finished my degree. I've just been working mostly. And doing lots of trail running. But I...lost my job last night." *Oh, for fuck's sake, Chastain! Stop spilling your guts to this guy.*

I raked my fingernails across my scalp, frustrated at myself for oversharing. I decided to blame it on the fact that I had a fever.

"I see. What is your degree in again?"

"Geology."

"Hmm." He paused, giving me more time to berate myself. "Why don't you come out to the academy this week and take a tour? It's a really great facility and I'd love to show you around."

The Tylenol must have started to wear off because my head throbbed, and my cheeks felt like they were on fire. Clearing my throat, I spoke through the brain fog that was closing the curtains on me. "Sure. Yes, of course."

"Great. I will email you the address. What's your email?"

"I-I don't have email. Or a computer."

"Okay, how about I text it to you?"

"Sounds good." I slumped in my seat, barely able to sit up.

"Okay, Vivian. Talk to you later."

"See you soon, Sarge."

I ended the call and rolled down the window, breathing in fresh air before I passed out and steeling myself for the short drive home.

*

I barely made it to my studio. I flopped down onto the unmade futon. I didn't even have the strength to kick off my shoes or undress. The fatigue and shakes took over and I fell into a dazed slumber that turned into a deep sleep once the sun set.

I woke mid-morning on Tuesday to the sound of someone knocking on my door. I opened my eyes slowly, expecting the hot throbbing to begin, but my eyes didn't burn. As the knocking continued, I sat up cautiously and found that my head didn't swim. My shirt was glued to me with old sweat.

I walked gingerly to the door, rubbing my eyes. Opening the door, I found Kate, hand up mid-knock, and behind her was Audre. I looked back and forth between them, wondering what was happening.

"Hi?"

"Viv. Wow, you look like garbage. Get inside," said Kate and she herded me back inside, with Audre in tow. She spoke to Audre over her shoulder. "Hey, Audre, can you please open up the window and get some fresh air in here."

"Of course." Audre opened the blinds and slid open the window.

Kate stood squarely in front of me, looking up at me. She touched my hands, the glands on my throat, my forehead, pulled down my bottom eyelid, and told me to open my mouth wide, which I did.

She nodded and patted my shoulder. "Vivian, go take a nice long shower. I'll have some soup ready when you get out."

"Uh…" I looked from Kate to Audre. Audre nodded. "Okay," I said and got myself in the shower.

I started out with cold water and realized that my fever had broken and a warm shower was what I wanted. Reveling at how good the water felt on my skin, I scrubbed shampoo into my hair, followed by lathering up my body with suds and rinsing it all off. The aches, shivers, throbbing head, and tired eyes had all left. What remained were sore muscles, fatigue, and a deep hunger.

I got out and put on fresh boxers and a T-shirt before slicking my damp hair back with a comb. The mirror was fogged up, so I did my best without a visual. My head was much clearer, and I was grateful for it. I opened the door and stepped out into my studio. It was bright with sunshine, fresh air flowed in through the window on a light breeze, and the room smelled like cleanser and soup.

Audre was spraying everything with Lysol while Kate was stirring a pot on the stove. I fed my fish, who frantically ate up all the flakes I gave them. Clearly, they hadn't been fed while I was sick, and I had a moment of guilt around that.

The futon had been stripped of the sweaty sheets and folded back up into a couch. The whole place, small as it was, was neat and orderly, just how I liked it.

"Thanks, you guys. Your timing is perfect. I've been down for the count, but I feel like I am back in the land of the living now."

Audre smiled at me as she tossed the rag into the pile of sheets by the front door and went to go wash her hands. Kate ladled up three bowls of soup and carried them skillfully to the coffee table, not spilling a single drop.

"Sit. Sit," Kate said, motioning toward the food.

I walked around to the far side of the coffee table and sat on the floor, so that Kate and Audre could sit on the couch. I sat with my legs crossed under the table, ready to tuck in to the soup. Audre placed three tall glasses of water on the table and Kate brought in a plate piled high with rosemary bread and a butter dish.

They sat down on the couch side by side, both appraising me. Kate spoke first. "Eat. Then we can talk."

I didn't need to be told twice. I blew on a spoonful of the soup, cooling it. I saw big chunks of carrot and potatoes, as well as green beans and onions. The first bite was amazing, and I couldn't bear to wait for the rest of it to cool down. I did my best to retain some sort of table manners while shoveling spoon after spoon of scorching hot soup into my mouth. After I had gotten the last drop from the bowl I turned to the plate of bread, lathering a big slice with butter and wolfing it down heartily. I loaded up a second piece of bread with butter and slid over to rest my back against the wall. I was full, so I took my time eating the bread as I watched Audre and Kate eat their soup and bread like civilized humans.

They finished at the same time and leaned back on the couch. I had four eyes on me, which made me flush in embarrassment at how I had eaten.

"I'm so glad to see you have an appetite. That's always a good sign," Kate said. "When my patients at work get their appetites back, it's usually a sign of good things to come."

I looked from one to the other as Audre crossed her legs. Then I glanced at the calendar on the wall, realizing it was a Tuesday. "Audre, don't you have work today?"

Audre nodded at me. "Yes, I do. But I was worried when I couldn't reach you."

"How did you guys know I was sick?"

"Ang," they both said in unison.

"Oh. Right." I had a foggy memory of running into her in the lobby. Then the memory about my conversation with Danny came in full force, slamming me back into reality.

"What's that look?" Audre asked, regarding me curiously.

"Nothing. I just remembered something that happened at work." *So, are you not going to tell them you lost your job?* I shook my head. Kate and Audre looked at me with tilted heads.

I made a weak attempt at diverting the conversation. "Thank you both so much for feeding me and cleaning up my place. Whatever I had totally knocked me out, and this was just what I needed. I hope coming over here doesn't get you guys sick too."

"I am around it all day at the hospital," Kate said.

"And I love ya, but I won't be kissing you today, Viv," Audre said, a twinkle in her eye. "Let's give it another twenty-four to forty-eight hours, and then it's on." We all had a good laugh at that.

I got up to clear the dishes, but the room spun, and I had to steady myself on the wall.

"Easy there, cowboy. You probably need another day or two to rest," Kate murmured as she got up to deal with the dishes. "Do you work tonight?"

"Nope."

"Oh good, get some rest. I've got to get to work myself." Kate placed the dishes in the sink and slipped her hospital clogs back on, then slid a cardigan on over her scrubs. "I'll save the hug for next time, see you guys later." And she showed herself out.

As Audre slid on her incredibly high heels, she gave me a seductive grin. "I need to get back to the office myself,"

"Not kissing you right now is proving to be a challenge," I groaned.

"Good." She blew me a kiss as she headed out of the door.

Chapter Nine

I spent the next two days recovering, moving between the bed, kitchen, and bathroom but not venturing outside of my studio except to wash the clothes and sheets I had used while sick. The laundry room was next to my studio and during the day everyone else was at work, so I had the machines to myself.

By Thursday I was stir crazy and raring to go as I jumped on my motorcycle and headed out to the Sheriff's Training Academy. Sergeant Brickhouse worked in an adjacent county, so I enjoyed a nice mid-morning ride. Though September, it was expected to only reach the upper 80s that day; the skies were blue and slightly hazy. After hopping off the freeway I cut my way through back county roads, enjoying the sight of recently harvested tomato, corn, and sunflower fields. A few last-minute combine harvesters were at work, kicking up dust and the smell of earth and diesel.

The academy was set apart from the nearest town, out in the fields. A secure compound with a typical government facility sign marking its driveway. I turned in and followed the signs to visitor parking. I found a spot in the shade of a small tree and shut off the engine, which ticked and pinged as it cooled. Inmate trustees were mowing and edging the grass while a deputy leaned up against a work van, watching them.

The grounds were well maintained, with close cropped green grass, shorn hedges, and a freshly sealed and painted parking lot. The administrative building was a long low complex made of concrete and glass in the 1970s federal modernism style. While aging, it was well kept. I pulled open a spotless glass door and entered the lobby, which had a sealed concrete floor and a clerk counter behind glass. I approached the glass window and waited. The woman on the other side of the window was reading a book and held a finger up to me, indicating that I should stand by. I waited, standing "at ease," my feet apart and hands clasped behind my back. Being in a paramilitary facility brought it out in me.

Once she finished the page she had been reading, she put a bookmark in place and looked up at me.

"How can I help you, sir?" she asked, as she removed her reading glasses. She was exactly what one would expect when picturing a dour, high seniority government employee.

Being "sir'd" was something that had happened a lot since I had cut my hair short, and it didn't bother me, so I took it in stride.

"Good morning. I have an appointment with Sergeant Brickhouse."

"What is this regarding?"

I paused, annoyed that she would ask such a question. *I have a fucking appointment, mind your own business.* Instead, I drew in a breath and smiled.

"I am not entirely sure. Sergeant Brickhouse called and said he needed to meet with me."

She frowned at me and tapped her fingers on the cover of her book. I stole a quick glance and saw that it was a romance novel, with a picture of a hunky guy carrying a despondent damsel out of a burning castle. She spotted my glance and flipped the book face down on her desk. I did my best to stop the smirk that wanted to come out.

"Very well. Have a seat," she said sourly and motioned to a low sofa across the lobby.

"Thank you," I said and strode toward the couch. Typical of any law enforcement facility, there was a large glass display case full of plaques, trophies, framed black-and-white photos, and government proclamations. I stood in front of the case and took my time looking over the items which memorialized officers lost in the line of duty, and competitions won.

I looked at the posed photographs of graduating academy classes. Old photos from generations ago. All white men, in uniform, standing tall. I rolled my eyes in annoyance at how exclusionary law enforcement had been for most of its existence. I got to thinking about systemic racism as I studied all those white faces and started digging my fingernails into my palms as I clasped them behind my back.

Footsteps echoing down a corridor broke my concentration. They sounded like the footsteps of a large, confident man. Sergeant Brickhouse's baritone voice came from behind me.

"Hello, Vivian."

I turned to face him, a smile on my face. When I was recovering from being attacked by Crystal Wylie and then attending her trial, Sergeant Brickhouse treated me in a very paternal way. Though the lead investigator, he was protective of me. Caring even.

He strode up, enormous hand extended. I reached out and took it. We shook warmly, his hand completely engulfing mine. He chuckled, a broad smile spreading across his face, his dimples popping and crinkles at the corners of his eyes creased. He hadn't changed a bit since I had seen him last. He was huge, built just like his name implied. He was in uniform, which clung tightly to his biceps, pecs, and traps. His neck was as thick around as my thigh. His lats tapered down to a solid core. His bald head gleamed like polished umber.

"Come on back," he said, motioning for me to follow him down a hallway that led off the main lobby. The clerk behind the glass window watched our entire exchange, her lips pursed. As we walked by, she put her glasses back on and picked up her book.

I followed him down the hall, recognizing that I was deferring to his rank and position, rather than walking at his side. I heard some murmuring down the hall, and as we rounded the corner, I saw an entire squad of recruits coming out of a classroom. It took a moment for one to recognize who was coming. When she saw us, her face immediately grew serious and she slammed her back against the wall, ramrod straight, before calling out, "Officer on deck! Make way!"

All the other recruits immediately stopped what they were doing and slammed their backs against the wall, clearing the way. The hallway was dead silent except for our footsteps on the concrete floor. I kept my eyes straight ahead as we walked through the gauntlet of recruits. Once we had passed them, Sergeant Brickhouse called out, "As you were." There was a collective sigh as they peeled themselves off the wall and went back about their business.

We turned another corner and passed through a wide doorway. Inside was a series of desks in a crescent shape, each adorned with the typical law enforcement décor. Police officer bobblehead dolls, shooting trophies, certificates of achievement, and each had a name placard. The desk chairs were all vacant. We passed through the front office and into his private office. He closed the door and motioned for me to take a seat. I sat in a straight-backed wooden chair that was centered in front of his desk. He took a seat in his massive black leather office chair, which creaked under his mass. His office was furnished with a C-shaped cherrywood desk and a big credenza, lined with framed photos of him with politicians and high-ranking officials. There were also grainy pictures of a much younger Sergeant Brickhouse, as a marine in various poses with other marines, all weighed down under a ton of gear and carrying weapons. I looked to his right hand and saw the familiar class ring with the Marine Corps emblem stamped just to the side of the big, burgundy-colored stone.

He watched me as I took in his neat and orderly office. No unkempt stacks of paper or file folders. Just a notepad, pen cup, blotter, and computer monitor on his desk. The side wall of his office was a long bank of windows looking out onto an exercise field and obstacle course. I took in a deep breath, fending off the anxiety that liked to sink its hooks in whenever I got around military and paramilitary facilities.

After taking stock of his space, I looked to him, and he nodded at me. "Thanks for coming down, Vivian."

I inclined my chin to him, waiting to hear what else he had to say.

"I'll get right to the point. In all transparency, the second you said you were unemployed, I knew that I'd like to invite you to apply to be a deputy sheriff." He paused as the statement hung in the air between us.

I watched recruits doing calisthenics and CrossFit style exercises in the grass outside while deputies shouted at them drill sergeant style. I stifled the urge to shift in my seat.

"What brought you to the conclusion that I would be a good fit as a deputy?"

He gave my question some thought, tracing a calloused thumb along his bottom lip. There was commotion in the front office as some deputies came in, chatting indistinctly.

"We first connected when I was working the Wylie case. You were straightforward and demonstrated integrity and grit. You did some things that were reckless, but they paid off in the end. I mean, you caught her for us, for Christ's sake. But beyond that, I can see you're solid." He stopped there, but I didn't reply. "Look, I know you are recently out of college and an army vet. You've got your whole career ahead of you, so why not join the department? The pay here is good, the benefits and pension are great, and things are good with the union. I see a lot of promise and potential in you."

I continued watching the recruits as they moved on to the obstacle course and practiced scaling over sections of six-foot-tall wood and chain-link fences held up by big metal frames. The taller men were able to pop up and over without any visible effort, while the females and shorter recruits had to get a running start, hook an arm and leg over the top, and heave themselves over. I was more than familiar with that exercise and knew I could do it with ease. But did I want to?

I looked back at Sergeant Brickhouse, who turned the Marine Corps signet ring round and round on his finger.

"I am flattered that you have put so much thought into this and that you feel I would be a good fit. I...need to think about it. Returning to uniformed service is a bit touchy for me."

"Fair enough. You've got time. Next academy class doesn't start until March. Applications are due in November. Normally we contact applicants by email, but I will have our recruiter mail you an interest card once recruitment opens in the fall. Okay?"

"Okay."

He pushed away from his desk and stood, so I followed suit. We walked through double doors to his front office, where the training officers sat. Two of the desks were occupied by uniformed deputies who were loading up semi-automatic magazines with flat topped ammunition, which I recognized as blanks.

"Vivian, these are two of my recruit training officers. They are the best of the best." The officers looked up from their work, nodding at me.

"Hey, Sarge, we are headed to the classroom to shoot the place up. Want to join us?"

Sergeant Brickhouse let out a booming laugh. "Of course! Vivian, you should come watch this."

I was intrigued to see the training environment from the trainer side, rather than as a trainee. We stood by while they finished loading up, and then stalked quietly down the hallway until we were outside the closed classroom door.

From within came the muffled sound of an instructor lecturing about radio codes. Sergeant Brickhouse opened the door quietly and we filed in and lined up against the back wall. The room was set up like a classroom. In front of us were rows of long tables with recruits in uniform diligently taking notes, all with their backs to us, and a uniformed training officer standing up front. Only one recruit turned to look at us, and as soon as she spotted Sergeant Brickhouse her eyes grew wide and she turned back to the lecture, subtly elbowing the person next to her.

The deputies, who had been hiding the pistols behind their backs, nodded to each other, stepped away from the wall, and raised the pistols, aiming them at the ceiling.

One shouted, "Fuck you, pigs!" They both rapid fired blanks, which were deafening in the confined space of the classroom. The deputy leading the lecture rolled his eyes as if this sort of thing were old hat, and we observed how the recruits responded to the ambush. The training officers stopped firing when they ran out of ammunition.

All the recruits had taken cover behind their tables and chairs, crouched down on the ground, and we had thirty blue mock Sig Sauer P226 pistols aimed at us.

Sergeant Brickhouse stepped away from the wall and walked across the back of the classroom, looking at his recruits. One wore a huge leg brace that was locked out straight. She hadn't been able to jump over the table like the rest but had overturned her chair for cover. Her flinty eyes were locked on me, and her pistol was aimed at my chest, dead center. Her red hair was styled in a flat top, with a spray of freckles across her nose to match, and she would clearly have shot me without hesitation, had it been warranted.

Sergeant Brickhouse spoke. His voice huge in the small space, commanding the room. "Recruits, I see that you were caught off guard with this exercise. I want you to each take a moment to consider what your *first* reaction was when you heard the gunfire. Did you respond automatically? Or did you look around to see what the other recruits were doing, and respond accordingly? If you hesitated, you have some work to do. You *must always* be ready. Heads on a swivel." He looked at the deputy in the front of the classroom. "Carry on."

With that, we filed out as recruits got up off the floor with a low murmur and righted the furniture they had tipped over for cover.

The deputies went back to their office and Sergeant Brickhouse escorted me to the main lobby. The clerk glanced up from her reading briefly, scowling at us, and returned to her book.

"Thank you again for coming out to see me today, Vivian," he said as he extended his hand to me. We shook.

"No problem. Thank you for inviting me to apply. I will think about it."

We parted ways, the heavy glass door shutting behind me with a gentle swish. While I had parked in the shade, I found that the shade had shifted, and the bike was now in full sun. I groaned and dug my helmet out from the hard bags. It was stifling to put on and as I straddled the bike, the hot seat burned my ass through my jeans.

I was starving and realized it was just about lunchtime. I thought about what towns were nearby, and Winters came to mind. I made sure to obey traffic laws until I was off the Academy's property and then opened up the throttle, rocketing myself along the empty country roads.

I pulled into downtown Winters, which only spanned a couple of blocks, and parked at Rotary Park. I walked up the main drag and found a café that had woodfired pizza, which I hadn't had in years. I decided to treat myself and snagged a seat on the outside patio. The food came quickly, and I devoured it, along with savoring a cold, sweet Arnold Palmer.

The place started to get crowded, so I used the restroom, paid the bill, and walked back to my bike, burning my ass yet again as I climbed on to the hot seat.

There was a very clear delineation where the town ended and the farm fields started. The day had warmed, and dust devils kicked up in the breeze. I opened up the throttle again and shot along for a few miles, slowing only to pass a tractor. I approached a T intersection and gaped when I recognized an abandoned warehouse on the Northeast corner.

I slowed and pulled into the gravel lot. I rode around to the far side of the building and stopped with my feet planted squarely on the gravel. I flipped open the visor of my helmet but didn't shut off the engine. In front of me was an empty gravel lot, to my left the rusted-out old metal and concrete warehouse. I spotted a spigot near the building and recalled that just a couple of years before, I had stopped there to go pee and check for geocaches, but what I had found was Crystal Wylie scrubbing blood off her hands at the spigot. She had attacked me. We had fought hard. In the end I had let her leave, not knowing I was about to discover her dirty deed in the warehouse. She had used a machete to hack the hands off a man and left him there to bleed out and die. No wonder she had been surprised to see me and had tried to kill me too.

All was quiet. A person passing by would have no idea what had occurred there. I was barely affected myself. I should have felt something, right? Being attacked during a bio break and fighting for my life against a stranger. That should leave a lingering something, but there was nothing. I scuffed my boot in the gravel and slammed shut the visor before pulling out in a spray of gravel and dust.

*

On the ride back to Sacramento I wondered if I had been a recruit sitting in that classroom whether I would have been one to respond immediately to the gunfire, or whether I would have hesitated. I had been out of the military for a while and knew that my reflexes had slowed. I thought some more about Sergeant Brickhouse's invitation for me to apply to be a deputy sheriff recruit. So many parts of me immediately said "No." I was still unpacking all the damage my time in the military had done. I had a hair-trigger temper and didn't trust myself not to lose my temper on the job. Hell, I could barely keep my cool as a bartender, how would I be while armed and dealing with the kind of stuff cops dealt with? I decided I didn't want to operate in a paramilitary environment again. So, those were my concerns about me.

But there was an entire ethical dilemma that I grappled with around law enforcement in general. I recognized that I was in a relationship with Ang, who was a deputy sheriff. That was on a personal level. But the profession as a whole was so problematic in a way that I was just waking up to.

Later that evening I stopped by the Lavender Library to visit with Audre during her shift as a volunteer. She was busy when I arrived, so I browsed the stacks and pulled a few books about the history of law enforcement. Settling in a chair in the corner, I read until Audre was free.

After her shift at the library, we walked to a café around the corner, the same place we had gone to on our first date, and settled into a couch in the back.

With trepidation, I looked at her. She placed her palm on my cheek lovingly.

"What's the matter, Vivian? You look...hollow."

"I was fired from the nightclub."

She sat up, her bracelets jingling as her eyes opened wide. "What? Why?"

I explained what had happened with Sheila, and then about my conversation with Danny. The clench of Audre's jaw and the angle of her brows showed that she was outraged, though she just listened, and only offered very reserved comments when I had finished, placing her hand over mine.

"You look mad, and I find myself feeling very self-conscious right now."

"I am mad, but not at you."

I ran my thumb along the top of her hand. "So, do you remember me talking about the investigator from the Crystal Wylie situation?"

"Sure."

"He gave me a tour of the Sheriff's Training Academy today. And, well, he asked me to consider applying to be a deputy. Or at least a recruit, anyway."

Audre nodded slowly but didn't say anything. I sipped my tea, which had grown lukewarm. I wanted to ask her what she thought about it but wanted to share my concerns first. Since she wasn't giving anything away with her facial expression, I dove in.

"From being in the military, and just how I was raised, I have always respected law enforcement as some sort of authority never to be questioned. My interactions with cops have almost always been good, even when I've done something bad like beaten the tar out of a customer. But..."

Just the thought of talking about race and speaking against the police made my stomach hurt. I had no idea what Audre's experiences, as a Black woman, had been when dealing with law enforcement.

I grit my teeth and glanced around to make sure nobody was in earshot. "I've got to be honest; this topic makes me very uncomfortable."

Audre raised her eyebrows at me, her expression still a tight poker face.

"Please forgive my ignorance if I say something stupid. I'm trying to make the right decision, so I did some reading, and I will do more. But it all comes down to me suddenly not trusting cops. Not individual cops, per se, but more like the institution as a whole, if that makes sense."

Audre nodded, her expression relaxing just a bit.

"Is it okay that I talk this through with you? If not, I can work it out myself or talk it through with someone else."

"Go ahead. I'm listening."

I blew out a gust of air and went on. "Okay, so what I learned just in the reading I did today was enough to turn my stomach. And maybe you already know all of this. I am not here trying to mansplain or whatever, so much as I just kind of need to say it out loud to fully grasp it." I sipped my tea again, which was cold and bitter. "I was reading today about the history of law enforcement in the US and how the origin of police is that they were used in the early 1700s as southern slave patrols. Their whole purpose was to catch enslaved persons who had escaped. I...had no idea. And then later in the north they were used by businessmen as union busters and by politicians for voter suppression. One book even said that the Texas Rangers slaughtered Mexicans and Native Americans. It wasn't until like 1838, in Boston, that a formal law enforcement agency was started, and it was deeply corrupt too. I just... I'm actually pissed off at the school district for not teaching me these things as a kid." I wiped at spittle on my chin and realized I was angry.

Audre raised her chin just a hair, but still didn't speak.

I pushed down the anger, recognizing I needed to change my tone. "I'm sorry. I figure this is stuff you already know, and I can see now that I've been living in a big-ass bubble."

"And why do you think that is?"

"Why do I think what is?"

"That you are so uncomfortable about this, and that you are just now learning about it? Why do you think that is the case?"

I looked down at my hand resting on top of hers, our fingers entwined, the color of my skin so different than hers.

"Because I'm white." I said it in a whisper, more to myself than to her.

We sat quietly for a while, people watching and thinking our separate thoughts. Eventually I turned to her and she gave me a gentle smile.

"Thank you for allowing me to fumble through that. I'm just learning what I now know so many other people have lived with their entire lives, and I don't intend to place any of the burden of my learning curve on you. So, I apologize if it came across that way."

She gave me the same gentle smile. Audre was compassionate. She had listened and witnessed, which I recognized afterward was a lot to ask of her.

Chapter Ten

By Friday I was beyond restless. I had recovered from the flu, hadn't worked all week, and hadn't done anything about trying to find a new job. Rather than going to the public library to use the computers to search for jobs, I waited until noon and called Jared during his lunch hour. He answered right away.

"Hey, Viv!"

"Hey, Jared, you on lunch? Is this an okay time to talk?"

"Ah-yup. I'm sitting on my usual bench looking at the water. Having a sandwich. What are you up to?"

"Not much. I need some advice."

"Of course. What's up?" The sound of seagulls cawing and waves breaking came to me through the phone.

"I lost my job."

"Oh. Wow. What happened?"

I sighed. "Not sure. They told me they needed to cut back for the slow season. But it was bullshit."

"That's terrible. What kind of advice is it you need from me?"

"I dunno. Maybe it's not advice I need."

"Well, I'm happy to just chat, if that'll help," he chuckled, and I smiled as I stared out of my studio window at the street and pool below. "Hey, you wanna come down for a visit this weekend? I don't have anything going on, so we can just hang out. Maybe go for a run or hike, eat some good food, like the old days back when you lived here."

My heart squeezed and I realized that was exactly what I wanted. "Yes. Thanks. I would love that. Can I come down today?"

"Of course. I'm not off work till six tonight. Do you still have a key?"

"Yup, I do. I'll pack up and head down. Thanks, bud. I'll let you get back to eating your lunch. See you tonight!"

We ended the call, and I was elated, instantly cheered up and excited. I decided to ride my bike down. I popped up from the windowsill and grabbed two small travel bags that would fit on my bike and began packing the basics. I had always traveled light and had no problem throwing stuff together quickly. I saw my copy of Clement Salvadori's *Motorcycle Journeys Through California* and tossed it into my bag. I also fished around in the safe stashed under the bathroom sink and pulled out a few hundred dollars.

I texted Audre to tell her I was going away for the weekend and to ask if she would feed my fish while I was away. She agreed. I also said she could stay at my place to take a break from her busy house if she wanted.

Fish settled and bags packed, I locked up and bounded down the stairs with arms full of riding gear and bags. I couldn't get on the road fast enough. My heart beat wildly with the excitement as I strapped down one bag and jammed the smaller one into one of the hard saddle bags. I fired up the engine and hopped on, strapping my helmet on as the engine warmed up.

I nearly jumped out of my skin when someone tapped me on the shoulder. I spun in my seat and saw Ang standing next to my bike, a bag of groceries in one hand and a gallon of milk in the other. She motioned with her hand for me to shut down the engine. I drew in a deep breath and shut the engine off. Silence filled the underground garage.

"Hey, Vivian," she said as she looked over my bike and spotted my travel bag strapped to the back seat.

"Hey, Ang."

"Are you going on a trip?" She shifted her weight from one loafer-clad foot to the other.

"Yeah. I'm going to spend the weekend in Morro Bay with Jared. I need to get out of town for a little bit. Stuff got weird at work."

"Oh. Did you forget that we have a date tonight?"

"I. Uh...oh." I had indeed forgotten. "Shit."

"Well, this feels shitty. You've totally forgotten our date? This is not the Viv from two years ago, that's for sure. You never would have forgotten a date back then."

That pissed me off.

"Well, Ang, the relationship we were in two years ago is not the relationship we are in now. We used to be primary partners and you were my main focus. But, as you may recall, when you declared you were solo poly and no longer wanted me as a partner, that totally restructured our relationship. Now we are sex only, at your choosing. So yeah, I forgot our date."

Ang raised her eyebrows. I was resentful that she had sidelined my excitement, leaving behind anger and discontent.

When she didn't respond right away, I turned back in my seat and fired up the engine of my bike. I saw in the side mirror that she had stepped out of the way, so I backed out of my parking spot and pulled up to the gate sensor. Ang stood by the lobby door, groceries in hand and a disappointed look on her face, and I did not feel bad about it.

*

It took me just over four hours to get to Morro Bay. During the ride I spent a lot of that time trying not to get hypnotized by the repetitive landscape along Interstate 5, though once I passed through San Luis Obispo and turned onto Highway 1, the excitement had returned, and I focused on the weekend ahead. The tension in my chest released as I passed Camp San Luis Obispo and Cuesta College. I had many fond memories of my time at Cuesta College, where I had taken classes after being discharged from the army, when Jared and I had lived as roommates.

The closer I got to his house, the happier I was and the more centered I became. I turned off Highway 1 onto San Joaquin, then took a quick left onto Jared's street, and pulled into his driveway, making sure to park off to the side so there would still be room for Jared's truck. I looked up at his house and felt like I was home.

Once I'd offloaded all my stuff, I raced up the creaky wooden steps to his front door, which was on the second floor. My key slid into the lock. The smell was exactly the same as I remembered it. Clean. Like fabric softener and bleach, with an undertone of masculine musk and cologne.

Before I could take a step out of the tiled entryway, I heard the telltale sound of a dog door flap, followed by a giant golden retriever skidding out around the corner from the kitchen. He paused and tilted his head to the side, not moving any closer.

I made my voice as sweet as I could. "Hi, Baxter." His tail did a tentative wag. "Hey, buddy! How are you! You're such a good boy. Are you guarding the house for your daddy?" I put my bag down and squatted, holding out a hand to him. He sauntered over and sniffed my hand. Recognizing me, he panted and barreled into my chest, knocking me on my butt with his enthusiastic greeting. Laughing, I sat up and petted his head and back. His tongue lolled out as he panted in excitement, while his tail whacked against the island of cabinets that separated the kitchen from the living room. *Whap. Whap. Whap.*

"Okay, buddy. I am getting up now. Good boy." *Whap. Whap. Whap.* Then he ran off into the kitchen and drank noisily from a water bowl.

I grabbed my stuff and went into my old room, which had been turned into a guest room. I opened the sliding glass door and let in some air before flopping down on the futon and breathing in the smell of the tide. The view of the Pacific was one I had spent countless hours looking at during study breaks and moments of contemplation.

Baxter came in, jowls dripping water, and lay down on the floor next to me with a huff. I lowered an arm and gently stroked the fur on the back of his neck. Baxter had had a rough life and he'd come a long way since Jared had saved him. The last time I'd seen Baxter he had been covered in blood after attacking his abusive owner, right there in the living room.

I watched the ocean until the vibrations from the long motorcycle ride finally left me, then I went into the kitchen to scout out the food situation, Baxter on my heels. It was the end of the week, so there wasn't much to be had. I recalled that Jared did his grocery shopping on the weekends. I had hoped to have dinner ready when he got home from work, and while I was pretty skilled at throwing random items together to make a meal, his supply was seriously lacking.

I had about thirty minutes until he would be home, so I walked a few blocks down to the Mexican restaurant. I got a big order of rice, beans, tamales, al pastor, and tortillas. They couldn't sell me bottles of beer to go, so I jogged over to the convenience store and bought a few bottles of Corona. The cashier carded me, which made me chuckle, given that I was a bartender...or rather, I had been. I had served alcohol for years and there I was getting carded for booze.

Beer in hand, I returned to the restaurant and picked up the food, listening to the soft rock piped in through overhead speakers. Jared was just getting out of his truck when I walked up, hands full. He gave me a massive grin as he slammed his truck door and slung a lunch bag over his shoulder.

He looked like he was doing well. His hazel eyes had their usual spark, his physique as fit as ever, his skin tan and his jaw sporting a five-o'clock shadow. He smiled, the small chip in his front tooth gleaming.

"Viv, you made it!" He chuckled as I tried to wave with my hands full. "What have you got there?"

"Dinner and beer."

"Excellent. Well, let's get on upstairs and dig in. I'm starved."

Out of the corner of my eye I spotted a small gap in the downstairs blinds snap closed as we walked by. Once inside, Jared washed his hands, plated up food, and opened beers all while trying not to trip over Baxter, as I set the table. It was the same old beat-up, secondhand wooden table he had had since we'd left the army. But he kept it clean and polished. Jared always took good care of his stuff.

He put on an old Kenny Rogers record. We sat down and shoveled in our first round of food without saying a word. After he piled seconds on to both of our plates, we struck up conversation as we ate slowly. Baxter lay under the table quietly, waiting for a stray bit of food to fall.

"So, who have you got living downstairs these days?" I asked in a hushed voice. Jared owned the whole house, but the downstairs was converted into a separate living space, which he rented out.

He took a long pull on his beer, washing down a mouthful of rice and beans. "Some guy who works out at the nuclear power plant in Avila Beach. He's an engineer of some sort. Keeps to himself, so I don't know much about him." He took another bite of rice and another sip of beer and dabbed at his mouth with a paper napkin that made a sandpapery sound against his stubble. "So, you want to talk about your job?"

I pushed back from my plate and looked out at the ocean through the big picture window. "They took me off the schedule, said it's the slow season and they are cutting back. But they replaced me with some other chick, so I know that it was a bullshit excuse. The bar manager had started having issues with me recently, and I think she just wanted me gone. So, I'm gone. And now... I dunno."

I watched a massive cargo ship slink along the horizon far out in the ocean, then looked back to Jared, who was eyeing me intently. He didn't try to offer any suggestions or solve my problem for me, which was one of the things I had always appreciated about him.

"And oddly enough, yesterday Sergeant Brickhouse invited me to apply to be a deputy sheriff recruit at his department. He runs the academy now."

"Oh wow. A personal invitation. That's kind of a big deal, Viv. Are you going to apply?"

"I don't think so."

"Hmm." He looked down at his plate, pondering his food, or my predicament, or both.

I pushed a tamale around on my plate for a bit before taking a bite. "I don't think it'll be a good fit for a variety of reasons. My temper would be a safety issue, for starters." I tossed a small scrap of tortilla down to Baxter. Jared gave a small nod. "And the more time that passes from when I separated from the army, the more I know I don't align with uniformed service anymore." While I knew Jared wouldn't pursue that, I still needed to say it.

We finished up the meal in quiet contemplation, while Kenny Rogers sang on the record player in the background about eyes that see in the dark. Jared washed the dishes and I dried them. The sun had begun to set so we took some beers outside and sat on the top step, which had a view of Highway 1 and the Pacific Ocean. We clinked beer bottles. "Cheers, Vivi. I hope things work out for you the way you want them to."

"Thanks for inviting me down on such short notice, and for having my back."

We sipped on our beers and watched as the sun cleared the horizon. As soon as the sun disappeared a cool breeze chased us back inside.

"Want to play cards?"

"Why, so you can kick my ass at Hearts? I don't think so," I said with a laugh, leaning my hip against the kitchen counter. I was slightly buzzed from the beers. More so than I had been in a long time, and I hated it. I had always hated the feeling of my body and mind being loose, not as quick to respond physically or mentally.

Annoyed, I padded over to the sink and drank a large glass of water. I slid the half full beer bottle across the counter toward Jared. He downed it and moved to the media stand, where he switched out the Kenny Rogers record for a Van Morrison album.

"I think I am going to hit the rack. I'm super tired," I said. Jared was so gentle and careful with his albums, so he didn't turn back to me until he had finished putting away the Kenny Rogers record and the Van Morrison sleeve.

"Oh yeah? It's still early. You okay?"

"Yeah. Just tired and buzzed. And you know how much I hate being buzzed."

He nodded knowingly. "You sure you don't want to play cards or something? Till it wears off?"

"I'm sure. Thanks though. Hey, why don't we go for a run in the morning? I haven't run in over a week, due to being sick. I need to get moving again."

"Sure thing, Viv. Sleep well. I put sheets and blankets in there for you, and there's a towel in your bathroom."

I gave him a smile. "You're always so thoughtful and such a good host."

He gave me a lopsided grin and turned back to the record player.

*

I woke early, the slightest hint of sunrise touching the sky outside. I kicked at the blankets grumpily, trying to untangle myself while remembering the flashes of bad dreams. Stress dreams of the battlefield, and of ducking behind a mud hut to avoid gunfire with my name on it and straining my ears for the sound of a hummer coming to extract me.

The blinds were open, so I looked out of the sliding glass door at the ocean, barely visible in the predawn darkness. I tasted blood in my mouth and ran my tongue along the grooves I had chewed on the inside of my cheeks. A good run was exactly what I needed, so I sat up and swung my feet over the side of the futon. Startled, I jerked them back up, and peered down at the floor. Baxter had made himself comfortable on the floor next to where I had slept. He looked up at me with sleepy eyes and gave a big yawn before shaking his head, ears flapping and collars clinking.

"You're the best, Baxter," I said as I reached over the side and stroked his fur. He panted and laid his chin back down on the floor. I laid on my side and pet him, listening to his contented sighs, until the sky and room lightened a bit.

I got up, careful not to step on the dog, and I slid into my running clothes: a ratty old T-shirt, lightweight running shorts, dual layer slippery running socks, and my worn-out running shoes. Those shoes had pounded out countless miles on the pavement of midtown and the trails of Briones. It was probably time for a new pair.

I opened the door gently, trying not to make any noise. As I did so, Baxter hopped up and gave a big stretch and shake before nearly taking me out at the knees as he headed for the water and food bowls in the kitchen.

I headed across the hall to the bathroom and peed for what felt like an eternity. I washed my hands, brushed and flossed my teeth, and tried to get my hair to lay down. One thing I missed about having long hair was being able to just slick it back into a ponytail or bun. But now that I had short hair, it required a lot of work in the mornings to get it to behave. I gave up and wandered out to the living room, looking for one of Jared's hats. I found his Cal hat hanging on the coat rack by the door and slid it onto my head. Baxter whined, his tail thumping on the floor.

"I can't feed you, dude. I don't know what or how much? You have to wait for your daddy."

He whined some more and then lay down, tail still thumping. I stood in front of the big picture window and watched the low waves of the ocean, beyond the freeway and tree line. The sky lightened quickly, and traffic increased on Highway 1 as I listened to the faint sounds of Jared getting ready from behind his closed door.

When his door opened, Baxter immediately sat up and began whining.

"Good morning, Viv. Hiya, Baxter!" Jared strode into the kitchen and gave Baxter plenty of pets and scratches before pouring a combination of dry and wet food into the bowl, sprinkling shredded cheese on top, and pouring a cup of warm water. Baxter danced around the kitchen, his nails clacking on the tiles. Jared waited until Baxter sat next to him and quieted down. He placed the bowl on the floor and straightened up.

"Eat!"

Baxter attacked the food with gusto.

"He's such a good dog," I said. Jared nodded.

"How'd you sleep?"

"The usual," I groaned.

"Damn, I had hoped that would improve after all the therapy you've done."

"It did. Just a little regression, I think. Hey, you mind if I borrow your hat? My hair wasn't cooperating."

"Sure, sure. No problem. You remember the last time you borrowed it?"

"Shit. How could I forget? Your kitchen was a bloodbath." I pointed to where he stood. "Martina had damn near had her throat ripped out by Baxter, but not before beating my ass and slicing my bun off like someone gutting a fish." After the last word rolled off my tongue I paused, a bit shocked by the reality of what we had been through.

"Yeah. That was a rough night." He looked at me wistfully. "I miss your long hair. I'd never seen hair as dark and shiny as yours. Like a raven. I mean...it looks nice short, too, but I'm still not used to it."

I adjusted the hat, snugging it down on my head a bit more. "Ready?"

"Yeah."

"Should we bring Baxter?"

We both turned to look at him as he frantically licked the last few morsels from his bowl, a piece of cheese stuck to his snout.

"Nah. If we take him on an R-U-N right now he'd hork up his breakfast."

"Good point."

Baxter lapped up some water and, muzzle dripping, headed out to the backyard through the dog door.

"Now's our chance, let's go," Jared said with a chuckle. We snuck out the front door and walked down the nineteen wooden steps I knew well, and then stood in the driveway warming up.

"Where to?" Jared asked as he pulled his heel up to his butt to stretch out his massive quad, a comical strained look on his face.

"We could run the beach down to Morro Rock. Or maybe drive out to Montana De Oro and run the Coon Creek Trail. What sounds good?"

We agreed on running down the beach to Morro Rock. I caught the flick of a crack in the downstairs curtains closing as we left. We ran across Highway 1 and down to the packed, damp sand on the beach. It was a route we had done countless times when we lived together. Running was always therapeutic for me, even more so with Jared at my side. In the early morning hour, the beach was abandoned aside from the occasional person fishing. We got into a good rhythm and I let myself drift.

*

My boots slapped on the pavement as I sprinted down the sidewalk and turned into the park.

Lungs aching for more air, I hollered. "You better stop and face me, you little bitch!"

Adults at the nearby playground looked at me, startled, and quickly gathered their toddlers.

I spotted the back of her black Megadeth T-shirt as she darted behind a utility building just ahead. My boots slid on the slick concrete as I followed hot on her heels around the side of the cinderblock building.

"Coward! Come and face me! You want to talk shit about me? Say it to my face!" I huffed as I closed in on her. I spotted my brother and some other kids from the high school cutting class in the park. They had caught sight of us and were cheering me on.

"Get her, Viv. You show that little bitch!"

So close, her hair and the tail of her shirt blew back behind her as she ran from me. I threw my hand out and lunged forward, grasping. Sure enough, I got a handful of hair and shirt. Victorious, I dug my heels in and pulled back on her until we were both on the ground panting. She immediately scrambled, trying to escape.

My brother and his friends had hustled around the corner of the building. One of the senior girls, who was with Joey, blocked off the escape route and caught the girl as she tried to get away. He put her in a full nelson.

I got up, wiping blood from my lip, which I had bitten through when we fell. We both panted, adrenaline exploding. I coughed loudly and spit blood into the grass.

"Well now, looks like we get to have our little chat after all, eh, Jude?" I panted, swallowing hard through a dry mouth. I had skipped every day of PE where we had to run and had taken up smoking in eighth grade, which I was questioning as I struggled to catch my breath. "Listen up. Here's the deal. You don't talk about me or my family. Ever! Got it?"

Jude breathed heavily and nodded vigorously. She had stopped struggling with the senior who held her tightly, her arms pinned over her head. The senior sneered. "Kick her ass, Viv. Pound that snotty little face in."

I looked at Jude and saw sheer fright on her face. Her whole body shook to the point that her teeth clacked together. I felt bad for her as I realized how utterly scared she must have been. Surrounded by bigger kids, unable to defend herself. It wasn't right. But I had to save face, otherwise the others would see my weakness and pounce on me too.

Joey, standing behind me, shouted. "Come on, Viv, do it! You're a Chastain." He rumbled up a loogie and spat at Jude, the phlegm splatting at her feet. Joey gave me a big shove and I stumbled forward until I was within arm's reach of Jude. I didn't like how the situation had escalated. It went from my losing my temper at Jude's shit talking, to her being in real danger. I had to figure a way out for us both.

I stepped up close, until we were nose to nose, and growled at her. "Jude. Don't you ever talk about me or my family again. If you do, you're dead meat. Got it?"

She nodded vigorously again and squeaked out an apology. "Sorry, Viv. Sorry."

I stepped back, hoping that was enough to appease the older kids. "Jesus, Viv, do it already," came a girl's voice from behind me. A blur passed by me and the girl jogged up and kicked Jude square in the hamstring. Jude slumped and bit her lip as she tried to hold in a squeal of pain. I knew I needed to think faster to get us out of there.

"All right, all right. Y'all just back up. This is my beef, not yours."

Joey and his friends backed up a pace. Jude clenched her eyes closed as I balled up my right hand into a fist, stepped in, and punched her in the gut. I made it look like a big punch, though I pulled it at the last possible second so I hit her with minimal force. Jude stepped back into the girl holding her and coughed hard, playing up her role as she recognized what I had done.

One of the girls behind me hooted and shouted. "Yeah, Viv, do it. Get her!"

I waved her off. "Nah, nah. We've got an agreement. This was her warning."

"Ahhh, booo." The senior holding Jude released her and spat on the ground at my feet. "Jesus, Viv, you're such a pussy." She turned to look at Joey. "Your sister is a pussy, Joey." Joey grumbled in return.

The bigger kids lost interest and sauntered off back toward the benches, lighting up cigarettes as they went.

"Thanks," Jude said as she rotated her neck a few times and shook out her arms.

"Yeah," I replied. "Sorry. That got out of hand."

"I'm sorry too."

"You want to go get high?"

"Sure," she said, and we walked across a big grass field to the far side of the park, where we slid behind some deep bushes that backed up to a wooden fence. We sat in the dirt and leaned against the fence. I pulled a pipe out of the deep pockets of my baggy jeans and a dime bag of weed from my boot. I opened the bag and took a fragrant nugget out. I spent a moment picking out the seeds and stem and packed what was left into the pipe. Jude watched me go through the motions, clutching her lighter. Putting the pipe up to my lips, I nodded toward her lighter, which she handed over. I lit it and placed it over the pipe, drawing in smoke as the pot crackled. As soon as it hit my lungs, I had a massive urge to cough, but did my best to stifle it and hold the smoke in as I passed the lighter and pipe to Jude.

She took them and repeated what I had done, taking a huge toke and holding it in. I blew out a huge lungful of smoke and leaned my head against the fence as I coughed. Jude blew her smoke out coolly, not coughing. She passed the pipe back to me and smiled. We paused, hands in midair, each with a hand on the hot pipe and lighter. Her smile gave me pause, because it included a raised eyebrow, and finished off with a tilted head and smirk. Was she...flirting with me?

Breaking eye contact, I took the pipe and dug my fingertip into the hot embers, stirring them up. I looked back to Jude, in her Megadeth shirt, flannel tied around her waist, baggy jeans, and combat boots, almost the exact same outfit as me. Strips of her hair were dyed purple. The sides were shaved to the skin and the top natural and picked into a mohawk. Her deep-brown skin shone.

I put the pipe to my lips, flicked the lighter, and drew in smoke from the crackling dregs of the last bit of weed. My lungs ached to cough, but I resisted, instead leaning toward Jude and crooking my finger at her. She leaned in until we were nose to nose. Her lips grazed mine as she opened her mouth and I blew the smoke into hers. She sucked it in and held it for a moment before blowing it out her nose.

The buzz of the high hit me and I wondered what to do, since we were still nose to nose, staring into each other's eyes. I took a chance, leaning in a centimeter closer, and kissed her. I expected her to punch me in the face, but to my surprise, she kissed me back, sliding her hand around the back of my neck. Thrill rose in my chest, fighting with the mellow of the pot high. My body buzzed from my scalp to my toes.

I had never kissed a girl before. Never even known that it was an option. But there I was, deep in a kiss with Jude, who I had known for years as a friend, but had terrorized not thirty minutes prior. She ran her deep-gray painted fingernails along the back of my neck, sharply, and it was amazing. I groaned and kissed her harder. I felt her smile against my lips. We broke off the kiss, leaning against the fence, dazed.

*

"Viv...Viv," Jared spoke my name gently. "We're almost there."

I blinked hard into the stiff ocean wind, looking at Jared. He grinned at me, his head bobbing as he ran by my side.

"Wow, you really went deep that time. Where'd you go?"

"Uh." I shook my head a bit, trying to clear it and transition back to the beach. "Davis, when I was a sophomore. You remember that story I told you about Jude?"

"Yup, sure do. She was your first girlfriend, right?"

"Yeah. Though we were both in the closet, so we had to keep it quiet. I wonder what ever happened to her."

"Why don't you check out MySpace?"

"My what?"

"Ha-ha. Jesus, Viv, you really do live under a rock. It's a website where people connect."

"Oh. You know I don't have a computer."

"Yeah. We should probably do something about that. You wanna turn around here or run around to the other side of the rock?"

I craned my neck, looking up at the massive Morro Rock as we approached it from the north side.

"Let's take a breather here and then head back." I didn't want to run around to the parking lot on the west side. The last time we had been there, Jared had propositioned me, asked me to move back in with him as his girlfriend. It had forced me to come out to him, and made things really strained between us for a while.

When we reached the end of the beach, where a rocky path led up to the road above, we slowed to a stop and walked around in circles as we caught our breath and cooled. We stood and watched a handful of surfers in full wetsuits paddle out and catch small waves back in, before we jogged out back toward Jared's house.

When we returned, Baxter was bouncing around excitedly, sniffing our shoes, licking our sweaty legs, and whining.

"Oh boy, I am in trouble. He knows I went running without him." Jared opened a cabinet in the kitchen and told Baxter to sit, which he did. "Hold." He placed the biscuit flat across Baxter's snout. Drool dripped from Baxter's jowls. "Okay," Jared said, and Baxter flipped his muzzle, the biscuit landing in his mouth. Nails clicking on the floor, Baxter trotted to his bed in the corner and laid down, munching on his treat.

Jared and I stood at the island that divided the kitchen and living room, downing some sort of protein shake he had mixed up in the blender. It tasted like chemicals and chocolate and had the texture of a gritty milkshake. After I gulped down the last bit, I washed my glass and wiped my mouth on a paper towel.

"I'm going to jump in the shower."

"'Kay," Jared said as he rummaged through the refrigerator.

I started the water and stripped out of my sweaty running clothes. I looked down at my body, which sported tan lines, some freckles, and a variety of scars. I had come to a point in my life where I accepted my body as it was, though some scars had deeper memories than others. I ran my fingertips along the deep, jagged scar on my left cheekbone. I had gotten that nasty gouge in Jared's living room during the same run-in with his ex-girlfriend, Baxter's former owner, when she had lopped off my bun.

The scar was tender, still somewhat new. Steam began pouring out of the shower, prompting me to adjust the temperature and get in.

After a good, cleansing scrub I got out, dried off, and went across the hall to the guest room, where I slid into some comfy jeans, long-sleeved T-shirt, socks, and well-worn boots. I grabbed a book from my bag, sat on the futon, and looked out of the sliding glass door at the ocean.

My cell phone vibrated in my bag, and I realized I hadn't checked it since I had arrived the day before. I grabbed it, looking at the screen. It was a 928 number that I didn't recognize. *Nine-two-eight?*

"Hello?"

"Viviana!"

I laughed when I recognized Bear's voice. "*Bueno, bueno,* my Oso. What's up!"

"Oh, you know, just living my best life out here in the badlands of Arizona."

"To what do I owe the honor of a call from you?"

"Ahh, the universe said it was time. Hey, you still riding that Honda ST1300?"

"Yeah. I fucking love that bike."

"So, what do you say to taking a nice long motorcycle trip with me, just bebop around, no timeline, no itinerary, just go where we want?"

"Uh."

"Vivi, you need to cut looooooose! You've been so rigid your entire life. It's time. You're done with school, go now while you can. Where you at?"

"Uh, I'm visiting Jared, in Morro Bay."

"Did you ride your bike or drive your cage?"

"I rode."

"Perfect! Load up your bike and get your ass down here to Bullhead City."

"I only brought enough gear for a quick weekend trip. I didn't bring any of the gear I'd need for a long road trip."

"Pfft. I've got plenty of extra gear. Load up, hit an ATM, and get your ass down here. You remember how to find my compound. I love ya!"

And with that, the call ended. I sat, first staring down at my phone and then out at the ocean. I shifted and the book in my lap slid to the floor. Staring up at me was a picture of Clement Salvadori, perched on a red Ducati, in the Marin Headlands overlooking the Golden Gate Bridge.

"Fine. Message received."

I hoisted myself up from the low futon and went out to the living room. Jared had showered and shaved and was setting up his ironing board. A pile of wrinkled clothes and hangers lined the back of the couch.

"Who was that?" he asked as he bent down to plug in his iron with a grunt.

"Bear."

"Oh! She's resurfaced?"

"Yup. She's back down in Bullhead City."

"Oh wow. How's she doin'?"

"Well, she wants me to ride down there and go on a big road trip with her, on our bikes."

Jared nodded, considering what I had said as he laid a dress shirt flat on the ironing board. "And are you going?"

"I-I think so." I ran my hand through my damp hair, flattening it down. "I mean, I'm in between jobs. The hot season is almost over. Now's probably the ideal time to go."

The iron hissed as Jared ran it over the collar of his shirt. He took his eyes off his work for a quick moment, looking right at me. "You should go, Vivian. When have you ever been totally carefree in your life? My guess would be...never. Tell you what, I know you packed light for your trip to see me. Let me loan you a few essentials. Rain poncho, sleeping roll, tent, thermals, stuff like that. I don't ride so I don't have any riding gear, but you'll need stuff for camping for sure and I can help with that." He walked out from behind the ironing board and pulled his Cal hat off the back of a kitchen chair. He put it snugly on my head and placed his big, warm hand on my shoulder. "I want you to take my hat. But you have to bring it back and stay long enough to tell me your stories from the road. Deal?"

Tears welled up in my eyes and my throat grew thick. "Yeah. It's a deal. Thanks, Jared," I said quietly.

I went to pack up my stuff, the sound of Van Morrison singing about a wild night drifting from the living room.

Chapter Eleven

After packing up my bags, I spread a big road map out on Jared's kitchen table. We plotted out the route to Bullhead City, which was right on the southern border of Nevada, snug in the corner where Arizona, Nevada, and California met. By my figuring, if all went well, it would take somewhere between seven and eight hours to get there.

Jared went out to get groceries. When he returned, we sat down to a lunch of big ham and swiss sandwiches, crunchy kettle chips, and some late season strawberries. He washed his down with a beer, and I stuck to water. A comfortable silence fell between us, the kind that we had enjoyed many times in the past. Baxter was in his usual spot under the table, happily sniffing around for dropped crumbs.

We pushed back from our plates once we had finished eating.

"I shoved a bunch of protein bars, nuts, bananas, and high energy snacks in your bag, plus a couple bottles of water. You'll need it all while you're on the road today."

"Thanks, bud. You're the best. You sure you're okay with me cutting our visit a day early to go gallivanting off in the desert?"

"You deserve it, Viv. You've had a rough go of things, and I think you'll have a good time. And, while Bear and I haven't always seen eye to eye, I know you are in good company with her. She'll take care of you in her own way."

I smiled at him and stood up. I cleared our dishes, used the bathroom one last time, and shot a quick text to Audre letting her know I'd had a change of plans and would call her later. I sent a text to Bear, telling her that I'd be rolling in around 9:00 p.m. if all went well.

Coming out of the bathroom I found Baxter leaning against my bag. I got down on the floor with him and gave him a big hug and lots of pets, stroking the smooth, golden fur along his neck and back. "I'll be back soon, Baxter, and we can go for a run or hike. I promise." His tail thumped on the floor and he raised his ears up at the word "run." We had a deal.

Jared helped carry my bag and gear down to the driveway. We jammed what we could into the hard bags and strapped the rest to the back seat and rear rack. He used painters' tape to secure the directions to my gas tank, where I could see them. The route I plotted out would have me weaving my way along CA-41, CA-58, and I-40.

I started up the engine, which was whisper quiet, and gave Jared a big hug as I waited for the bike to warm up.

"Text me now and then to let me know where you are. Have fun and be safe." He ended the hug but left his hand on my shoulder.

"Yup, agreed."

"What is it bikers say? Shiny side up and rubber side down?"

I chuckled. "Yeah, that's it. I'll do my best."

I checked my load to make sure everything was secure, straddled the bike, put on my helmet and gloves, and gave Jared a wave. I righted the bike, flipped up the kickstand with my heel, and popped the bike into first gear. Baxter was in the big picture window upstairs, keeping an eye on us. The downstairs tenant was also watching. I saw a twitch as a small gap in his curtain closed.

Checking that the street was clear, I rolled the throttle gently and pulled out. A quick glance over my shoulder showed Jared, standing squarely in his driveway, waving. I got onto CA-41 North and made my way out of Morro Bay quickly, stopping on the edge of town to top off the gas tank.

It was a mild day as far as September in California goes, and it was a Saturday so there weren't too many cars on the road, which made for smooth sailing. The vistas of brown, dry hills and fields stretched on mile after mile as I motored along CA-41, and eventually CA-58. I was reminded of the vastness of the state as the road rolled out before me.

The temperature rose as I came down the coastal mountains into a long stretch of hot, dry valley. Dust and sand blew across the narrow two-lane road in thin beige waves. I swallowed and realized I had grit in my teeth, which reminded me that I ought to take a break to hydrate. The road reminded me of riding Highway 1 on the coast, though as I rounded the many tight curves of CA-58, there was no vast ocean to be seen. Just more low hills covered in scrub brush and sage, dotted with oil derricks pumping slowly.

I enjoyed the thrill of the narrow curvy road, speeding along it, leaning into the turns and chasing my shadow as it sped along ahead of me. I saw a faded tan and brown sign that read: Brea Pits. I rolled off the throttle when I saw another sign informing me that the speed limit dropped down to 45 mph. A third sign informed me I was entering a town with a population of one hundred and sixty. An old rusty pickup truck ambled along ahead of me, which forced me to slow down and take in the sites, limited as they were. It was a dusty little town that stretched for maybe blocks. Low buildings edged the two-lane road. I pulled into the parking lot of a market and parked in the shade cast by the low stucco building.

I dismounted carefully, finding that my legs ached, but were somehow also numb. My entire body still vibrated from the bike engine and road despite being on still, solid ground. I peeled the helmet off my sweaty head and gratefully dug a bottle out of my bag that Jared had tucked away. I walked in a small circle in the parking lot, trying to get my legs back, while sipping on the water.

A taller brick building next door had a yellow and red sign spinning on the sidewalk out front. I squinted my sun blind eyes and saw that one side of the sign said "Penny" and the other side said "Bar." Penny Bar, Penny Bar, Penny Bar it advertised as it spun on and on. A hot breeze blew down the main road, bringing rivulets of dust and sand with it.

Curiosity piqued and bladder bursting, I locked up my bike as best as I could and strode across the small lot to the Penny Bar. I found that the façade of the entrance was covered in hundreds of carefully placed pennies. *Hmm.*

I opened the door and stepped inside. It was dark, as I expected of most bars. After the door closed behind me,

I stood stock still in the entry, allowing my eyes to adjust. When I could see, I looked around the room and found that the sign out front was no lie. The entire place was covered in thousands, maybe hundreds of thousands of pennies. The bar top, the pool table, the walls, the floor. Every square inch was covered in pennies that had been glued and lacquered down. A low murmur came from a separate room that housed what looked to be a diner. There wasn't anyone behind the bar, and only one sleepy looking gentleman propped up on a bar stool gazing down into a glass of beer. I walked around and found a hallway that was also covered floor to ceiling in pennies. It was really something to take in. Despite the lack of lighting in the place, the copper pennies shone.

I found the restroom, grateful for that little oasis of a town. After washing my hands and splashing some water on my face and the back of my neck, I walked outside to be blasted by hot wind and bright afternoon sun. Squinting, I ambled back over to my bike, legs oddly sore, and gave it a once-over to make sure none of my bags had been stolen and that my tires were still roadworthy. I finished off a bottle of water and rolled out of the little windswept town only to find more rolling hills dotted with oil derricks and scrub brush. And so it went, mile after mile.

I eventually made a dogleg on I-5 to CA-43 and zipped into Bakersfield to top off my gas tank. The bike could go about three hundred miles before needing fuel, but I was aware that what lay ahead was about five hours of barren open road. I fueled up, used the restroom again, and then moved my bike into the shade. I sat on the curb sipping water and pulled out my phone. I scrolled to Audre in my contacts. I hit the call button and the phone rang a couple of times, though it was hard to hear over the road noise.

"Hello?"

"Hey! Audre. How are you doing, my love?"

"Vivian! Great to hear from you after that vague text earlier. What are you up to? Or better yet, where are you?"

"Heh. Yeah. I am currently sitting on the curb behind a gas station in Bakersfield."

"Bakersfield? What are you doing in the armpit of California?"

"Hey now. Bakersfield has a bad reputation, but it's..." I looked at my surroundings, spotting a homeless encampment in a deserted lot, an overflowing dumpster behind the gas station, the filthy curb I was sitting on, and caught the distinct smell wafting from the slaughterhouses. "...it's lovely."

Audre chuckled with mirth. "Okay, fine. But really, why are you in Bakersfield?"

"Change of plans. I am going to take a motorcycle trip with Bear. Destination unknown."

"Bear! Oh, please send her my love. That sounds like the perfect thing for you right now."

A big drop of sweat dripped from the tip of my nose onto the pavement at my feet. "Yeah. Good timing. I'll be sure to give her a hug from you. What are you up to tonight?"

"I'm seeing Shae. We haven't had a proper date in a while, so she is taking me wine tasting and to a paint night."

"That sounds great. I hope you two have a great time."

"I will. Keep me posted when you can. And please be safe."

"You know it. Love you, babe."

"Love you too."

With that, I flipped the phone shut and put it in my pocket. An unbelievably loud hot rod bombed down the road, and I decided it was time to get the hell out of town. I hopped back on to CA-58, which was a wider four lane road, instead of the narrow two lanes I had been on earlier in the day.

Once out of the city the vista opened up again. Centered on the highway was Bear Mountain. I grinned inside my helmet when I recognized the correlation that I was on my way to see Bear, in the flesh.

It wasn't lost on me that Audre going on a nice date with Shae made me happy, and I genuinely hoped they had a good time. Whereas, when I had been in a relationship with Ang, I was always sick to my stomach and heartbroken whenever she had dates with others. The stark contrast was obvious, and I could only figure that with Audre I always felt full and loved, while with Ang there was a constant sense of scarcity...of emptiness and always feeling like she didn't share enough of herself with me. I reminded myself that I was not entitled to anything from anyone, and that I just needed to remember how each felt and move forward with that in mind.

I passed big rig after big rig. Huge caravans of them took up the slow lane. Soon enough the low rollers started as the highway began the climb up to Tehachapi Pass. The road passed by the North side of Bear Mountain. Up and up I climbed. One thousand feet elevation. Two thousand feet elevation. Big rigs in the right lane crawled their way up with their hazard lights on. The scrubby brown hillsides screamed for rain.

The road lost some elevation and I enjoyed bombing down the grade, praying there wasn't a highway patrol officer hidden around any of the bends. Then the steep climb continued. Three thousand feet. To my right, between more slow-moving big rigs, I saw the Tehachapi Mountains. And soon enough I buzzed right by the town of Tehachapi before finally making it to the top of Tehachapi Pass, at four thousand feet of elevation. Along the ridgeline ahead I spotted a wind farm. Countless massive white windmills spun in the wind.

As I passed the ridgeline and the wind farm, the landscape changed, the hills dropping out to a wide-open view of the Mojave Desert. The road straightened out, with berms of sand bordering it. I spent the next four hours trying to stay alert on the mind-numbing, hot stretch of road. My eyes burned, sweat dripped down my belly under my riding jacket, and my hands went numb.

I took a brief break in Needles to refill the gas tank, pee, chug a bottle of water, and get blood flow back to my legs, hands, and ass. My pee was almost the color of apple juice, which I knew was bound to happen since I had hardly had anything to drink and had sweat a ton. I made a mental note to hydrate when I got to Bear's place. I shook my arms out and stretched, hoping that the throbbing in my left shoulder would subside. Dusk was settling in as the sun sank lower in the sky behind me.

I checked my map and sent a quick text to Bear, letting her know I would be there in about thirty minutes.

I wanted to arrive at her place before dark and needed to get moving. I slid the helmet back on. The fresh hotspot on my scalp protested loudly. The cheek pads inside were damp with sweat. No time to deal with it. I got onto Mohave Valley Highway, which promptly turned into a bridge over the Colorado River. I shot quick glances up and down river but focused on not getting overrun by a jacked-up, lifted pickup truck that was on my tail. As I came down the other side, with very little fanfare, a sign declared that I had entered Arizona, the Grand Canyon State.

I scooted over and made room for the truck to pass, which it did, spouting huge plumes of black smoke from the massive smokestack exhaust pipes on the back of the cab. I glimpsed a decal on the back window that proudly advertised for Rolling Coal, so those huge smokestacks belching out clouds of black smoke were quite intentional. I rolled my eyes and held my breath as I drove through the exhaust.

Thankfully, the truck turned off a few blocks later, and not long after that I was out of town and back out in the open, irrigated fields, which soon gave way to the open desert. I fought with myself to stay alert and focused. Fatigue and dehydration had started to take over, making my eyes burn, head pound, and muscles scream to get off the bike.

I made it to Bullhead City, a low-slung town that had an abundance of strip malls and palm trees to balance out the dusty gaps in between. I skirted through town along the Colorado River, and then back inland until I was out in the boonies. Just as dusk faltered, I made it to Bear's compound, which was tucked into a crevice between two foothills.

The entry gate was wide open, and Bear sat on a low post, a paperback book resting on her knee, waving me in. She had a huge grin on her face; the gap between her front teeth and her wild, dark brown hair flashed into view as my headlight passed over her. I rolled slowly through the gate, following the hard-packed dirt and gravel driveway, and into the wide-open bay door of an outbuilding Bear had motioned toward.

I gingerly dismounted, not trusting my legs to support me, numb as they were. With great relief, I pulled off my helmet and gloves and watched as Bear closed the gate and walked over to me. Bear was built like, well...a bear, and was never in a hurry. I shook out my arms, legs, and hands, and stretched out my jaw and neck as I waited.

She chuckled as she approached, skate shoes kicking up dust, arms open wide. "Viviii! Come get this hug, bitch!"

I gave her the biggest damn smile I could muster, and our bodies came together into a rough embrace, which was followed by much laughing and back slapping.

"Look at-choo, Viv. You made it! Damn, I am so proud of you. I know spontaneity isn't your thing, and yet, here you are." She motioned to the vast expanse of the desert.

I faltered, my fuzzy brain made finding words difficult, and realized just how fatigued, hungry, and dehydrated I was. Bear saw it, too, and tsked at me.

"Grab yer shit, let's get you inside." I unlocked the hard bags and lifted them off the sides of my bike and fumbled with shaky, numb fingers to try to unclip the bungee cord holding my bag to the rear rack.

"Here, lemme," Bear said and had the bungee cord off with a flick of the wrist. "Let's go." Between the two of us we carried my gear across the dirt lot from the outbuilding to her house, which was a low, whitewashed cinderblock structure.

She pushed the door open with her foot and ushered me in. It was just as I remembered from earlier visits. Low ceilinged and furnished with mismatched, dinged up furniture. A massive TV took up one wall, with a couch and coffee table lined up front and center.

Her ancient dachshund got up from his bed and waddled over to me. "Hi, Clive, baby. How have you been, pup?" I asked him as he sniffed my pant leg absently before laying back down in his bed with a sigh.

"He's deaf as a post nowadays." Bear shook her head.

I shifted my weight, the bags growing heavy in my tired grip.

"Come on, come in dammit. You're in your usual room." She led me down a dark, narrow hallway. She flicked the light on in the room. I squeezed through the doorway and put everything on the floor.

"Why don't you take a quick shower and get settled? Dinner will be ready soon. There's a towel in there for you." With that she stepped out and closed the door. I shed my riding jacket and sat heavily on the soft bed, removing my boots with a gasp of relief.

I dug some sweats and clean underwear out of my bags and stumbled to the bathroom. I didn't bother turning on the light, and stood under the hot streaming water, waiting for my brain to perk up. Eventually I scrubbed myself down with Bear's shampoo and body wash, since I had forgotten to bring my hygiene kit into the bathroom. When I gingerly scrubbed at my hair, the hot spot on my scalp protested. Clean enough, I got out, toweled off, and dressed shakily. My sweats and warm socks were just the right amount of looseness and warmth that my body needed, and I sighed as I allowed myself to relax. When I opened the bathroom door I was met with the smell of dinner, and I groaned as my belly rumbled. Checking my watch, I saw that it was after 10:00 p.m. My last proper meal had been sandwiches with Jared in Morro Bay ten hours earlier, and I had burned a hell of a lot of energy and calories riding all day.

"Viv, get your ass in here and eat," Bear hollered. I wandered through her living room and took a seat at the kitchen table. It had been recently painted black, the top of it a bit tacky still. "You like it? I painted it last week. It looks so much better. After I get back from our trip, I am going to paint the universe on it and then seal it." She slid a massive bowl of beef stew in front of me and placed a plate of rolls in the middle of the table.

"I know it'll look great when you're done." I struggled to hold my head up as I spoke.

"Eat, dumbass, you look like you're about to pass out." She got up and came back with an enormous plastic cup of water and placed it next to my bowl. It was one of those massive soda cups you get at the gas station.

"Let me guess, you wanted to get here before dark, so you rode like a machine and didn't stop. Now you feel like shit, and your body hurts all over. Am I right?"

I nodded as I spooned some stew into my mouth. The flavors hit my tongue and I smiled at her. The broth was the perfect blend of beef and salt with hints of bay leaves and veggies. The next spoon had a big bite of potato and carrot on it, which I chewed greedily, ignoring the fact that the inside of my mouth was being scorched by hot potato. Bear ate a few bites, watching me.

"You remember the last time I made this for us?"

I pondered the question while I had a few more bites. Then it came to me. "Yup, car camping at Lake Solano. Somehow you convinced me to go camping in fucking February. It was so cold overnight, but the sunrises were amazing, and you kept us fed really well."

She nodded at me. Clive made his way over to the kitchen and lowered himself onto the floor at Bear's feet. I took in the white whiskers on his muzzle, and his patchy fur, remembering how he had looked in his younger years.

"Wow, he sure is hanging on, isn't he?" I said before chugging half the cup of water.

"Yeah. He's got it pretty good here and he lurvs me, so he hasn't given up the ghost yet."

I nodded and forced myself to eat slowly so I didn't make myself sick. I grabbed a roll and dipped it in the remnants of the stew.

"So, I think tomorrow while you are resting up, we can talk about where we wanna go on this trip. Sound okay?" I nodded at her. She got up and topped off my cup of water. "Drink up."

"Dude, I'm gonna be up all night peeing."

"Your body needs it, and besides, we don't have shit to do tomorrow, you can take a nap. Drink up."

I finished up the stew, rolls, and water. My body was happy to have some liquid and hearty food on board. The shakes wore off as we cleared our plates and I followed Bear into the living room, my eyes already drooping. She turned on the enormous TV and grabbed a game controller before sitting in an odd little chair, smack dab in front of the TV. The chair was low on the ground and shaped kind of like a padded pilot's chair, with a big headrest and armrests. Clive made his way slowly to his bed, which was within arm's reach of her chair.

"What's about to happen?" I asked as the light from the TV filled the dark room.

"Gaming."

"And the chair? I've never seen anything like it."

"Have you been living under a rock, dude? It's a gaming chair. See?" She demonstrated by resting her head on the headrest and leaning back in the chair. It had a round bottom so when she rocked back, she ended up in a position where she was gazing up at the huge screen. I scratched my head.

Her game began its opening sequence, the music blaring out of the speakers. She grabbed a headset and plugged it in, silencing the TV speakers. "You wanna watch?" she shouted into the silent room.

"Sure," I said and lay down on the couch, pulling a blanket over myself. The huge screen was a blur of color and flashing light as Bear's character ran through an urban combat scenario, shooting at snipers and blowing up cars and buildings. Warm and cozy under the blanket, supported by the well-worn couch, I fell asleep within minutes.

*

"Gas! Gas! Gas!"

I pulled off my helmet and dug in the pouch strapped to my leg. I ripped out my M40 gas mask and yanked it down over my head and face roughly. With practiced hands I tightened the straps, placed my palm over the filter canister, and drew in air, sealing the mask to my face. I slapped my helmet back on as best I could and peered out the side window of the Humvee. A cloud of smoke enshrouded the vehicle, and I clutched my M16, hoping like hell that the canister on my gas mask was capable of filtering out whatever the hell was in that smoke. Chemical and biological warfare were a threat we had been warned of and had trained for, but this was my first time potentially being gassed by the enemy.

"Ramirez," I hollered, the air hot and muggy inside the gas mask.

Jared turned in his seat, his eyes wide behind the lenses of his mask.

"You're not scared of a little gas, are ya?" I chided, trying to cut through the insanity of the moment.

Jared blinked at me and shook his head as his eyes narrowed and regained focus.

The roof gunner began scrambling and shouted down to us. "Dismount!"

We were in an up-armored Humvee which meant the doors were cumbersome. I struggled to get the heavy door open and rolled out onto the gravel. A sharp pain bloomed in my lower abdomen.

*

I woke with a thump as I rolled off Bear's couch and onto the hard tile floor. Gasping, I scanned the dark room and recognized I was not in danger. I sat up slowly, registering that the room had grown cold. The walls creaked against the gusting desert winds outside. The only light was from a lava lamp in the corner that cast bizarre shadows on the ceiling. I rubbed my shoulder and the side of my head that had hit the floor. My bladder signaled that it was near bursting so, hands outstretched, I shuffled gingerly to the bathroom. Afterward I made it to the bed, snuggled up under layers of blankets, and fell immediately back to sleep, praying not to relive the memory that had made its way into my dream cycle again.

Chapter Twelve

Unfortunately, the dream picked right back up where it had ended when I hit the floor. It cycled over and over until I woke again, sweating and gasping for air. I found that I was burrowed down with the blankets over my head, which were damn near suffocating me. I popped my face out and squinted my eyes against the bright sunshine piercing the sheer curtain.

"Fuck," I groaned. I was exhausted and my clothes clung to my damp skin. I stood, realizing I needed to piss immediately. As my feet hit the floor, my head swooned and throbbed. I shuffled to the bathroom and let out a massive amount of pee. After washing my hands, I splashed water on my face and in my hair and then fluffed my sweatshirt, circulating some air to my skin underneath. Rubbing my burning eyes, I looked in the mirror with a grimace.

Clive was waiting for me in the hallway, wagging his skinny tail slowly. I followed him through the living room to the kitchen. Bear opened the oven and pulled out a tray of bacon. She put it on the counter next to a plate piled high with waffles. She transferred the bacon to a plate covered in paper towels, while she shook her hips and kept raising her hand, singing the high notes to a Prince song that I recognized but couldn't hear. I spotted a wire and realized she was wearing earbuds.

I sat down at the kitchen table quietly and watched her finish up making breakfast between dance breaks. She rinsed her hands and turned to grab the towel hanging off a hook at the end of the counter when she saw me and burst out in laughter. Her laugh, unique as it went from a chuckle to a cackle, was contagious. I broke into a smile and clapped as she pulled out her earbuds and curtsied. She wore an oversized, faded Batman T-shirt and baggy flannel pajama bottoms. Her outfit was accessorized with a pair of huge fluffy Pac-Man slippers.

"You sleep okay? You passed out so hard on the couch I couldn't bring myself to wake you."

"Yeah, I slept okay." No point in reliving the shitty PTSD cycle I had been stuck in the previous night.

"You sure? Cuz you look like shit, Vivi."

"Thanks. You always tell it like it is, Bear. I appreciate that about you. Yeah, I'm okay aside from a pounding headache."

"Seeeee. Dehydrated. I know coffee isn't your thing, so I picked up some of them peppermint tea bags that you like. How 'bout that?"

I nodded and watched as she filled a Star Wars mug with water, plunked a tea bag in, and nuked it in the microwave. She placed the steaming hot mug in front of me.

"Let's eat," she said and clapped her hands. We piled our plates with waffles and bacon and scrambled eggs. All conversation stopped as we plowed through the food. My body sucked up every calorie with gusto. I wiped the final bite of waffle through a puddle of maple syrup, cleaning my plate, and ate it with joy. My tea had finally cooled down, and I sipped it as we looked at each other across our empty plates.

"So, what's up? You've got something big hanging around you. Spill it, Viv."

"Dammit, I can't ever keep anything from you."

"My ancestors, Viviana. They tell me." She pointed to the ceiling, her expression dead serious. "So, what is it? Girl problems? Money problems? Is it your mom again?"

"Work problems actually. I got fired."

Bear raised her eyebrows. "Damn. I thought they liked you there."

"They did. I don't know what's up. But it's a done deal."

"Fuck."

"Yeah."

"Well, if you need a change of pace, you can always come stay down here. I have more than enough room. My mom and dad put in a modular home behind the car barn on the backside of my property, but they are gone on some round the country RV trip, so their place will be empty for months. You're welcome to it. My mom loves your dumb ass."

"Thanks. I'll think about it. But hey, let's talk about our moto trip. Where are we headed?"

"We can check out the Grand Canyon, that's pretty close by. If we are going north that'd be a good place to start. Or did you want to go south, down into Mexico?"

"I didn't bring my passport, so I need to stay in the US. I think I can manage about a week. So, let's start with that."

Bear scoffed at being limited to one week.

"Ey. I gotta get back and find myself a job. The rent isn't going to pay itself. Which they raised, by the way."

She nodded and grumbled. I cleared the table and Bear spread out a road map of the US. She also produced a notebook, pen, and purple highlighter. I sat next to her and took in the vast options that lay before us.

We spent the entire morning in our pajamas, poring over the map, talking through road conditions, weather, timing, where to stop and sightsee, what gear we would need, how far our bikes could go between refueling, and the other myriad things one has to consider when planning a motorcycle trip. By noon we had agreed to a route, jotted it down on scratch paper, and highlighted it on the map. We broke for lunch and showers.

After eating I gave myself a head and neck massage in the shower, grateful that my headache had subsided. Clean and dressed in jeans, a T-shirt, and riding boots, I was ready to venture outside. I found a motorcycling magazine on the coffee table and sat, reading, until Bear came out dressed, tucking her damp hair under a flat billed Nintendo hat. Clive followed right behind her, waddling.

"You wanna go give our bikes a looking over to make sure they're ready for this trip?" I asked, settling the magazine down.

Bear scratched the back of her neck. "Sure."

She lifted Clive, who wouldn't be able to keep up with us outside. I opened the front door and was blasted by the midday Arizona sun. Squinting, I stepped onto the hard-packed dirt outside. About fifty yards away was the car barn, and I caught a peek of the home her parents had built behind it. Otherwise, there was nothing but open, windswept land and the two rolling hills that her land was situated between. I thought of the post-apocalyptic wastelands in the Mad Max movies but recognized that this was just Arizona.

We walked to the barn, the sun immediately biting into the bare flesh on the back of my neck and arms. I slid the big bay door open and stepped into the cool shade with a sigh of relief. I ran my hand over the gas tank and seat of my bike before looking around the barn. Bear's classic Beetle Bug was parked in its usual place. It had cream-colored paint, and leopard print upholstered seats.

Big, rolling tool cases lined the walls, and in the middle of the barn was an engine lift. Her welding cart was parked next to a rack of scavenged scrap metal. Wood pallets were stacked up high. I knew Bear picked pallets up whenever she found them and broke them down for firewood.

Projects at various stages of completion were spread out. Art projects. Motorcycle builds. The walls were decorated with graffiti art, murals of the universe, and cyborg women. The car barn summed up Bear pretty damn well.

I scanned the place, looking for Bear's bike, which was a 2001 Yamaha Road Star 1600, lovingly named Champagne.

"Ey. Where's..." My words were stopped in my throat as I spotted the skeletal remains of Champagne. The fenders and gas tank were laid out on a work bench. Electrical wires poked out from the frame here and there. The bike was stripped to bare metal, the inner workings exposed. It took me a minute to digest what I saw as I stood there on the concrete.

Bear stepped up next to me, groaning as she set down Clive. His nails clicked on the concrete as we walked over to an old open crate with a blanket inside.

Bear straightened and I turned to her. "What happened to Champagne?"

"Doing an engine rebuild and fixing the electrical." She scuffed the toe of one of her Vans on the floor.

"What are you going to ride on our trip?" I looked around the barn for another bike. She usually had at least one spare, but I didn't see anything complete and road ready aside from a dirt bike that sure as hell wasn't street legal.

"I'm not."

Confusion bubbled up in my chest. I was baffled.

"I...what?" Anger released and I raised my voice just a hair. "I don't understand. You asked me out here to go on a motorcycle trip with you. We literally just spent all morning planning out the route."

"Yes. And it's a great route. You're going to have a blast. I'll tail you in the Beetle Bug to the Grand Canyon. After that it's all you, babe."

I clenched my teeth and balled my hands into fists. We stood there staring at each other as hot wind gusted by outside. Bear didn't flinch and didn't back down. Her dark-brown eyes solidly met my gaze and held it. My mind raced, trying to figure out what to do next, but it was logjammed because I simply didn't understand at all what was going on.

"Why?" It was all I could squeeze out between my tight lips. My throat grew thick as I realized tears were about to start falling.

"I said it before. My ancestors told me." She said it without blinking, her face dead serious.

My temper snapped and the tears disintegrated into anger. "Bear! Your ancestors told you to mislead me and lure me out to this godforsaken fucking desert? You know my world doesn't work like that. My life is *very* black and white."

"And mine isn't. I live and commune with the spirits. And here you are."

The tears threatened to come back. I looked away from Bear to Champagne and at my bike, and then at the scuffed-up toes of my boots. Heat flushed up my neck and face as tears rolled down my cheeks, splatting on the floor and the front of my shirt.

Bear placed her hand on my shoulder, which I shook off, caught between anger and...what was it? I closed my eyes and thought about what Alexia had taught me about feeling my feelings and really dissecting them, finding the root. I focused on where in my body I felt it, and once pinpointed, I talked to it. To my six-year-old self, actually, and there it was: rejection. I thanked the rejection for trying to protect me and told it I would take it from there. I'd spent a lot of time in therapy to learn how to do that and was glad I had gotten the hang of it.

Bear stood in the same place, waiting for me. I turned my face to my shoulder and wiped my tears on my shirt sleeve, and then looked back at her.

"What am I doing here, Bear?"

"I don't know. But here is where you are supposed to be. And this trip, it's for you. Not for me."

Exasperated, I simply nodded and let all the anger and frustration go.

Quietly, I asked, "Okay. Will you help me give my bike a once-over? Make sure it's ready?"

"Of course."

In silence, like the team we were, we inspected my bike from top to bottom. Topping off all the fluids, adjusting the tire pressure, checking the horn, lights, and brakes. Washing all the bugs off my windscreen and face shield. I was pretty good about staying up to date on bike maintenance, so nothing major needed to be done.

We washed our hands in the shop sink and stood looking out of the bay door at her squat little house.

"Do you mind if I take your dirt bike out and ride around the property a little?"

"You remember where the property line is?"

"Yep."

"Have at it. The dirt bike is a bitch to start, but let's give it a whirl."

She rolled the bike out of its corner toward the bay door, and I took it. Straddling the seat, I flipped the petcock open and dropped the bike into neutral, then I unscrewed the gas cap and checked that the fuel tank had gas in it. I sealed the gas tank back up and gripped the lever that engaged the front brake and rolled the throttle three times to prime the engine. I swiveled out the kick start lever and placed my foot on, balancing the weight of the bike on my left leg. I lowered my right foot until it met resistance and then gave it a solid push. The engine whirred but didn't fire up. I gave a second, more explosive kick and the engine fired to life. I swiveled the kick starter lever so it was flush with the bike and rolled the throttle a couple of times to keep it running. The motor revved loudly in the barn and Bear hooted and patted me on the back.

"Have fun," she shouted over the ruckus as I rode out of the barn.

Bear's property was perfect for dirt bike riding because it didn't have any fences and was barren and wide open. I rolled the throttle and shot out a rooster tail of dirt as I took off toward the hills. Between the dust and bright sun, I immediately wished I had put on some sunglasses but carried on. I pushed the bike as fast as I dared, eating up the flat ground until a slow incline began. The crevice between the hills created a bowl, and I rode countless laps around the bowl, my knuckles white, heart pounding, dusty tears flowing down my hot cheeks. I almost never rode without a helmet, so there was a level of wild abandon and risk that brought a smile to my face along with the tears.

When I grew tired, I slowed to a stop and parked the bike in a strip of shade cast by the hillside, then I sat down in the dirt, legs stretched out. The open landscape in front of me was so foreign after having lived in Morro Bay and Midtown Sacramento since leaving the army. The lower layer of the horizon was yellow with distant dust storms, above which was a clear, deep-blue sky. There was a distinct absence of any smell to the air. A small lizard sunned itself on a rock just beyond my strip of shade.

I lay down on the ground, tucking my hands behind my head, pebbles digging into my back, and stared up into the sky. There was literally nothing to see besides uninterrupted blue overhead. No birds, no airplanes, no clouds.

The bike engine ticked as it cooled next to me, the heat of it radiating toward me. I closed my eyes and allowed the fatigue of the previous day and night to wash over me. My brain blanked out and I knew sleep would come at any moment. I was jerked back awake by vibrating and ringing from my front pocket. I pulled out my phone and slid it open, eyes still closed.

"This is Vivian."

"Hey, babe. How are you?" The smooth, even voice of Audre purred into my ear.

"Hellooo, Audre. I'm doing well."

"I was beginning to worry about you."

"Yes, sorry. I should have called, or texted at the very least, to let you know I made it. I was an absolute zombie by the time I reached Bear's place last night and today has been...weird. I apologize. I will try to be better at keeping you up to date. How are you?"

"I'm good. My family missed you at Sunday lunch and said to say hello. And...I miss you too. I've really enjoyed having you with us on Sunday afternoons."

"Thanks. It's good to be missed—if that makes sense."

"It does." She paused. "Are you sure you are okay?"

"Yeah. I'm good. Just didn't sleep well."

"Was it from sleeping in a new place, or are the dreams back?"

"Dreams. Memories, really. But yeah."

"Sorry. I wish I was there to hold you."

I chuckled. "You wouldn't want to hold me right now. I am covered in sweat and bike grease and am lying on the rough ground in the desert."

"That sounds about right. And I wouldn't change a thing about that. Though you are right that I'm not gonna lay in the dirt with you. Okay, I'll let you go. Enjoy your nap, sweetie."

"I love you," I said, and really meant it. My heart swelled up in my chest as the words crossed my lips. *Jesus, I must be tired.* I rubbed my eyes.

"I love you too. Keep me posted on your trip, please."

"I will."

We ended the call, and I slid the phone back into my pocket and rolled onto my side in the fetal position, tucking my hands under my face to keep it mostly out of the pebbles and dust. Sleep came swiftly, but rest and recovery did not.

*

"Gas! Gas! Gas!" I shouted as I fumbled out of the Humvee and ran low toward some soldiers who were taking cover behind a Quonset hut. They didn't have masks on, and the cloud of smoke was right on my heels. I shouted it again and made the arm signal for gas as I ran by. They bolted upright and ran behind me. I glanced

back and saw that they were putting on their masks while running, which was no easy feat, but better than choking to death on whatever chemical had been launched at us.

I skidded to a halt at the end of the long Quonset hut and peered around the corner. The road was clear, so we darted across and took cover behind the next hut. My M16 was slung over my shoulder. I yanked on the strap and got it into my hands.

Jared and a handful of other soldiers, unrecognizable behind their masks, darted across the road and took cover with us. Thankfully, one was our radio operator, and he immediately got to work ringing up the brass for me. Jared crouched low at one end of the hut, M16 at the ready. He signaled for another soldier to do the same at the other end. I appreciated how Jared always had my back.

The radio operator shook his head at me, indicating he hadn't been able to get through, and then went back to work trying to connect with our command team. I scanned the area, which had fallen eerily quiet. We were in an extremely vulnerable position and I needed to get us out of it.

The silence was broken by a fwoomp sound and then the clink of metal on metal overhead. I looked up and saw a small canister bounce over the roof of the hut. The cylindrical canister landed right between the radio operator and me. He was too engrossed in his task to notice, and I simply stared at it for a moment as my brain registered it for what it was: a chemical grenade.

"Grenade! Down! Down!" I shouted as I sprang up and kicked it away as hard as I could. The canister

skittered away and exploded, shrapnel and clods of dirt flying in every direction. My training kicked in and my body reacted without any thought as I dropped into a head-on prone position, face down in the dirt as debris rained down.

*

I woke with a start, panting, face down in the dirt. Something tickled the back of my neck and concern about long-ago shrapnel and dirt clods came to mind. I reached back and swiped at my neck. Shock ran through me as something small and furry responded to my touch. I slapped it off me and it landed on the ground next to my face... It was a tarantula. I lay still, my cheek on the ground, and watched as the spider walked away.

I'd been holding my breath and released it in one big gush. Standing up, I dusted myself off, and recognized that my mouth was gluey. Dammit, I hadn't brought any food or water with me. The sun was setting fast, and I didn't want to get stuck out in the pitch-black desert.

I prepped the bike and kicked down on the lever. The bike gave a faint whir but didn't engage. I tried again. Nothing. I closed my eyes and fought off the panic and frustration that was trying to rise in my chest. I ran through all the steps again. Bike in neutral. Throttle pumped to prime the engine. Front brake on. All good. I gave three more solid kicks, my leg tiring. I took a moment to rest and then kicked down again, the bike finally firing up. Relief flooded me as I aimed the bike toward Bear's house and opened the throttle up wide. She had turned on the outside floodlights, which helped me find my way in the settling dusk.

*

Bear cackled when I told her about the tarantula on my neck.

"Yeah, they are out in force this time of year. October is their mating season. That'll teach you to sleep out in the open in the desert. Plus look at your cute pink nose. You've got a touch of sunburn to top it all off."

I grumbled as I unlaced my boots. She brought me a massive plastic cup full of water, which I downed about half of before going to the kitchen and washing the dishes. She had cooked me several meals, so the least I could do was clean up. Bear sat at the kitchen table, coloring in a mandala coloring book, earbuds in her ears.

When I had finished, I tapped her shoulder and she held up a finger, indicating that I should wait. She pulled a slim silver device from her pocket, touched the screen, and popped her earbuds out.

"Listening to an audiobook."

I tilted my head, eyeing the thing she had pulled from her pocket. Pointing at it, I asked, "What is that?"

"It's an iPod Mini. Do you not know what an MP3 player is?"

"I've heard of MP3 players. But...you touched that circle thing to control it? How...what?"

"It's a click wheel."

I looked at her blankly. She sucked her teeth and fixed me with a stern look. "Really, Viv?"

She held the iPod up and poked at the wheel, which lit the LED screen up. She gave me a quick tutorial.

I was amazed and baffled at how far behind I was when it came to technology.

We had leftover beef stew and rolls for dinner, and she chatted animatedly about her former career as a body snatcher, picking up the bodies of dead people who had died from suicides and natural causes.

"One time I had to pick up a suicide from the train tracks in Sacramento. She had stepped in front of the train. I was so mad at her for it. She was such a pretty lady. Dressed in a pale-blue nightgown. The train barely left a mark on her. It just—*poof*—knocked the life out of her."

She went on to tell me about a man who had committed suicide in the bathtub and hadn't been found for quite some time. She referred to him as "chicken skin man" because when she tried to remove him from the tub his skin slid right off in her hands.

"Shit," was all I could say. She had told me all those stories before, and they never got easier to hear.

A long silence fell between us, each in our own thoughts. Exhausted, I got up and cleared the dishes.

"You going to head out tomorrow, or stick around? You're welcome to stay as long as you want," she said over her shoulder to me.

"I think I'll head out first thing. You still want to go with me to the Grand Canyon though?"

"Yeah. I'd love to see it with you. Super bummed I can't ride with you to get there, but it's not my time. You know how much I love riding with you."

"Yeah. Same."

We recounted how we had first met at a motorcycle poker run in Marysville, California and how motorcycling had been the bond that brought us together. We ended up sitting on the couch in the dim light of the lava lamp late into the night, talking about all our epic rides, camping trips, and trouble we had gotten into, and out of. At a certain point I was slurring and could barely keep my eyes open. Bear sent me to bed, and I did as I was told.

Chapter Thirteen

Up before the sun, I showered and packed up my bags. I joined Bear in the kitchen. She was shuffling around in her slippers making coffee for herself and peppermint tea for me. I prepared a big batch of scrambled eggs, toast, and fruit, which we obliterated in silence while Clive waited patiently on the floor, licking up crumbs.

Afterward I carried my gear out to the barn in the predawn glow. Loading up the bike, by flashlight, I made last-minute checks to tire pressure and fluids and stretched out my sore muscles. I peeled off the painter's tape and directions from my trip to Bullhead City, and then taped down my new directions for the day.

There was a flash on the horizon and the day dawned anew. With air cold enough that my breath bloomed in clouds, I wandered around the barn looking at all of Bear's artwork until Bear closed up her house and joined me in the car barn, wearing an insulated Carhartt jumpsuit, a beanie pulled low, and carrying Clive in his bed.

"You ready?" she asked, tilting her head.

"Yeah. Let's go."

She placed Clive's bed on the passenger seat of her old Beetle and buckled herself up behind the wheel. It took a few turns of the key before the engine fired up, belching clouds of gray exhaust. I started up my bike and pulled on cold weather riding gear as we waited for our engines to warm up enough to roll out.

The exhaust in the barn got to be too strong, prompting me to straddle my bike and pull out onto the driveway. Bear rumbled behind me, her VW engine far louder than the sewing machine hum of my finely tuned motorcycle.

I led the way out onto Highway 40. The sun continued to rise and expose the wide-open plains dotted with occasional scrub brush. We were riding straight into the sun, the bright light forcing me to squint, which gave me a slight headache. Just before the turn off for Highway 64 North little rollers started and all manner of pine trees dotted the land, though the underbrush was still dead brown grasses. On Highway 64 we passed through a couple of small towns, though for the most part it was just mile after mile of empty two-lane road. I was glad to have the sun off to my right, which allowed me to relax my eyes a bit.

I followed the brown-and-white signs to the Grand Canyon. Once inside the park, I rode on Desert View Road around until we reached the watchtower. I climbed off the bike on stiff legs and took my time removing a few layers of clothing, stretching out my legs, arms, and neck, and drinking some water. Bear took Clive into the shrubs so he could pee before putting him back in the car. I jogged over to the restrooms and used the toilet before splashing some cold water on my face.

We walked out to the watchtower and snagged ourselves a bench away from the groups of tourists making their pilgrimages to the rim of the canyon. We sat, buried in our own thoughts for a while. But eventually my curiosity about Bear's intentions returned.

"I'm trusting you that taking this ride by myself is the right thing, you know." I leaned into her shoulder.

"Yeah. I know. And I can't promise that things will go smoothly, but this is where you are supposed to be right now. That much I do know." She paused, swinging her legs slowly. "You know the root of the word travel? It comes from the word travail. And travail...that means something is going to be a pain in the ass. Like you." She chuckled, clouds of steam coming out in short puffs.

"You're not really selling this solo trip very well."

"Look. I've known you a long time. I've seen you go through a lot. And one thing I know about you is that you need to learn to be happy on your own."

I turned and looked at her as she continued gazing out over the canyon. Her profile was so distinct: a few dark hairs springing out from under her beanie, her freckled skin somewhere between tan and olive, sharp chin, and a nose like an eagle's beak.

Defensiveness rose in my chest as I sat back, leaning my shoulder on hers again.

"I'm alone a lot. I don't know what you mean."

"Yeah, you are alone a lot. And you keep a small circle of friends, that is true. You live alone in your studio. But think about what you do with your time alone. Viv, you are always on the move. Always filling every second with cleaning, hiking, running, riding, reading, geocaching, working. When do you allow yourself to just exist? To be in your own presence?"

I gave that some thought and couldn't fault her logic. She was right. I was always doing something to occupy my mind or body.

"What happens when you do find yourself with no activity to do? Do you sit in the silence and just...be?"

"I get immediately antsy and find something to do."

Out of the corner of my eye I saw Bear nod slowly.

"So, it's time to find a way to knock that shit off. Take time over the next week to just stop. Stop and look at the land. Think your thoughts and feel your feelings. Have your fun, too, but stop running from yourself, dammit."

"So, when did you become my life coach?" We both gave a small laugh and leaned on each other. The comfort of our connection returned, and we sat in silence.

*

We shared a midmorning snack of peanut butter and honey sandwiches, kettle chips, and a banana for me. I made sure to hydrate. Bear helped me tuck away the cold weather riding clothes since I wouldn't need them the rest of the day. My bike was laden with compact camping gear and supplies, and I looked at it with pride. I was ready. I reached through the window and pet Clive's smooth head. "You be a good boy for your mama," I told him gently. He licked my hand in acknowledgment.

Bear came around and gave me a proper bear hug, squeezing the air out of me and then thumping me on the back heartily.

"Thanks for everything. I appreciate you. You'll have to come visit soon so I can return all of the gear you're loaning me."

"You got it. I'll have Champagne up and running soon enough. And ey, don't take any shit from anyone while you're out on the road. You're gonna be passing through some small rural places with some backward-ass mindsets."

I nodded and patted her shoulder. "You know you don't need to worry about me. I can take care of myself."

"You're tough as fuck... I wouldn't eat you on Donner Pass. But you know I'll worry about you anyway. Now get your ass outta here."

With that I headed out to AZ-64 and made my way east to US-89 north. Despite being surrounded by what I knew were amazing vistas I didn't pay any of it much attention as I processed what Bear had said about me not being able to just be, about not being comfortable by myself. She was right that I kept my brain or body busy most of the time, but I was still pissed off that she had called me out on it. Had I not been working hard for the last couple of years in therapy, and didn't I have a better handle on my temper? I had better balance in my life, and despite it all I still wasn't comfortable with silence.

I nearly missed my turn to 89A but saw it at the last second and made a sharp left, cutting off an oncoming farm truck. My heart rate doubled and my brain refocused on the task at hand, which was to ride safely. Less than a mile after turning onto 89A, which was barren, I saw a structure. As I approached it, I groaned. It was a Mormon temple. One of the problems I had with the route we chose was that I would be passing through Utah and Idaho, both ultra conservative Mormon states, which were a safety issue for me as a butch-presenting lesbian. I had designed the route to avoid Utah as much as possible, so I would only be in it briefly, skirting just the bottom corner, yet there I was, in northern Arizona approaching the Utah border, and saw my first sign of the church.

I blew past the temple and opened the throttle a tad. The two-lane highway was lightly traveled. When safe, I'd pass slower moving minivans, big rigs, and old pickup trucks. Otherwise, it was just mile after mile of barren desert land punctuated by scrub brush and the occasional homesteads, which were situated far from the road. I wondered how the people who lived way out there made money to survive. There was nowhere nearby to work and none of the homesteads appeared to have livestock. It was far too arid to grow crops, so they weren't farmers or ranchers.

Eventually rock formations began to break up the landscape and the road hooked to the left where I spotted a bridge ahead. Before the bridge, I took a turnout and discovered a parking lot and information center. Signs advertised it as Navajo Bridge Interpretive Center. I parked and carefully dismounted, testing my legs. I found them numb but steady and shed my helmet and jacket before digging out a bottle of water and another peanut butter and honey sandwich and tucking a banana in my back pocket. I downed the water and sandwich while leaning on my bike, and then sauntered over to the information center to use the restroom and check the place out.

The structure was long and low, and built out of stones that appeared to be from the surrounding area. The visitor's center was as you expect from any state or federal park. Racks of postcards, shelves of books, and helpful staff. They informed me that running parallel to the current bridge is the old Navajo Bridge, and that I could walk on it. I went outside and was amazed. Sure enough, the bridge had been designated for pedestrians only. I walked through a metal gate where the sign informed me that I was on the ninth highest bridge in the US, and the Colorado river was 467 feet below.

Indeed, there were steep cliffs that dropped straight down, with the bridge connecting one side of the river to the other. I walked halfway across and leaned on the railing, looking upstream while I ate a banana. I had never seen anything like it, and I knew I probably never would again. The sharp drops of the cliffs, with layered rock formations, the river flowing so far below, and endless clear blue skies.

After I finished the banana, my instinct was to get going. After all, I still had many hours of riding ahead of me. But I considered Bear's words about allowing myself to be, so I did. I took my time examining the rocks and cliffs in the distance, paying more attention to the fine details, and began feeling something akin to longing.

My chest throbbed gently with the desire to share the moment with someone. In the past I would have had the urge to have Ang with me, but that was no more. Audre. That's who I wanted to share it with. To wrap my arm around her waist, feel her warmth beside me, and hear her thoughts on the view. I began to reach into my pocket to call her and tell her how amazing it was, but I stopped myself, remembering that it was good to be in that moment alone.

An internal battle was being waged between the anxiety to get back on the road and the desire to silence it and stay. I closed my eyes and breathed deeply. The desert air didn't smell like anything. I stayed there, suspended 467 feet above the abyss, and breathed until the sound of people approaching caused me to open my eyes and take one last look before returning to the parking lot. I tossed the browning banana peel in a trash can and used the restroom again before mounting up.

Back on the bike, I rode across the new Navajo Bridge, marveling at the fact that I was riding across a bridge so high. Another new and exhilarating experience and no one to share it with but myself. Immediately after reaching the far side of the bridge, I pulled into a gas station in Marble Canyon to top off my tank. I had plenty of fuel left, but knew I was getting close to the border with Utah, and I planned to blast through Utah without stopping.

I made quick work of the next stretch of road, which was straight until suddenly it wasn't. The road did a sudden S curve followed by more wide curves as the terrain began to change. Hills sprouted up all around, covered in trees. The farther I went the steeper the hills, the twistier the road, and the denser the trees. Just as quickly the trees disappeared. The barren landscape carried on mile after mile as my hands, ass, legs, and feet went numb while I sweated under my jacket, and noticed a throbbing starting up in my left shoulder.

Mercifully, the road led me to a town called Fredonia, where I stopped and rested under a tree until the throbbing and numbness began to wear off. It soon became apparent that people were watching me, and the vibes were bad enough that I left town while I still could. I hooked a left and got on AZ-389 to the Utah border crossing, which was uneventful.

The road continued to twist and turn and climb, and while my inclination was to haul ass through Utah as fast as possible, I made sure to watch my speed because getting pulled over was something I truly wanted to avoid. UT-59 melded into UT-17 and then blurred into I-15, which provided a nice straight stretch of road until I turned west on UT-56, skirting Stoddard Mountain. I started to see farmland and found it odd that the crops were planted in huge circular fields, rather than the rectangular plots back home in the Sacramento Valley.

After one last slow bend in the road, I breathed a sigh of relief as I crossed the border into Nevada. Then the road straightened out again and the ride was smooth until I had to make a turn in the town of Majors Place. It took me a few minutes to realize that the Highway 50 I had turned onto was *the* Highway 50. The same one that ran west right through Sacramento. It carried me upward as the elevation continued to climb. Thirty minutes later I arrived at a campground just before the city of Ely, Nevada, which was my planned stop for the night.

I flopped off the bike a dehydrated, underfed, and exhausted mess. Check-in was a blur. Setting up the tent and campsite was done by pure muscle memory. I had zero energy or motivation to ride into to town to find a proper meal, so I sat in the small vestibule of the low one-man tent and warmed up an MRE.

MREs had served me well in the military. They were designed to be calorie and carb dense, which was exactly what my body needed. I poured water in the sleeve, activating the magnesium powder inside, and sealed it. The pouch inflated as it began to boil. Waiting, I prepared the lemon-lime electrolyte drink and opened the giant cracker packet. I squeezed the contents of the peanut butter pouch on it. The concoction was similar to eating wallpaper paste, but it was familiar and I didn't care. I was simply happy to be eating and getting some energy into my body.

While I waited the requisite twelve minutes to ensure my food was properly heated, I thought about my visit with Bear and how she had never intended to ride with me. I got stuck there, wondering about why Bear felt the need to lure me out to Arizona and why I was so incredibly anxious.

Bear had always been steadfastly herself. She moved smoothly between daily life, her own personal demons, and her ancestry. Half Mexican and half Inuit, she had lived a life I couldn't relate to, but I had always accepted her for who she was, as she had also done for me. So, who was I to question if the ancestors had come to her about the journey I was on? Bear was known to pop mushrooms and peyote buttons, so she very well could have had a vision. I knew in my heart she always wanted the best for me, so I had to trust that her sending me out on the road alone was what she felt was right.

I closed my eyes in an effort to be in the moment, harkening back to what Bear had told me to do. The wind rustled the tent and raked over my exposed skin. I sat there, training myself to just feel and listen. To be in that one moment. I wanted desperately to open my eyes and do something or see something, but I kept them clamped shut. I relaxed into the wooden picnic bench, my hands clasped on my lap for warmth. It took some time for me to reach a sensation akin to being at peace in the moment and with how chilled to the bone I had become, while also calming my mind down to nothing but the physical sensations.

The timer on my watch beeped and I opened my eyes. Chow time. I slit open the hot food packets. Steam rose from the first spoonful of chicken stew. The smell and taste of it brought back many memories of eating while out in the field with my unit. I alternated between spoons from the stew packet and the rice packet until both were empty. I dumped out the rest of the MRE and found a pouch of cheese-filled pretzel bites and a bag of M&M's. I saved the pretzels for a roadside snack later in the trip and ate half of the M&M's. I ate candy so rarely that a whole bag would probably have made me sick.

I cleaned up the MRE trash and went to the communal concrete bathroom to brush my teeth and pee. By the time I made it back to the tent, darkness had fallen, and I was dragging my feet. I didn't even bother to change into pajamas, sliding in the sleeping bag fully clothed. Sleep found me immediately. I woke once during the night, ice cold and teeth chattering, my breath coming out in big white puffs. I was too tired to put more clothes on, so I tucked my head inside the sleeping bag, rolled up into a ball, and fell back to sleep.

*

"How'd ya sleep?" inquired the chirpy, young desk clerk as I shouldered open the door of the campground office.

I raised my eyebrows at her, knowing I probably looked like absolute crap because I felt like absolute crap. Though I had slept most of the night, I had a headache and was nauseous. I registered the warmth inside the office and was glad for it.

"What's the elevation here?" I asked with a croaky voice, running my hand through my messy hair.

She turned her green eyes to the ceiling, considering the question. "'Round about sixty-four hundred feet I think."

"Ah, okay."

"Why, you not feeling so hot?"

"Yeah. I don't do well at elevation; this is pretty high for me. Six thousand feet is usually my limit. Huh, well actually I got elevation sickness in Reno once, and that's more like forty-five hundred feet. Apparently, I don't do well in the high desert."

She nodded sagely. "Well, if you're sticking around a few days, it ought to wear off. And make sure you stay plenty hydrated. That'll help. You want some coffee or tea?"

"I'd love some tea, thanks."

"You're welcome to help yourself." She pointed to a side table set up with coffee and hot water jugs with pump handles on top. Sugar packets, creamers, and assorted tea bags were in a basket. With frozen fingers, I took a cup, filled it with hot water, and dug around in the tea bags assortment, but they were all caffeinated.

"Where you headed?" she asked me.

I wasn't in the mood for chitchat but couldn't just ignore her. "Um, not sure. I have a route planned out, but I wanted to check something. Do you have a road map I can look at?"

"Oh yeah, of course. You want to come back to my desk and use MapQuest?"

I looked at her blankly and my face warmed in embarrassed because I didn't know what she was talking about. I ran my hand through my hair again. "Uh. MapQuest?"

"Yeah, it's a website. Really cool. You can look at maps from anywhere you can possibly think of. All over the world!" Her face lit up as she explained the website to me.

"I...uh, that sounds really neat—" I squinted at her name tag. "—Jen. Thank you. I'm a little technologically challenged. I do better with paper maps. Do you have one I can look at?" The water had heated the paper cup to the point that my fingertips burned. I set it down on the table.

She looked slightly embarrassed, her eyes darting down to the floor as she hooked some hair behind her ear. "Yes. Sorry." She pulled a map off the rack and placed it on the desk, still looking down.

"Do you want to check it out with me, since you know the area?"

She looked at me and her face lit up. "Yes, of course!"

I spread the map out across the large counter and located Ely at the junction of highways 50, 93, and 6. I placed my grubby finger on the junction.

"I am supposed to be doing a huge arc from here up through Idaho, skirt by part of Montana, then on to Washington and down through Oregon and California back home in Sacramento. But—" I traced my finger along Highway 50 as it cut across Nevada straight to California, ending in Sacramento. "—I kinda just want to go home."

Jen looked at the map, scrunching up her lip gloss laden lips and stroking her chin as she pondered my predicament.

"So, go home then." She paused. "I mean, if you are having doubts about your trip, better to head home now while you have a clean shot. If you change your mind way the heck up in Butte, you're kinda stuck. It's barely even sunrise, so if you head out now and ride hard, you'll make it by early evening.

Relief flowed over me and I sighed. "Yeah. That makes sense. I guess I just needed to hear it from someone else. Like...I needed permission to make it okay. Thanks."

She tilted her head at me, tucking her hair behind her ear again. "You're welcome."

I drank the cup of lukewarm water I had set aside, since it had finally cooled. "I guess I'll go pack up camp and get going. Do I need to sign anything before I go?"

"Nope, you sorted out all of the paperwork and fees last night. You're good to go."

"Thanks, Jen."

She nodded and gave me a smile that carried a bit of pity in it, which I wasn't accustomed to, but my thoughts were too muddy to suss out how I felt. I pushed open the front door and walked back out into the icy morning. I packed up camp and loaded up my bike by the faint glow of the predawn sun. As I warmed up my bike, I was glad that the engine was so quiet, because I didn't want to wake the other campers. I rolled out just as the sun crested the horizon, stopping briefly in town for gas and to check my tire pressure before hopping on US-50 and heading west, instead of going north on 93 to Idaho as planned.

Even with the cold weather gear on and the heated hand grips on my bike, the wind chill was vicious, freezing me deep down to the core. Just outside of Ely the road became narrow and twisty and cut between hills. I was both surprised, and not, that the hills had snow on them. I recognized that I needed to be vigilant about black ice on the road, so I redoubled my focus and backed off the throttle a bit.

Soon I was out of the hills and back out in high desert with mile after mile of flat open road bordered by scrub brush and wide-open lands. I had heard that stretch of the highway referred to as "the loneliest highway" and I understood why.

I made a point to stop every hour to stretch my legs, drink water, and eat a little something. The nausea and headache from the elevation still held firm, so I knew that I needed to be extra careful with myself in the barren landscape.

I stopped in Fallon for gas and to find some lunch, though I didn't dawdle because I had a new surging urgency in me about getting back down to lower elevations and home. Just outside Fallon I chose to turn onto I-80, which would get me home about an hour earlier, if all went well. I passed through Reno where I shed my cold weather gear before skimming by the north side of Lake Tahoe with barely a moment's thought that perhaps I should stop and enjoy the lake scenery. But a knot had formed in my chest. It was tight and bound up in anxiety and frustration. I just wanted to be home right then, yet there were still eighty-five more miles to go, and I wanted to get into Sacramento before the commute started.

Around Colfax and Auburn, the elevation dropped significantly, and by the time I blew through Rocklin and Roseville I was gritting my teeth with the effort it took to maintain a safe and sane speed. The closer to home I got the more unraveled I became.

The last few blocks up *Q* Street were a test of my patience and stamina as a full panic attack threatened. I forced myself to do deep breathing as I waited for the security gate of the underground garage to slowly creak open. I zipped into my parking space, killed the engine as I hopped off, leaving all my gear and bags still strapped to the bike, and was still removing my helmet as I sprinted up the stairs.

Hands shaking fiercely, I unlocked the door to my studio. Inside I landed on my knees in the carpeted entryway before lowering myself down. The rough carpet itched my cheek as I lay on my side shaking. My head throbbed and hot tears flowed. I didn't fight it. Whatever was happening, I let it flow over and through me.

It occurred to me that I needed help and I fumbled out my cell phone so I could leave a convoluted voicemail for my therapist asking for her next available appointment. After the shaking subsided, I fell into a shallow sleep full of memories I had spent years ignoring. Heavy footsteps in the corridor outside woke me and I sat up slowly, resting my back against the cold white wall. My head throbbed and my stomach lurched.

I ran both hands through my messy hair and down my face. More footsteps in the hall. This time they were light and measured. A key slid into the lock and the door opened. Light from the corridor dug into my eyes.

"Vivian! Oh, honey." The door closed and the smell of Audre's lotion and perfume caressed me. The hall light flipped on, and I covered my head with a groan, head and eyes shattering. The light shut off.

Audre's knees popped as she squatted down at my side. Her voice came in a whisper. "Vivian. Let's get you to bed. Can you walk?"

I nodded and stood with her help. My legs stuttered and faltered as I made my way to the couch. Audre pulled the futon out into a bed and put the sheet down and then helped me lay down. Together we got me out of my boots and riding clothes and into sweats. The chill air of my studio hit my hot skin and the shivers returned. Audre propped me up with pillows, pulled blankets over me, and kissed me on the forehead.

I alternated between shivering and dozing as Audre turned on the wall heater and removed her high heels, moving about the studio on silent bare feet. She put on my favorite cello CD. Jordi Savall playing "Suite En Sol Mineur: Fantasie En Rondeau." I closed my eyes when she turned on the hood light over the stove and warmed up a can of soup. I heard her make a hushed phone call telling someone she would be home late.

Tears from feelings of gratitude and unworthiness mingled on my cheeks. Audre sat on the futon next to me and I opened my eyes. She had turned off the hood light in the kitchen and only left on the light in the fish tank, which cast a calming blue glow. We made eye contact as she gently handed me a bowl of soup and a spoon. Her eyes carried a heavy dose of concern.

"It's not nearly as good as my homemade chicken and rice soup, but this is what you had on hand. There is some tea on the coffee table for you, too, when you're ready. I certainly wasn't expecting to find you here at all, let alone in this condition. I just stopped by after work to feed your fish."

I nodded and smiled and took a few bites of soup, enjoying the warmth of it as it made its way down to my stomach.

"I'm lucky to have you in my life. Thank you," I said, my voice low and raspy. She wiped the tears off my cheeks and watched me eat, her hand resting on my thigh.

I put the empty bowl on the coffee table and picked up the mug of peppermint tea.

"What's going on, Viv?"

"I don't know. My road trip with Bear turned out to be a solo trip. Once I got on the road, I was fine at first. I started feeling sick when I got to elevation around Ely and it all fell apart from there. I just...was overcome by an urgency to get home. I mean, it was probably an anxiety attack that then brought on a panic attack and migraine. And from the time I left Morro Bay I was putting in too many miles a day without taking care of my body. So...I made it home just in time to collapse into a shuddering mess on the floor."

She nodded and chewed her lip as she considered what I had said, her eyes narrow as she thought.

"I left a message for Alexia to see if she can fit me in. Don't worry, I'll be fine. Just stressed out about losing my job. And I'm sure my body will rebound by tomorrow with some food and water and rest."

I reached out and took her hand, the skin smooth and warm. "I am so glad you arrived when you did. It is scary to me how completely incapable of taking care of myself I get sometimes. I never had this problem before. As a kid I had to take care of myself. And in the army, well...you just keep going no matter what. So, to just shut down the way I do sometimes. I dunno, Audre. I don't like it."

She gave me a gentle smile. "It may come as a shock to you, Viv, but you are really, truly a human being. It's okay to get sick, get anxious, fall apart, and need help."

"Hmph."

I wrapped my arms around her. She scooted closer and leaned her head on my chest. We sat like that for a while, watching my fish go about their business in the illuminated tank. Audre's presence next to me was so full of love and warmth, I couldn't help but start to relax, the core of anxiety in my chest slowly giving up its stranglehold.

The sound of thumping, low chatter, and footfall outside my door brought us both out of our contented stupors. Someone knocked on my door gently and Audre got up to see who it was. I blinked my eyes a few times to try to refocus and clear my head. From around the corner, I heard the door open and Audre speak.

"Hello, Kate. Hey, Ang."

Kate and Ang both greeted Audre warmly, then Kate whispered, "Is everything okay?"

"She needs some rest but will be fine. Here, let me help you," Audre said and then I heard some shuffling. Audre, Kate, and Ang filed into my tiny living room carrying all the gear and bags from my bike. Audre sat back down next to me and the other two stopped at the foot of the futon, hands full, and looked at me curiously. Ang spoke first.

"We got back from dinner and saw your bike parked all wonky and your bags had been left behind. That's not like you, so I figured something was up. Here's your stuff," she said, placing my bags against the far wall. She leaned against the entryway, arms across her chest and a scowl on her lips. Kate frowned, too, but came over and placed her hand on my forehead and then looked at the whites of my eyes and checked my hands, poking at my fingernails.

"Ah Kate, ever the nurse," I said with a smirk.

"Prognosis is: you're not gonna die, today. But you know the drill. Water, healthy food, rest."

"Yes. Yes. Thanks. Audre has got the first round covered. I can manage the rest."

"Can you?" Ang said with a grumble as she scuffed the toe of her shoe on the carpet. Kate and Audre both looked at her with surprise. "I'm just saying. You're kind of a mess lately, Viv. You seriously ran off last week and totally forgot our date. And you got yourself fired. And apparently now you're having a lapse with your mental health and can't even manage to listen to your body enough to stop and rest on a motorcycle ride—"

"Listen up, Ang," I said, my voice sharp and direct. "You've always been a bit of an asshole, but this is extreme even for you. Whatever you're upset about, let's talk about it like adults rather than you pout and lash out and say shitty things you don't actually mean."

Kate and Audre were caught in the crossfire and remained silent, their lips tight and eyes narrowed.

"Jesus. I don't have time for this. I'm on night shift and need to go get ready for work." With that, Ang pushed off from the wall and stalked out of the door.

"Thanks for bringing up my bags!" I shouted at her retreating back. The door closed solidly with a *thunk* and her footsteps faded.

"Well, that was awkward," I said to Kate and Audre, trying to lighten the mood.

"You rest up. I mean it. I better go talk to her," Kate said as she rose and blew us both kisses on her way out.

"Thanks for bringing up my stuff, and the free physical," I laughed.

"Any time."

And with that, Audre and I were left in my quiet studio, the air vibrating with Ang's anger still. Audre raised her eyebrows at me.

"Yeah. I know. I fucked up. I forgot I had a date with her and dashed out of town to see Jared. I left on bad terms with Ang and clearly we still need to talk about it."

I laid down and Audre cuddled up at my side, her arm across my chest.

"You're going to wrinkle your nice work clothes."

"Worth it," she said and cuddled up even closer.

I drew in a deep breath and the core of anxiety that had burrowed deep inside me relented, allowing me to drift off to sleep. I woke once as Audre slipped out quietly, no doubt to get home since it was a work night. I rolled over and smiled as I smelled her on my pillow.

Chapter Fourteen

After making quick phone calls to Bear and Jared to let them know I was back home in Sacramento, I met with Alexia to debrief. As I gave her a high-level overview, my throat grew tight. I drew in a shuddering breath and looked down at my shoes, my words petering off.

"That's quite a week you've had, Vivian. What would you like to focus on today?"

"Well, I don't like that this crazy level of anxiety has boiled up. I thought I was past this. I mean, I get it that big things are happening, like losing my fucking...uh, losing my job. Sorry."

She shook her head gently, forgiving the profanity.

"Go on."

"Okay, but what the hell is wrong with me that I can't just take a road trip and enjoy myself? I nutted up on the first day and crawled home with my tail between my legs."

I raised my hand to my mouth to bite a hangnail but tucked my hand under my thigh instead.

"You ask what the hell is wrong with you, and my initial thought is that there is nothing wrong with you. In fact, given the circumstances not just of the last few weeks, but of your entire life, I'd say you are doing pretty darn well. But what I want you to consider is why *you* think the anxiety is back. And what's underneath the anxiety?"

I was kind of hoping she would tell me, rather than make me figure it out. I looked past her, out of the window behind her chair. The building across the street was still under construction, as it had been for years, and I watched as a carpenter scuttled along the scaffolding. He had a job.

"I'm pissed off at losing my job. I loved that job. It isn't just about no longer having a paycheck coming in, but the club was my social circle too. I am friends with some of my coworkers, and I enjoyed my regular customers coming by to tell me about their lives. And then, *bam*, gone. I guess I'm mostly angry about how it happened. Just a total blindside."

I gave up watching the carpenter and went back to looking at Alexia, who was as patient and serene as always. I had a squirming tightness in my chest, and tears threatening to rise up, so I closed my eyes and homed in on whatever it was that I was feeling. After a moment of digging around, I figured it out, but I didn't think I could say it without crying, and I didn't want to cry in front of Alexia. I kept my eyes closed and lowered my head.

"I think I figured it out," I said quietly, and cleared my throat.

"Go ahead. It's okay, Vivian."

I clenched my eyes closed even harder and tried to swallow down the lump in my throat. "I, uh, I think I'm upset because I feel...rejected." The word rolled off my tongue and I snapped my lips shut, stifling a sob. I took a deep breath and waited a few seconds before going on. "I am taking it very personally that Sheila fired me, especially because she didn't give me any warning. I had no idea I wasn't doing a good job, or whatever the issue was. And then Bear not going with me on the ride... rejection again. Or at least, that's how it feels to me."

I sniffled and raised my head, opening my eyes. Alexia was beaming at me.

"I am so proud of you right now."

My eyebrows shot up and I sniffled again. "What? Why?"

"You are doing great work, and you are able to look inward now and really get to the root of things. Two years ago, you never would have been able to do that. So, yes, I'm proud of you."

"You are the one who taught me, so you should get the kudos."

"No, no. I am merely a resource, you have done all of the heavy lifting."

"Thanks." I swiped at the dampness around my eyes. "So, now what? I've figured out that I am coming unraveled because I feel rejection, which sounds lame to me now that I say it out loud. What do I do with that?"

"I think you will find that just figuring this bit out is a massive thing in itself. Now, I'd like you to think farther back to other times in your life that you've felt rejection and been upset by it."

"Alexia, we've already spent so much time talking about my childhood, I really don't want to circle back around to that again."

"Okay, so you've identified that the times you felt rejection were during your childhood. Keep going."

She'd caught me. I stifled a sigh.

Irritated, I went on. "Fine. Here's the highlight reel. Mom made me feel like a burden. Big brother terrorized and beat the tar out of me on a regular basis. I was isolated and had very few friends. I grew up in fear."

"What I hear is that you are irritated and you'd rather rattle off a few bullet points instead of fully delving into this topic."

"Yup."

"Hmm. Well, I am not going to force you to talk about something if you don't want to. Though I would like you to give this some thought over the next week. Okay?"

I nodded, annoyed at myself for not being willing to dig deeper that day, and also relieved that she let me off the hook. We adjourned soon after and it took me hours afterward to recalibrate, which I did while reading at the café.

When I finally checked my cell phone, I had voicemails from Sergeant Brickhouse and Ang. Sarge wanted to know if I had given any more thought to applying for a position as deputy sheriff recruit and Ang wanted to talk. I sent her a text in reply.

Almost home. Want me to come over?

She replied immediately.

Yep

I huffed and walked home. It was a mild day for mid-September in Sacramento, and I took my time enjoying the quirky yards and houses in Midtown. I stopped at a thrift shop to see what was on offer and purchased a tattered copy of David Mitchell's *Cloud Atlas*. I had been meaning to read it but kept forgetting to check at the library for it.

Eventually I let myself into the dingy lobby of our apartment building, climbed the stairs, and knocked on Ang's door, which she opened and walked away without greeting me. I stepped in hesitantly and closed the door behind me. Her apartment was spotless and had the usual smell of wood polish and leather. Compared to my utilitarian studio, her apartment looked as if it had been appointed by a skilled interior designer. High-end furniture and well-placed accent pieces conveyed a welcoming feel. Too bad their owner did not.

"Hey," I said, lingering by the door.

She leaned against the kitchen counter, legs crossed at the ankles, drinking a large glass of water. She was dressed in sweatpants and a faded T-shirt, and her hair was styled in the tight bun that she wore for work.

"You working tonight?"

She nodded as she continued gulping down water. I waited and tried to remain open even though her behavior was less than open. She placed the empty glass in the sink and motioned toward the couch. I walked into the living room and sat as far on the end of the couch as I could. She sat at the other end, sideways, so she was facing me. I turned to face her, placing my books on the gorgeous hardwood coffee table. I continued to wait. She gave me an appraising look, as though she were also waiting for me.

"Are you waiting for an apology from me?" I tried to keep my voice even.

She crossed her arms and leaned back. "Yes."

I pondered that briefly, choosing my words very carefully.

"I apologize for forgetting our date." It took a lot for me not to make a shitty comment about her conduct during our argument, knowing it would not help things. I sat in silence, wondering if she would apologize for her outburst in front of Kate and Audre the previous night.

"Apology accepted," she said and opened her arms, beckoning me with a smile. I hesitated. She registered the delay and dropped her arms and her smile.

"Since we are making apologies, Ang, I think you owe me one as well." It was my turn to cross my arms.

She narrowed her eyes and tilted her head. "Just what is it I should be apologizing for?"

"You were unnecessarily cruel last night. And with an audience, no less."

A long pause followed, and her face was so still I couldn't read which way she was going to go with it. I prepared myself for her to say something shitty.

"Yeah. That's fair. I'm sorry I ripped into you. I was still hurt about you forgetting our date." She swallowed and looked away for a moment. "And I am sorry that you lost your job. I recognize what a huge impact that will have on your life."

I had expected something petty from her, so I was surprised by her thoughtful apology.

"Can we agree to make an effort to be more kind to each other in the future when there is potential conflict? This really didn't feel good, and I know we are both capable of doing better."

She nodded and opened her arms back up to me. I shifted across the couch and we held each other in a long hug. Once the embrace ended, I sat back.

"Would you like to reschedule our date? My calendar isn't too busy right now."

She shifted across the couch toward me. "Fuck scheduling a date, let's go to my room now."

"Wait, don't you have to go to work?"

"Yes. But we have enough time to have some fun."

I took her hand and led her to the bedroom. I had some pent-up angst from the last week and would gladly take it out on her. I'd be sending her off to work with red, hand-shaped welts on her ass, and I knew she'd be happy about that.

*

"Vivian, this is your mother."

I ran my hand over my face as I checked my watch and sat up in bed.

"Hello, Bernadette. Good morning."

"Please don't call me by my first name like some coworker. I'm your mother for Pete's sake. And don't tell me you're still in bed. Never mind, I don't want to know. I'm calling about your brother."

I blew out a puff of air. "Mm-hmm." I swung my legs over the side of the futon and stared at my fish darting about in their tank.

She let out a long sigh. "Well, in case you care to know, he is in rehab again."

"Okay."

"And I'd like you to go visit him. Support him. He needs family right now."

I bit the inside of my cheek, holding back the pile of profanity that wanted to spout forth. "Mother. We went through this when he was in rehab last year. I don't owe him anything and am not going to support him while he is in rehab."

"Why are you being so difficult, Vivian?"

"Why have you enabled him all of these years, Mother?"

There was a long pause as that statement hung in the air. I shifted and checked my watch.

"I will tell you exactly why I am being so difficult. I feel no desire to support my childhood abuser."

She scoffed. "Abuser. That's a bit extreme."

"No. It's not. It's completely accurate. Just because you want to ignore everything that went on under your nose when we were kids doesn't mean it didn't happen."

"You're exaggerating. Anyway, I thought you two had mended fences last year."

"Yes. He actually saved my life. But he was shit-faced drunk when he did it. We had a bonding moment afterward, but the fact is he's never acknowledged the abuse when we were kids, and I don't feel like he is entitled to my support right now."

The line dropped. I pulled the phone away from my ear and looked at the blank screen. "She fucking hung up on me," I said to the fish in disgust.

I got in the shower and considered what to do with my day. It occurred to me that I should probably talk to Ang about her experience as a woman in law enforcement before I called Sergeant Brickhouse back. I had a resource at my fingertips who would give me her truth about her career. But as I rinsed the shampoo out of my hair, I decided against it. I knew Ang loved her job and she would be offended if I opted out. After educating myself on the underbelly of law enforcement I wasn't too keen on working there.

I decided to wait to call Sergeant Brickhouse back and opted for a trail run at Briones instead. I puttered around getting dressed, packing my day pack, and eating breakfast so that I would miss the morning rush hour traffic. I was still a tad saddle sore, so drove my truck instead of riding the motorcycle, and made good time to the trailhead. It wasn't lost on me that I was doing exactly what Bear had pointed out, by staying busy instead of sitting with something.

I started at the Bear Creek staging area and did an especially challenging loop that took me up to the ridgeline and back down again. The run was uneventful, and I still felt a little sluggish after my overexertion on the road trip. When I made it back to the parking lot, I walked a few laps as I cooled down. I sat on the tailgate to change out of my running shoes and pull on some track pants over my lightweight running shorts. I got into the truck, rolled down the window, leaned the seat back, and cracked open my lunch cooler. I propped one foot out of the window and relaxed as I ate my sandwich and carrot sticks. There was absolute silence aside from the wind rustling trees and the *thunk* of acorns falling onto the wooden picnic benches.

There was only a handful of cars parked in the lot, so I was slightly annoyed when a large pickup truck parked near mine. It was one of those big trucks with a full-sized back seat in the cab. I watched as the driver got out of the front seat, stumbled a bit, and got into the back seat, which had tinted windows. I couldn't see him clearly but could see his silhouette through the dark glass. I had gotten changed in my truck many times, so assumed he was just changing into his hiking or running clothes. I focused back on my sandwich and watched the oak trees sway. The mild breeze blew through the open window, and I closed my eyes with the pure, perfect peace that I often experienced when at Briones.

The sound of muffled sobbing came through the window. I opened my eyes and looked over at the truck, wondering what was happening over there. The sobbing grew louder and then the back door to the cab opened. The man leaned out and threw up on the pavement. I sat up, watching him carefully. He held onto the door weakly, resting his forehead on the crook of his elbow. That's when I saw the blood dripping from his arm in a steady stream. I leaned forward and looked at the puke. It was a mush of undigested pills. *Shit.*

I jumped out of my truck and ran around to him.

"Hey. Hey."

I placed my hand on his shoulder. He flinched and mumbled something incoherent, his grip on the door slid and he started falling out of the truck head-first. I lunged forward and caught him under the armpits. My sneaker slid as I stepped in his vomit.

I pulled him out of the truck, gripping him under the arms, and laid him on his side in the shady grass of the parking lot island. He gagged and mumbled again. I checked the cuts on his arm, and they were damn deep. I unbuckled his belt and yanked it out of the loops, then put the belt around his upper arm and cranked it down, creating a tourniquet. I checked the time so I could tell the first responders how long it had been on, and pulled out my cell phone to call 9-1-1, but found that I had no signal in the deep valley.

"Hey. I'm going for help. Stay here."

He grunted in return and gagged into the grass. I took the keys clipped to his belt, just in case he got any ideas about trying to drive away. I slammed the door to his truck and locked it up to make sure everything inside was secured, and then sprinted across the parking lot and up the road to the hut where a park employee collected entry fees. There weren't any cars at the hut, and I ran right up to the window. The young man was leaning back on a stool reading a chemistry textbook. He sat up and put his book down quickly.

"Whoa, you okay?"

I looked down and saw that I had blood on my shirt and probably looked a little crazed. He leaned out through the open window and looked up in the direction I had come from.

"I'm fine. But do you have a phone or radio? There's a medical emergency and we need an ambulance."

"Uh. Yeah. Okay. I've got a phone in here. What did you say the emergency was?"

"Someone needs an ambulance. Please, it's urgent."

He turned and picked up the receiver of an ancient landline phone and dialed 9-1-1. He spoke to the dispatcher briefly and then turned to me.

"They want to talk to you since I don't know what's going on."

He held the receiver out of the window, the springy cord stretched to its limit. I took the receiver and leaned in the window.

"What's your emergency, ma'am?"

"Hello. We are at the staging area parking lot. There's a gentleman here who is bleeding profusely and is quite sick."

"Do you know how he got the injuries?"

"I-I don't know him, didn't see what happened, and don't want to make assumptions about what's going on with him. Just...I put a tourniquet on his arm but seriously, you guys need to hurry. I know we are kind of far from any main roads, so there's not a moment to waste here."

"Ma'am, help is on the way. What is your name?"

I handed the phone back to the park employee and told him I'd be with the man and pointed to where the trucks were parked. I sprinted back and found the man on his back, choking. I rolled him on his side and pounded on his back until his airway cleared, though his lips remained blue.

"Hey, dude. Hang in there. Help is on the way."

"No," he said, quite clearly.

I sat on the ground and rubbed his back and wondered if I had done the right thing by calling for help. Clearly the guy had made a suicide attempt, but for some reason I wasn't able to say that out loud to the dispatcher or the park employee.

I clenched my jaw and continue to rub his back. His skin had turned a sickening shade of blueish white, which I knew damn well was bad news. Very faint at first, I heard the sound of sirens in the distance. I did some deep breathing to try to keep myself calm amid the flood of adrenaline coursing through me.

Hoofbeats approached quickly from behind us, and I turned to see a police officer on a horse. I stood to greet her as she dismounted and tied the reins off on a tree limb. Removing her sunglasses, she looked at me and the man on the ground.

"Hello, officer. I'm the one who called."

"Do you know this man?" she asked as she squatted down to check his pulse.

"No, ma'am. He parked next to me and...well." I pointed at him, to indicate his condition should speak for itself. The sirens grew closer, and I saw a fire truck and paramedic rig driving up the park road. I stood and waved to catch their attention. The driver of the lead vehicle acknowledged and pulled into the parking lot.

The firefighters and paramedics climbed out of their trucks and gathered some gear at what I considered a leisurely pace. I tried not to make assumptions about them but in the moment, I wanted to holler at them to hurry the fuck up. The police officer spoke to them, and the paramedic got to work assessing the man, who was no longer mumbling. The fact that he had fallen silent was concerning. I focused on watching the crew from the fire department go about their work, and the police officer watching over them. All the mounting anxiety faded away and pure curiosity took over. I tried to sidle up closer to watch the paramedic work, but the police officer shook her head at me. So, I watched what I could from where I stood. The paramedic spoke in low tones to his partner.

I was so focused on what they were doing that it took me a moment to register the smell of smoke. Everything stopped as they noticed it too. All their radios squawked to life and a bunch of codes I didn't know were being called out between bursts of static. The pace picked up rapidly from there. The paramedics loaded the gentleman up on a backboard and gurney and rolled him into their truck before driving away. The firefighters jumped in their rig and took off, which startled the police horse.

I looked at the mess on the ground and wondered who would clean it up. The police officer was looking in the windows of the man's truck and I recalled that I had his keys. I pulled them out of my pocket and held them up.

"I have the keys," I said.

She took them from me. "I thought you didn't know him."

"I don't. I took them from him so he didn't try to drive off while I went for help. Can I go?"

She took down the information from my driver's license before releasing me. I gave a wave to the man in the hut as I pulled out of the park. On my way down Bear Creek Road, I saw smoke pluming up not too far ahead and then I came upon the scene of a grass fire that was quickly eating its way up the side of a hill of dead grass and oak trees. A fire engine blocked one side of the road and a firefighter was directing traffic. As I stopped, waiting for my turn to drive, I watched the firefighters go about their work on the hillside and at the engine. They busted their asses with a level of focus and determination I admired.

The car in front of me began rolling forward and I saw it was our turn to go, so I tore my eyes off the scene, though my mind remained on the paramedics assessing the man at Briones and the firefighters jumping from the medical aid call right to fire suppression. The entire drive home I thought about it, wondering if I had what it took to be a firefighter or paramedic or both, what it took to qualify, and how to go about getting the training.

Instead of going home when I reached Sacramento, I diverted to a branch of the library and took a seat at one of the public computers. I didn't know where to start so I typed various things into the search engine: "California firefighter," "how to become a firefighter in California," "female firefighter," along with things like "firefighter-paramedic in California."

I spent the afternoon clicking on link after link and reading up on all of it. I got some scratch paper and a little golf pencil from the librarian and jotted down notes. I learned that some departments hired firefighter recruits and put them through an academy, and realized I met all the requirements except for having an EMT certification. So off I went in search of how to get an EMT certification. I learned that a few of the local community colleges offered the required course, which was one semester long. But I also learned that I had just missed the cut-off to add classes by a week and the semester had already begun. I wrote down the phone number for the admissions office and checked the dates of the spring semester. I also noted phone numbers for departments that were hiring for seasonal fire control worker. If I could get picked up by one of those departments, I could get some experience and earn some money while I waited for the next semester to start in January.

My heart raced with excitement as I put the pieces together and realized if I worked hard on it that getting on eventually as a firefighter trainee was something attainable. After that it was a matter of passing the academy and probation.

On the back side of the scratch paper, I drew out a timeline of what I needed to do and when, to make sure I had everything complete. Fire season was in full swing, so I knew I needed to get cracking on applying for fire control worker jobs, and that's what I did. Some departments had online applications, and others you had to call and request paper copies. Those I could do online I submitted that afternoon.

Afterward I sat in my truck and called the others. I had such an incredible adrenaline high that my palms were sweating. I couldn't recall the last time I had been so excited about anything and took it as a good sign. Once all the calls were made I stared at my phone for a while, procrastinating on calling Sergeant Brickhouse.

As the sun started to set and the surrounding office buildings began to empty, I dialed his number.

"This is Sergeant Brickhouse."

"Hello, Sergeant Brickhouse, this is Vivian Chastain returning your call."

"Vivian, hello. Good to hear from you. How have you been?"

"I've been away on a road trip, sorry for the delay in getting back to you. I have been doing really well." I knew that was a stretch, but I wasn't about to spill the issues to him.

"Great. I'm glad to hear that. Keeping up on your training?"

"Yes, sir. I just got back from a trail run up in the hills."

"Good. Good." He paused and I could hear him rubbing the stubble on his jaw. "Have you had a chance to consider applying for the sheriff's academy? I only ask because the application window isn't open very long, and it's for the January academy."

"Yes. I have given it a lot of thought. I've gone back and forth about it and I've come to a decision but am afraid to disappoint you, sir."

"Oh? No need to worry. What did you decide?"

"I am going to try for the fire service, rather than law enforcement." I cringed as I said it but tried to keep my voice steady and strong, though I had a moment of shame, as if I were going to let him down.

"Don't you worry, Vivian. I am not disappointed in you. In fact, I am proud of you. Good for you for giving it plenty of thought and deciding what is right for you. I would have loved to have you here at the academy, but I am sure you'll be brilliant at fire academy as well. If you would like to use me as a reference, please don't hesitate."

My eyes grew wide. "Thank you, sir. That means a lot to me. I appreciate your support."

"Happy to do it. Okay, you take care and keep up on your fitness training. Trust me, you'll need it to work in the fire service."

"I will. Thanks again."

I ended the call and cried. Fat tears dripped on the front of my shirt, and for what? Because someone I looked up to respected me back? I wiped the tears off my cheeks briskly and drove myself home as the streetlights came on.

Chapter Fifteen

I spent Saturday with Audre meandering around Midtown, looking in shops, and enjoying the milder weather. We stopped by the nightclub where I had worked, and Buck pulled me into a rough hug. She was never one to speak much, but she whispered in my ear, telling how upset she was that I had been let go. She wiped at a tear gruffly and slapped me on the back so hard I stumbled, then she took Audre's hand and bowed, kissing her knuckles as if she were royalty. "Good to see you, Audre," she said in her low Marlboro Man voice. Audre gave her a sweet smile.

We rounded the corner to the front bar, and I saw the place only had a few Happy Hour customers. The staff were preparing for the upcoming rush of people. I spotted Jen filling the huge ice bucket and someone I didn't recognize was cutting lemons. Audre took a seat in one of the booths and I sauntered up to my old station and gave a friendly rap on the bar with my knuckles. The bartender looked at me and put her knife down.

"Hey. What can I get for ya?"

"A glass of the Chardonnay and a bottle of water, please." She rolled her eyes at my cheap tab and went about pouring the wine and grabbing a bottle of water from the cooler.

I put some cash on the bar. "Keep it," I said, meaning for her to keep the change. She nodded and swiped the money off the bar, her lips pressed into a thin line. I picked up our drinks as Jen walked through the service door behind the bartender. When Jen saw me, she let out the most animated shriek I had ever witnessed. The new bartender flinched and looked at her in annoyance. Jen set the ice bucket on the floor and hopped up and down, her arms reaching out toward me. Her wallet chain rattled, and her blonde dreadlocks bounced. The cigarette wedged behind her ear came loose.

I grinned and put the drinks down. "Jen, baby! How are you?"

She ran around the bar and grabbed me in a huge hug, her head nearly burrowed in my armpit. I laughed and patted her on the back as she squeezed me harder. "Easy there, Champ," I squeaked out. She released me and stood back, giving me a smile so massive that her hazel eyes crinkled up behind her glasses.

"Dude! I am so happy to see you! I cannot even begin to express how much I miss working with you." She looked me up and down and then peered around the bar until she saw Audre, who gave her a little wave. "I've missed you, too, babeyyyy," she said to Audre with a laugh.

The new bartender was trying to look busy, wiping down the bar and filling garnish trays, but she was clearly eavesdropping and sizing me up. I grabbed the drinks and we walked to the booth. I sat next to Audre and Jen scooted in across from us, leaning in conspiratorially.

"Can you believe this shit?" she asked as she poked a thumb toward the new bartender.

"No. I truly cannot."

"Didja go talk to Danny or Maggie about it?"

"Yup. They totally shut me down. So, is that Amy?" I pointed in the direction of the new person.

"Yeah. She'd never poured a drink in her life when she got here. Sheila spent an afternoon showing her a few of the popular drinks and left her to figure the rest out herself. Apparently, Amy is someone's cousin, so clearly they took her on as a favor."

My blood started to rise, along with my temper. I leaned across the table and whispered harshly through my teeth. "But what the fuck? Why cut me off the schedule? I worked here for fucking years and was a favorite of the customers."

"Don't I know it. Sheila has gotten an earful from plenty of our regulars when they learned you got fired. But she just gives them vague bullshit responses. Believe me, you have plenty of people who miss you. What're you gonna do? Maybe try to get picked up at some of the other bars in town?"

"Nah. I'm taking this opportunity to do a career change. I'm gonna try for the fire service."

Audre squeezed my thigh to show her support.

"Whoaaaa. That's badass. Good for you!"

"Yeah? You think so?"

"Dude. Yes. Go for it. That's perfect for you. You've got ovaries of steel and you're hella fit and nothing scares you. Yes, do it." She slapped her hand on the table for emphasis. I grinned at her, and Audre rubbed her hand up and down my back warmly.

I heard knuckles rapping on the bar loudly followed by "Hey! Jen! Get your ass up here. You've got work to do." The voice did not belong to Sheila, who was the only person in a position to talk to staff like that.

My temper flared again. "Please tell me that wasn't the new bitch."

Jen shrugged. "That's the new bitch. Gotta go. Good to see you. Don't be a stranger." And with that she slid out of the booth with a jingle of her wallet chain, and she was gone.

"I need to test out the new bartender."

Audre's hand tightened on my thigh. "Babe."

"Don't worry. Just gonna give her a proper newbie initiation. I'll be nice."

Audre smirked at me as if to say *yeah right.*

I walked up to the bar and waited for the bartender. When she finally approached me, I hesitated, rubbing my chin with my thumb, to test her patience for indecisive customers. She shifted and rolled her eyes, so I made her wait a bit longer. The old school bartender at the other end of the bar, who had been pouring drinks longer than I had been alive, and was a salty bitch, perked up and stopped wiping the bar to watch.

"What can I get you?"

"Um. Hmm. I just can't make up my mind. What do you recommend?"

She huffed and listed off some beers on tap and the simplest mixed drinks. Clearly, she wasn't confident in her mixed drinks skills. Anybody could pour a beer or make a rum and Coke. Pfft.

"Okay, I think I'd like a Grasshopper."

Her face showed a split second of fear and I knew I had her. Not only that, but I had ordered a drink I knew she couldn't make with what the bar stocked. Grasshoppers were a shaken drink made from green crème de menthe, white crème de cacao, heavy cream, and a grated nutmeg garnish all served in a chilled cocktail glass. The bar didn't stock heavy cream, white crème de cacao, or nutmeg.

I watched as she ducked down under the bar where I knew there was a shelf for personal belongings. She was no doubt leafing through a bartender recipe book. After a moment she popped up and grabbed the shaker and poured in the wrong quantities of the wrong types of liquor with a dash of milk. She shook it up and poured it into a room temperature tumbler, which she had rimmed with granulated sugar. She slid the drink toward me.

"That'll be seven dollars."

I looked at the drink and heard the other bartender chuckle. Without paying, I carried the drink down to her and offered it up.

"You remember when you pulled this same shit on me when I was a baby bartender? This is supposed to be a Grasshopper."

"Yeah. Let me taste this train wreck." She sipped it and spit it out in the bar sink before turning to Amy.

"You call this a fucking Grasshopper?" She dumped it down the sink and, with a measured hand, slid the empty glass all the way down from her end of the bar to where

Amy stood. The glass stopped square in front of Amy, who turned and walked away.

"Good luck with that one. Her personality sure as hell isn't winning her any tip money. And if her drinks are on par with her attitude, she is in for a rude awakening about life as an uppity, shitty bartender. See ya."

I went back to Audre. "See? I was nice. It was just a little pop quiz."

We chatted while Audre sipped on her wine and I finished off my bottle of water.

Audre put down her glass and straightened her blouse. "I'm excited for your change in career, and I can see you are too." She reached her hand across the table to me, her bracelets making a delicate clink. "I haven't seen such a spark in your eyes before, except for maybe after our first kiss." She gave me a little wink. I smiled, running my thumb along the top of her hand.

"Thanks. It means a lot to me to have your support in this. It's going to be a long road and I'm going to be gone a lot, especially during fire season. But I will do my best to minimize the impact on our relationship and time together. I promise."

"Thank you. I do recognize that the next year or two are going to be a challenge and will take you away a lot, but I am okay with that if it's what you want to do and especially if it means you'll eventually have a job you love. We've got nothing but time." She reached up and stroked my cheek. Such a simple gesture but it carried behind it so much support and love that I choked up. I tried to swallow back the tears, but a few fell, nonetheless. Audre wiped them away and kissed my cheek.

"I love you, Audre. I probably don't say it enough, but I mean it truly and deeply. I am so grateful to have you in my life."

"Don't you forget for one second how we met. Literally at that bar back there." She pointed to my old station. "The care and concern you showed for me when I hit the floor with a seizure, while I don't remember much of it, my friends assured me that you handled me, a perfect stranger at the time, with love. You're going to make an amazing firefighter paramedic. You have more grit and determination than damn near anyone I know. Whichever department gets you will be lucky to have you." She placed a delicate kiss on my lips, careful not to get her dark-purple lip stain on my lips.

I had no words, but she didn't seem to expect any in response, so we sat there in the little bubble of the moment, holding hands and looking out of the window at Twenty-First Street.

*

My first Sunday back in town since my trip, Audre's family welcomed my return to their Sunday luncheon with open arms and many questions about the brief adventure. I gave them the high points and talked mostly about the amazing scenery. I left out the parts about my meltdown and rushing home to land in a heap in my entryway. I did, however, share with them how grateful I was for Audre and her showing up at just the right moment. Her family seemed to really respect and adore her, so I got a lot of nods around the table when I carried on about her. She held her chin high and smiled as I spoke, not shying away from the praise, which made me even more proud of her.

The conversation flowed on as everyone shared their favorite moments from the week and discussed what acts of kindness they had seen and done. It was a practice that they repeated every week and was something I aspired to include in my life moving forward. Focusing on the positive. Going out into the world with intention and kindness. Shedding the pessimism that had been ingrained into me by my own family.

A tinge of sadness clung to me, though, as I reflected on the fact that I lacked any sort of connection with my family, and for having grown up in fear in a sterile and dysfunctional household. Seeing the example set by Audre's family gave me something to strive for but also placed my own family under a glaring spotlight in my mind. I had worked through it plenty with Alexia, but some days were harder than others. I held Audre's hand under the table and sat back to shift my focus back on her family and remain in the moment with them rather than letting my shitty past take away from it.

After I had finished washing the dishes, I sat on the back patio with Audre's father. He was more stooped than usual, and his wrinkled hand shook just a bit on his knee.

"Are you okay, Mr. Williams?"

"Call me Frederick. Yes. Just a little more tired than usual. I'll be fine."

"Can I get you anything?"

"No, no. Oh say. I heard you were considering trying to get into the fire service. Is that right?"

I drew in a breath, worried that losing my job and flailing around without a career was going to place me in a negative light in his eyes.

"Yes. I've done some research and have a plan. I just hope it all works out."

"Would you consider that a career change?"

I paused, wondering where he was going with that question.

"Yes. Most definitely. I've never been a firefighter before and have had no training."

"You ought to ask if the VA will give you retraining funds to get you through whatever program you need."

"Hmm. I don't know. I used the GI Bill not that long ago for my Bachelor's degree. I figured that's the end of what they'd offer me."

He shook his head. "Vee rap."

"Vee rap?"

"Yes. VRAP. Veterans retraining assistance program. Well wait, you may not be old enough to qualify for that one. You've got to be at least thirty-five. How old are you?"

My heart sank a bit. "I'm twenty-eight."

"Hmm. Okay. There's also something called the VR and E. Vocational rehabilitation and employment program. But cha need a disability rating for that one. And you may even be able to get more through the GI Bill. You may want to make an appointment with the VA benefits office to see what's available to you. No point in paying for retraining if there's a program out there already that'll cover it."

"Thank you. I'll see what I can find out from the VA." I cringed inwardly because I loathed asking the VA for anything.

Audre stepped out onto the patio and I had to remind myself to close my mouth. She had changed out of her loose, flowing church dress and put on a tight cocktail dress that hugged her curves.

"You ready, Viv?"

I tilted my head, trying to remember what our plans were. We didn't have any that I knew of. She bit her bottom lip ever so slightly and I got the message.

"Yes. I am indeed ready." I turned to Frederick and shook his hand. "Great to see you, sir. I always enjoy sharing Sunday lunch with you and your lovely family."

He nodded and, when he saw Audre's dress, he waved us off.

"Good night, Daddy," Audre said and blew him a kiss. He blew her a kiss back, his hand still shaking.

We drove our separate cars back to my place. That way she could drive herself back home later.

Audre looped her arm through mine as we climbed the lobby stairs, her heels clicking on the tile. At the top we ran into Ang as she was heading out.

"Hey, guys," she said, smiling as she took in Audre's outfit. "Have fun." She waved over her shoulder at us and made her way down the stairs. We chuckled and walked down the corridor to my studio.

As I unlocked the door and welcomed Audre inside, I couldn't help but comment. "There I was trying to behave, having a civilized conversation with your father, and you show up looking like this." I ran my hand over her ass for emphasis, the smooth fabric whispering under my palm. "It took everything I had not to look like a bumbling idiot in front of him. And I am totally objectifying you right now."

"Good. I like it when you objectify me."

She led me over to the futon, sat on my lap, and wrapped her arms around my neck. I buried my face in her neck and slowly ran my hand up her thigh, listening to her breath quicken. She smelled like lotion, lightly floral with a hit of shea butter. I placed a very gentle kiss in the spot I knew drove her wild, right where her neck and trap muscle met. She shivered. Then I gave her what I knew she was waiting for, another gentle kiss in the same spot followed by sinking my teeth into the muscle. I had learned exactly how hard to bite that gave her pleasure but would not leave a lasting mark. She groaned in my ear and her arm tightened on my neck, as her hips began to roll.

I gripped her hip firmly, angling her off my lap and onto her back. Her arm still around my neck, she pulled me down on top of her, a grin on her lips.

*

When I woke, Audre had gone, no doubt to get ready for work. After going pee, I washed up and laughed when I saw myself in the mirror. I had her dark-purple lip stain all over my mouth, jaw, and throat. I had learned when we first started dating that I needed to keep makeup remover on hand for this exact issue. After we had made out for the first time, I had no idea how to get the stuff off and darn near rubbed my lips off trying to remove the stain left behind by her lipstick. I had since learned and smiled at myself as I went about removing it.

Despite losing my job, things were starting to feel good. I had fixed the issue with Ang, sort of, and my relationship with Audre was fulfilling on so many levels. I had a plan on the next steps for changing my line of work. I just needed to keep the lights on and a roof over my head until things got rolling.

I knew bar managers all over town and got busy calling them, asking if I could pick up shifts at their establishments. Those who answered were happy to have me on call as a bartender, which was better than nothing. I landed a shift that night at a sports bar in Midtown.

After that was settled, I begrudgingly called the VA Benefits office and requested an appointment for an assessment but learned that the first one available was not for four months. By then the semester would have already started, so I decided to just figure it out on my own.

I went into the bathroom and squatted in front of the cabinet under the sink, pushing aside a bottle of lotion and a small basket of tampons and pads. Behind all of that was a fireproof safe where I stored important documents, my pistol, and all my tip money.

I pulled out the box where I kept the cash and carried it to the kitchen table. And removed the lid. Inside was a sheet of paper with handwritten entries for when I put money in and took money out, plus stacks of bills separate by denomination.

If my log sheet was correct, and if I was careful, I had enough cash there to pay my rent and bills for two months. I had already paid off my truck and motorcycle, and it was a relief not to have loan payments to make on top of everything else. I counted the money to make sure the amount I had was the same as what was on the sheet, and everything balanced. I ran my hands over my face and let out a big sigh. Having a two-month cushion was nice, but I had to be very careful and not get complacent. I still needed to hustle and work every chance I got.

Satisfied, I put the money back in the safe and went out for a run before doing laundry and cleaning. I kept myself busy the entire day until it was time to get ready for work. While I had been to the sports bar as a customer before I had never worked at it, so I headed down a little early to get set up, meet the staff, and become familiar with the layout of the station I would be working at.

I started getting dressed in my usual work outfit, the outfit that showed off my tattoos and earned me the most tips: black beater, black Dickies, boots, wallet chain. But it occurred to me that I was not going to work at a lesbian nightclub anymore. I was going to work at a straight sports bar. I swapped out the beater for a black fitted polo shirt, the Dickies for some khaki slacks, and the boots for black loafers. I skipped the wallet chain. Looking in the mirror there was no hiding that I was a dyke, with my hair styled in a short men's cut. But toning down the outfit would hopefully divert any negative commentary or attention. At the end of the day, I was a damn good bartender, and I knew it. But customers tend to get weird when they see someone different than them handling their drinks, or food, or whatever service it is that is being provided.

I took a cab to the bar and stood out front for a moment, watching the bouncer and the customers who were on the sidewalk talking. The front of the place had a massive wooden door, and no windows. As someone walked out of the door the sound of sports commentators and cheering spilled out. It was very different than the dance music and style of club I was used to.

I waited until the bouncer was alone. "Showtime," I whispered to myself as I walked up to him, heart racing. I craned my head back, looking up at him. "Hey. How's it going?"

"Good. ID, please," he said in a deep voice. I pulled out my wallet and showed him my ID.

"I'm here to work tonight. Subbing in as a bartender. I'm Viv." I stuck out my hand and his massive paw swallowed it up as we shook.

"Okay. Yeah. I heard we were down a few. I'm Bronson." He adjusted the black beanie that was pulled snugly down to his eyebrows and over his earlobes.

"Anything I need to know before going in?"

He rubbed his hands together, his massive pecs and traps shifting as he did so. "They get a little rowdy. But you look like you can handle yourself." He pointed at the dark-purple scar that ran down my left cheekbone and the other one on my temple. "Bar fight?"

"Something like that," I said with a smirk.

"If they get loud with you don't back down. Some of them in there will try and test you."

"The customers or the staff?"

"Both."

"Great. Sounds like I have a fun night ahead."

"You'll be fine. Come find me if shit goes sideways."

"Thanks."

Sound spilled out as Bronson pulled open the huge door for me and I stepped in, allowing my eyes to adjust to the darkness inside. The place was huge. Easily twice the size as the nightclub I had worked at. The middle of the room had rows of big tables with benches, kind of like massive picnic tables, and the wall along one side was all booths. In the back near the bathrooms, they had pool tables and video games. On the other end was a kitchen with a counter that you could walk up to and order food. Along the other long wall spanned a bar that had at least four stations at it. It appeared my choice of a black polo shirt had been good, since that's exactly what the other bartenders were wearing.

Above all of that there were at least a dozen different widescreen TVs suspended from the ceiling playing every sort of sporting event you could imagine: horse racing, golf, dirt bike racing, reruns of classic football games, boxing. I could tell which of the screens had a live event on it because people were crowded around the tables underneath those TVs and were eagerly watching and letting out bursts of cheers and groans.

I approached the friendliest looking bartender and introduced myself, letting him know I was there to sub in for the night. He didn't seem to know anything about it and didn't appear too thrilled. Whether he was mad about not knowing or put off by me as a person, it was hard to tell. So, I took a seat on a bar stool while he huddled up with the other bartenders, which led to a lot of whispering and then a phone call. Eventually the manager walked up to me, greeting me warmly and shaking my hand, which shut the bartenders up. He introduced me around and took me behind the bar to show me the station I would be working at.

Everything was standard. The soda gun, types of alcohol in the well, garnishes, what alcohol they had on the back shelf. The only thing that made me nervous was the cash register. It was a computerized thing that on first glance seemed really overwhelming, given my inexperience with computers. I soon learned, with great relief, that it was much easier to use than the registers at my old job.

The other bartenders warmed up to me fairly quickly and we got busy as the Happy Hour and dinner crowds rolled in. I poured a hell of a lot more beers than I was used to—it was definitely a beer drinking crowd. And the requests for mixed drinks were easy: rum and Coke, Red Bull and vodka, and the occasional Cosmo.

After the dinner crowd cleared out there was a lull, followed by a DJ coming in and, to my chagrin, I learned that the bar was hosting its weekly country night. That meant cowboys. I didn't mind the country music or line dancing so much. It was the general attitude of cowboys on top of how shit-faced drunk I knew some of them were prone to getting.

Back when I was still in the service, I went to plenty of country bars while off duty. There wasn't much else to choose from where I was stationed in the South. Back then I had looked like all the other female soldiers, and blended in with the straight crowd, because I had to. It was still Don't Ask Don't Tell back then and I could have been kicked out of the army if I showed my true colors as a lesbian. But times had changed, and so had my appearance. And there I was working behind the bar on what promised to be a full-fledged country night.

Several people showed up early for free line dancing lessons. After ten the crowd began pushing up to the bar and the DJ got going full swing once the manager turned off all the TVs. The room was full of men in cowboy hats, tight Wrangler pants, boots, and fancy plaid button-up shirts. The women wore a variety of pink, blue, and white tight pants with sequins decorating the back pockets, plus boots, tight tops, and big hair. The room smelled of perfume, cologne, chewing tobacco, and beer.

Things started out fine. I only got a few people giving me a double take before ordering their beers and wine coolers. Things got more hectic after midnight as the beer drinkers moved on to doing tequila shots and the first fist fight broke out.

Bartenders see a lot, and I saw that fight brewing earlier on in the evening. Two guys had been tossing insults back and forth, something about a girl. The drunker they got the louder they got, until one finally walked up and sucker punched the other behind the ear. I could hear the smack of flesh over the music and all hell broke loose as they pounded on each other, then their friends and girlfriends started scuffling. Bronson and his crew moved in quickly and pried them apart, kicking them all out to the street to sort it out there. That fight set off a domino effect of tussles, arguments, and inevitably another fight. Bronson and his crew handled it all well, and everyone not fighting carried on with their dancing and chatting as if nothing had happened. Completely different than when the rare fight broke out at the lesbian club, which cleared the room and killed business for the rest of the night.

One guy had been sitting at my end of the bar most of the night nursing beer after beer and watching the crowd. He wore the standard plaid shirt, cowboy hat, and had calloused knuckles and a deep tan on his wrinkled face. To top it off, he had a Fu Manchu style mustache. Tiring of his beer, he ordered a double shot of Jägermeister. I had to hold my breath while pouring it because I hated the smell of Jägermeister. He downed it in two gulps and ordered another. He sipped on the second one and turned his seat so he was facing me instead of the crowd and proceeded to watch every move I made, a stern look on his face. When one of the barstools closer to me opened up, he took that seat. I was well aware he was watching me like a bug under a microscope, and I kept tabs on him with my peripheral vision. My hackles were up, and I couldn't shake the feeling that he was going to be trouble.

I saw Bronson walk into the back, so I tailed him back there.

"Hey, Bronson. Things going okay?"

"Oh yeah. Just the usual bullshit when we have hick night."

"Hey, can you see that guy sitting on the fifth stool down?"

Bronson leaned past me, peeking around the corner of the doorframe out to the bar. "Yeah."

"I'm getting bad vibes off of him. Have you had trouble with him before?"

"Yeah. He's a creep. All the complaints we get about him are from women. But he also seems to know exactly where the line is and doesn't cross it, at least not in here."

"Lovely. Well, now that you're inside can you keep half an eye on me? I can see him getting ugly."

"Yeah. This place is packed, but I'll try and stay close unless some dumb shits decide to brawl again. Although, one thing I appreciate about this crowd is they fist fight. They don't knife or shoot each other. They just get drunk, give each other bloody noses, and then do it all again next week."

"Well, I'm gonna give that creep a bloody nose if he crosses any lines with me. Fair warning."

Bronson laughed heartily and clapped me on the back. "I don't doubt it."

I made my way back behind the bar and Bronson waded into the crowd. He was much taller than everyone else, and was built like a Buick, so he was easy to spot. I carried on pouring drinks and chatting up customers sitting at the bar. Meanwhile the man continued to watch me. He finished his drink and slid the glass down the bar so it hit my hand. I excused myself from the person I was talking to and turned to him. He crooked his finger at me in a "come here" motion, a nasty sneer on his lips. I smiled as I bit back my rising temper and made a quick glance into the crowd looking for Bronson but didn't spot him.

I walked down to where the man was sitting and wiped up a ring of sticky Jäger with a bar towel.

"Ready to close out your tab?"

"I was wondering. You look like one of them dykes. Is that right?" He said the word dyke with such disdain that his eyes narrowed and his jaw flexed. A slight slur to his words and the hooded look of his eyes told me that he was more drunk than not.

I smiled at him. "I don't talk about my personal life at work, sir."

"You are, aren't you? I can tell by that stupid haircut and how you carry yourself like a man." He jabbed a finger at me, pointing at my hair.

I looked at him evenly, holding back all the snarky comments I wanted to make. Even harder was not punching him in his bigoted fucking face. I used to find it fun to poke at dangerous people. But de-escalation was what I had been trying for since starting therapy, and that took a lot of effort on my part.

I smiled at him, folding the bar towel into thirds. "So, are you ready to close out your tab?"

"Yunno what? I don't like your kind. Always out there waving your queer-ass rainbow flags and shouting about equality and pride. And for what?" He jammed his meaty finger down onto the bar for emphasis. "So, you can bugger each other and molest kids and fuck animals? Oh, yeah. I've heard all about it. Bunch of perverts."

He had started to raise his voice and people sitting on the bar stools near him had begun paying attention, watching me to see how I would respond.

As much as I wanted to take the high road, my old tendency to pop off pushed through. "Fuck animals? Hmm. And how the hell would I do that? Maybe you can tell me all about that. How many sheep have you raped? How many kids have you groomed and molested? Cuz you sure as hell put out that drunk-uncle-molester vibe."

He sputtered and his face turned bright red. He scrubbed at his mustache.

"I'm right, aren't I? Are you drunk Uncle Chester the Molester?" As the words rolled off my tongue, I scanned the room for Bronson because I knew I had stirred the pot a little too hard.

"Now you listen here, you stupid bitch! I—"

"No, you listen here, fucker. You take your drunk, obnoxious, bigoted ass right on out of here."

"Who the hell do you think you are, coming in here..."

"Out! You're eighty-sixed." I waved at Bronson over the crowd, letting him know I needed him at the bar. He gave a nod, but he was on the far side by the front door and had to wade through the tightly packed crowd.

"The hell I am. Get me the manager."

"Get him yourself."

The people sitting to each side of him had gotten up and moved away, looking back and forth between us as our voices rose.

"You all ought to be lynched. That's the only solution," he growled, spittle forming at the corners of his mouth.

"Are you threatening me?"

"Make of it what you will." He picked up an abandoned pint glass and rolled it back and forth between his hands. I looked up to check on Bronson's progress and in that split-second pain exploded on top of my skull. The son of a bitch had slammed the pint glass on my head. It didn't shatter, but rather worked as a bludgeon to crack me on the head. Sparks bloomed in front of my eyes, and when they cleared, he was standing across the bar from me grinning, flecks of chewing tobacco in his teeth. I shook my head to clear it and felt a giant hand grasp the front of my shirt, pulling me against the bar.

I hooked my loafers under the counter so he couldn't pull me up and over, and I swung my fist out wide, hitting him squarely on the ear with all my might. He howled and his grip loosened on my shirt. I took that opportunity to jam two fingers into the dip of his clavicle at the base of his throat. He immediately began coughing and gagging. He bent forward and grabbed another handful of my shirt, though he was coughing too hard to do anything about it. I let him grab it so I would have an excuse to bring my elbow down full force on the bridge of his nose, which I did. His nose gave way with a satisfying crunch. I threw a bar towel at him so he wouldn't bleed all over the bar.

Bronson reached us at that point and yanked the guy's hand off me before dragging him across the room and out of the door by his shirt collar, the man cupping his nose and howling the whole way out. People who had stepped away came back and took their seats at the bar. I poured a new beer for the person whose pint glass had been used to clobber me. Adrenaline still surged, so I was able to go about working for another few minutes before the manager came by and demanded that I join him in the office.

*

I sat in the back office, a bag of ice resting across my knuckles, and holding another bag of ice to my head. The manager was pacing and grumbling to himself. I looked around and saw that it was pretty much like every other bar office I had seen: cramped, stacked full of boxes of seasonal decorations and supplies, and an untidy desk. The manager stopped pacing directly in front of me. His worn-out sneakers had holes in the mesh tops and no doubt the soles did too. His jeans were baggy, but gave way to a perfectly round pot belly, which tested the limits of his faded polo shirt. He looked dead tired and unhealthy with the whites of his eyes yellowed and bloodshot, and tiny red veins showing on his nose and cheeks. He had missed patches of hair under his nose shaving several times over.

He released a big sigh. "Look. I know you were just protecting yourself. And I know that guy is a jerk. But...a bartender pounding the hell out of a customer is bad for business. I'm sure you could have handled it differently. I can't have our customers feeling unsafe with the staff." He paused. "I can't have you back here, even as a casual on-call."

I wanted to go into a long soapbox speech about victim blaming and how, even as a freelancer, it was his responsibility to provide me with a safe work environment, and that the staff already were aware that the guy was trouble. But I left it all unsaid because I didn't trust myself to remain professional and he didn't seem open to a different point of view.

Without a word I stood to leave, but the narrow door swung open, and Bronson squeezed in followed by a police officer. Bronson rolled his eyes and shrugged his shoulders at me as he scooted back out of the room, closing the door behind him. I remained standing as the officer gave me a hard look, scanning me from head to toe. There I stood with a bag of ice in each hand doing my best to keep my face neutral.

The officer had a clipboard with some forms on it and held a pen in his hand. He asked for my ID, which I gave him, and then we all waited while he called in my ID to make sure I didn't have any warrants. Bass from the music out front thumped through the walls. Once he got the all-clear, the officer told me to sit, which I did. He informed me that the man had filed a complaint against me and the police department was investigating.

"Ha. *He* is pressing charges against me? On what grounds?"

"Assault and battery. Says you attacked him."

I nodded, biting back my temper.

"Officer, the gentleman was using hate speech, saying that all gay people should be lynched, and he didn't like my retort, so he smashed me over the head with a pint glass." I pointed to the swelling lump on my scalp. "When that didn't knock me out, he grabbed my shirt and tried to pull me over the bar. So, I boxed his ear. He kept grabbing at me, so I gave him an elbow to the nose, and that's when a bouncer intervened." I showed him my swollen knuckles and elbow. "Plenty of people were standing right there and heard the whole conversation and saw the resulting tussle. And something tells me your department is probably already familiar with him."

The officer nodded and I waited quietly as he wrote notes for a few minutes, diligently filling out a form. The manager paced behind his desk. When the officer stopped writing he looked at me and clicked his pen a few times.

"Officer, am I free to go?"

He hesitated and sighed. "Yes. You are free to go. I don't see any merit to his complaint."

I looked at the manager. "Can I go back up to the bar and grab my stuff?"

He nodded at me.

The officer cleared his throat. "Why do you need permission to get your work supplies from your workstation?"

I shifted, considering whether to be diplomatic or not.

"Well, sir—" I motioned toward the manager. "This distinguished gentleman has terminated me from my temporary position here, due to me defending myself from his lecherous customer."

The officer swiveled his gaze from me to the manager. "Is that correct?"

The manager blew out his cheeks and muttered, "Yes." Then he found his voice. "But this is a privately owned establishment, and I can do what I want as its manager. I decide who works here and when." He placed his hands solidly on his hips, feet planted on the floor.

The officer *tsk*'d and narrowed his eyes. "I may not be an employment law attorney, but I do know that you have a responsibility to keep your staff safe from harassment and abuse—"

"Thank you. After seeing how things are run around here, I have no interest in returning to this place. I am just going to call a cab and grab my stuff, if that's okay with everybody." They both nodded. I smirked. "So, should I take my pay out of the till then? Seven dollars an hour times six hours. That's forty-two dollars."

The manager's eyes bulged and shot sideways at the police officer. "I...uh. We can talk about that once we are finished with the officer here."

"Are you paying her under the table?"

"She's, uh, freelance. She manages her own taxes and stuff."

I had a feeling he was not going to pay me for the work I had done, so I used the police officer's presence to my advantage. "So, should I take it out of the till, or are you going to pay me now from the safe?" He eyed us both and grumbled, squatting down to open the safe. He stood, his knees popping loudly, and thrust forty-two dollars in cash at me.

"Thanks. I'll be on my way." I stepped out and called a cab from a pay phone in the back hallway before returning to the bar to get my stuff. I grabbed my shaker and wine key, and as I placed my hand on my tip bucket, I saw that it was empty. I turned and saw the other bartenders scurry, trying to look busy. *Motherfuckers.* I took a deep breath, reining in the rage that wanted so badly to lash out.

People stealing from me had always ended in somebody getting bloody in the past. But I knew there was a police officer somewhere on the premises and I just needed to get the fuck out of there. But...staff stealing tips from other staff in the industry was so dirty. We all survived on our tips.

I put down my stuff and grabbed the soda gun from its holster on the bar. There's an old bartender trick where you take your fingertips and place them over the nozzle of the soda gun to make it spray super far. I had used that trick plenty of times at my old job to spray down the crowd with water when it got too hot in the bar.

I placed the fingertips of one hand tightly over the nozzle, leaving a gap just the right size, and turned toward the other bartenders who were still trying to look busy, probably hoping I would just leave. I unleashed an unholy river of cranberry juice on them and the floor and the back-bar bottles of liquor. The bartenders scrambled, trying to get away, but in such a narrow space behind the bar they didn't have anywhere to go. It took them a moment to realize I was spraying juice instead of water.

As soon as they realized what an enormous mess I was making for them they began cussing and turned toward me.

I placed the soda gun back in the harness, grabbed my stuff, blew them some kisses, and sauntered through the crowd to the front door. My cab was waiting at the curb and so was the jerk whose ass I had kicked earlier. Bronson placed his enormous body between the man and me and gave me a nod. As I was getting in the cab, the guy began hollering a bunch of garbage at me around Bronson's bulk.

"Bye, Chester," I said and waved as the cab pulled from the curb. On the short ride to my apartment, I took stock of the evening. I had picked up a shift to make money between jobs. Gotten into it with a hater. Let my temper get the best of me and I knowingly injured that man more than I needed to. I got fired from picking up any more shifts there. My tips got stolen, but I didn't leave totally empty handed. Overall, not a great night. As I climbed the stairs in the apartment lobby I smiled, thinking about how many hours it would take those thieving, bitch-ass bartenders to clean up all the cranberry juice before it dried and attracted fruit flies and other critters that would be bad for business.

*

After I showered and cleaned up my knuckles, I lay on the futon, ice pack on my head, in the glow of the fish tank and wondered why my entire life had been so full of violence. I knew plenty of people who had never been exposed to any sort of violence up close and personal. But I thought back and saw even from early childhood that physical violence had always been there. My constant companion. Even recently, when I had been making a conscious effort to change how I responded, violence was still there.

I ran through the entire evening and what it was exactly about me that the guy seemed to fixate on. My hair, for starters. Which sent me on a long debate on whether I should grow my hair long again. I had only cut it short in the first place because of a previous fight I had been in where the woman sliced my bun off before adorning me with the scars I still carried on my face.

The long black hair, always worn in a precise tight bun, had been one of the last things I clung to from my time in the military. Losing the bun had been the final step in fully transitioning to being a civilian and had also allowed me to really come into my own as a butch lesbian. I had gotten so many disgusted and disapproving looks and nasty comments from random people on the street once it became much more obvious that I was gay. I went from looking like an athletic, clean-cut woman, to standing out as different.

Most of the time I ignored it, but what had happened that night was the first outright physical attack due to my sexuality and it had chilled me. I ran my fingers through my hair and down the scars on my temple and cheekbone, then up to my head, running my fingertips around the huge lump that had formed where I had been hit. He had really rung my bell, but I didn't feel like I was concussed, which was a relief.

I knew I had a choice to make. Continue to be myself, and take whatever consequences came with it, or grow my hair out and retreat into a somewhat safer anonymity.

I fell asleep on the futon, fully dressed and undecided. But when I woke to sunlight streaming in through my blinds a few hours later, I had made up my mind. I got showered, dressed in running clothes, grabbed some cash, and jogged across Midtown to see my barber.

Tash was opening up for the day, unlocking the shop door, and grinned when she saw me.

"Viv-ee-an. What's up? And you are right on schedule. Every two weeks like clockwork I know you'll turn up on my doorstep." I followed her into the shop, grateful that the heater was on since I was dressed in lightweight running clothes. She slapped the seat of her chair. "Hop on up."

I sat in her old-fashioned barber chair, the kind with black leather, and an ashtray built into the arm. As she put the cape around me, she asked, "What are we doing today? The usual?"

I paused, looking at myself and at her in the mirror. "Yeah, the usual. A one on the sides and a quarter inch off the top," I said with a smile.

"What was that about?" She lifted her chin at my expression in the mirror.

"Ah. Just been thinking about making a change, but decided I like the look I've got going at the moment."

"You should keep it. You're fucking hot with this cut. And I'm not just saying that because you tip well." As she ran the clippers along my scalp she laughed. "You remember the first time you came in, with Buck, right? What a mess you were. Your hair all hacked up and those cuts were fresh on your face."

I smiled at her, feeling the scar on my cheek crinkle. "Yeah, I remember. That was a rough time. Things are better now. Oh, except, careful on top. I've got a decent sized goose egg up there."

She nodded and went about cutting my hair, concern on her face, being careful not to press on the tender spot. She looked around before speaking. "Viv. I know it's probably not my place. But are you okay? More often than not, when you come in here you've got split knuckles, cuts on your face, or are busted up somehow. Are you, maybe, in an abusive relationship? And...you totally don't have to tell me. But if you need resources, I can help."

"Thank you, Tash, I appreciate you saying something. But it's not that. In fact, my partner is amazing. I just seem to find trouble a lot. And hey, a few of those marks have been from wiping out while trail running. But yeah, I'm trying to have less physical violence in my life. I'm even changing careers, which I am excited about."

"Oh yeah? Nice!"

"I know you have a ton of clients. Are any of them female firefighters?"

"Yeah, a couple. They are all total studs. Aside from that they are really solid individuals. It seems like they really like their jobs, and it pays well. Is that what you're going for? Firefighting?"

"Yes, that's the goal. But I have to start at the very bottom and work my way up."

"Ey, now's the time. Right? On my thirtieth birthday my dad said to me: 'You're old enough to know what you want to do, and young enough to do it.' So, I am passing that little tidbit on to you, Viv."

"Thanks."

I considered what she had said while she finished cutting my hair and cleaning me up, then I jogged to McKinley Park and ran the path for a while before making my way back home to shower again. After eating I checked my cell phone and found that I had voicemails from a couple of different fire departments that I had applied to for fire season.

The first one I called back was a department I had been able to apply to online. Thankfully, the woman who had left me a message was at her desk and answered right away.

"Mesa Verde County Fire District Human Resources."

"Yes, ma'am, my name is Vivian Chastain. I received a message earlier today about my application for fire control worker."

"Okay, let's see." I heard some papers shuffling and a keyboard clacking. "Chastain. Yes. There you are. Okay, your application looked good. We'd like you to come down for an assessment and a pack test."

"Sure. Okay. What's a pack test?"

"Oh. Well. It's technically called the work capacity test. It's pass/fail. You have to hike three miles with a forty-five-pound pack in under forty-five minutes. We are technically supposed to give you four weeks to train and prepare for the test, but you applied late, and we are administering the test over the next couple of days. I know that sounds pretty treacherous—"

"Am I allowed to run?"

"What? No. You cannot run the route. Huh. I've never had anyone ask me that question before."

"I'll do it. Just let me know when and where to be, and what to bring."

The woman and I talked through the logistics and by the end of our call I was excited. I loved testing my endurance and trying new obstacles. It was one of the reasons I had loved being a soldier, because there was no end to the challenges I could put myself through. The more I wanted, the more they could, and would, dish out.

I sent out a flurry of texts to Audre, Bear, Jared, Kate, and Ang letting them know about it. And in return I got lots of excited texts back. It was so great to be loved and supported and, for once, finally be in a place to absorb that support rather than deflect it. I looked out of the window, watching a light-rail train whoosh by, and smiled.

Chapter Sixteen

My cell phone rang, and the screen showed a number I didn't recognize. Assuming it was another fire department calling me back about my application, I answered.

"This is Vivian."

"Viv. Hey. It's Joey."

I blew out a big sigh, wondering what he wanted, because he always wanted something. "Hey there, big brother. What's up?"

"I wanted to let you know I graduated from rehab. And I'm going through the twelve-step program."

I pursed my lips. We had had this same conversation plenty of times before.

"Well. Congrats for graduating. Are you staying with Mom?"

"Um. No. Not this time. I'm renting a room in a sober group home. It's good. We hold each other accountable here."

I tried to muster up some enthusiasm. "Great. Great. I'm glad to hear you are trying something new this time."

"Yeah. It's good. And I owe the county a bunch of community service hours due to some past indiscretions, so I am serving out my hours and giving back to the community. It's really helping me to refocus on the rest of the world. To give back rather than always take, like I used to."

That sounded promising. I had never heard Joey speak about giving back and serving the community. Or even admit that he had only ever cared about himself. Maybe he was making actual progress.

"So. I'm on step eight."

"Okay. I don't know what that means."

"It means I've made a list of everyone I have harmed, and I am reaching out to make amends."

That must be one long-ass list. I stifled my cynical laugh. "Hmm. That must have been an eye-opening experience, making that list."

He sighed. "Yeah. It was. So anyway. I wonder if we can meet up some time soon. I can come to your place or maybe we can connect at a park or something?"

I decided to give him a little test. "I have time today. How about today?"

"Oh. Uh."

"Yeah, that's what I thou—"

"No, no. I am not trying to wiggle out of it. It's just that I am not allowed to drive right now, so I was thinking about whether to take the bus or ride my bike."

"Oh."

"But yeah. Today is good."

We worked out the details and ended the call. I made myself a simple lunch of a peanut butter and honey sandwich, a green salad, and a banana. I sat at the rickety card table in my kitchen eating my lunch and reading, enjoying the relative silence of a weekday afternoon. I took a bite of sandwich and turned the page when my upstairs neighbor, who was normally nocturnal, began pacing.

"Jesus, this fucking guy and his pacing," I grumbled to my fish.

After lunch I walked the ten blocks down to the café and settled in on the patio with some peppermint tea and *Cloud Atlas* until my brother eventually showed up. He walked up to the table and stood there awkwardly, as if he wasn't sure about giving me a hug or not. I did not get up, instead motioning to the empty chair across from me.

He didn't order anything, saying that aside from quitting alcohol he also was off caffeine for the time being. I suggested some herbal tea, but he declined. And then we sat there, staring at each other across the cold metal table in the shaded, chilly courtyard. I wrapped my hands around the warm mug and waited. It was his show, so I wasn't about to try to take the reins.

"So, uh, I know you probably think this time through rehab will be just like all of the other times. With me relapsing and doubling down on my alcoholism. But this is it. I'm ready. It's time. No more going back to how I have been living my life."

I raised my eyebrows at him, not convinced, and annoyed that it was expected of me to be supportive and amazed by his revelation. I just couldn't be that person for him.

"I can't be your cheerleader, Joey. I hope it all works out, but I am not the one to come to for support with this.

I am not doing any emotional labor for you and your recovery."

"I know. And I understand. It's okay." He picked at a hangnail on his thumb and chewed his lip for a moment. His usual unkempt brown hair hung in his eyes, and he hadn't shaved in a few days. His hands were scarred and calloused from years of doing construction labor and from untold drinking accidents.

"I'm not here to ask you to do anything for me or support me through this process. I understand why you can't. I recognize, now, how terrible I was to you...and have been from the first day they brought you home from the hospital as a baby. I just..." He ran his hand across the rough tabletop. "I just, at the time, couldn't stop myself. I knew that what I was doing was wrong while I was doing it, but I just couldn't stop. All of those times I terrorized you, beat you, trapped you, tricked you, stole from you, made you bleed. Year after year of it. I just want to say that I am sincerely sorry. None of it was your fault, not even when Mom said it was. It was all me. You didn't deserve any of it."

A quiet moment fell between us as a gust of wind blew the first leaves of fall down the sidewalk. "I cannot express how truly sorry I am. For all of it. And I thank you for agreeing to meet up with me today to talk. I wouldn't have blamed you at all if you had told me to fuck off. I hope someday you can forgive me, and that we can work toward building trust. But I know I have a lot of work to do on my end for you to even consider that."

I did my best to absorb everything that he had said. I told myself to acknowledge what a monumental moment it was. And yet, I felt nothing. I knew that the words he was saying were a big deal, but I just sat there looking at him blankly. I knew that when I talked to Alexia about it later, she would probably tell me my lack of emotional response was me trying to protect myself from further harm and disappointment by my brother. But...I realized that I wanted to feel something. And then frustration boiled up over having such high levels of internal defenses. I looked my brother right in the eye, knowing he was a big part of the reason I was wired that way.

Words tumbled out of my mouth before I had a chance to consider them. "You know what? I am really glad you have made it this far through the steps, and that you seem to be taking things more seriously this time. You have clearly put a lot of thought into what you wanted to say to me." I paused, taking a breath.

He continued to hold my gaze, not flinching or looking away.

"I need you to know how fucked up I am as an adult because of how you treated me as a kid. I need you to know that during those super-important formative years when I should have learned how to have secure and loving relationships, I was just trying to survive. I broke a guy's nose last night when I didn't have to." His eyes flicked down to my swollen knuckles. "I am filled with so much rage and am so ready to fight at the slightest sign that someone is trying to do me harm. It served me well in the military. It is not a good thing in the civilian world, or when trying to have relationships as an adult. And now...now I spend a fortune every month on therapy because I am trying to fix it. To undo all of the messed-up ways my brain is wired because of you."

Joey looked down at his hands and sighed heavily. "Yeah. That's fair. And I acknowledge and accept all of it.

I wish I could go back and undo it all, to go back and protect you and love you instead of abusing and terrorizing you. I am truly sorry."

Another breeze blew through the patio and I shivered, cold to my core. With that, I went from feeling nothing to feeling everything. "Thank you." I stood, grabbed my book, and strode out to the street. The impulse to run itched inside my veins, and I did. I ran the ten blocks home and kept going, book in hand. I ran a zigzag of Midtown streets, turning every time I came to a red light or anything else that tried to slow me down. My lungs and legs burned. I had already gone running that morning and taking a second run with no warm-up or stretching, while dressed in jeans and a fleece, was rough.

The frenzy in my brain and chest slowly wore off and I made my way back home, where I climbed into a hot bath and stared at the wall while my brain went through an emotional triathlon, the events being rage, frustration, and finally sadness.

I was suddenly so tired I wanted to curl up on my side in the tub and sleep, but didn't want to risk drowning, so I got out and dressed and curled up on the futon, which was still folded up into a couch. I layered myself with blankets and stared out of the window at the canopy of the trees across the street, watching the thick branches and leaves sway in the wind until I drifted off to sleep.

Chapter Seventeen

The pace of life picked up. I passed the pack test, as I knew I would. I also passed the background, medical, psych, and drug tests, and dove into my job as a seasonal fire control worker. I was on a hand crew and was rarely home.

I worked rotating twenty-four-hour shifts digging fire lines, literally clearing away flammable grasses and brush and digging down to the soil so there was no fuel for the wildfires to spread to. It was the most grueling and intense work I had ever done, and I loved it. I fell in easily with the crew, which were mostly young men from a variety of backgrounds. We sweat and bled side by side, breathed in the smoke and ate rations together, slept in the dirt and joked together. It was us against the terrain and the fire, and we were determined to win. We left behind wide swaths of land stripped down to the dirt.

My hands blistered and then calloused. My skin sunburned and then tanned. My eyes and lungs burned from the smoke and then became accustomed to it. The hot spots on my scalp from the hard hat eventually calmed. I worked myself until I could barely stand up after each shift and then slept deeply on my days off. It was blissful in that all I had to think about was not dying.

I went from one huge wildfire to another until the rains came in late November and fire season ended. I had saved up almost every penny that I had earned and had a nice cushion when I returned home.

Audre and Ang had kept my fish alive, which I was grateful for. When I got back, I immediately went up the hall to the laundry room and started several massive loads of laundry. My clothes were all filthy, stained with dirt and sweat rings, and smelled of woodsmoke. I checked the fridge and cabinets to see what I needed to get from the grocery store and discovered that someone had stocked me up with fresh fruits and veggies, yogurt, and all my favorite foods. I leaned against the counter and smiled, tracing over the smile on my lips with my fingertips.

I recognized that I had a lot of work to do. I needed desperately to get back into therapy and I wanted to reconnect with Audre and Ang, and I had to prepare for the EMT class that would start in January. While away I had ignored all calls and texts from my mother and brother, using what little energy I had between shifts to call and text with my core people.

The following day was Thanksgiving, and Audre's family had invited me to join them. I ran out to the store, braving the crowds of shoppers to get the ingredients I needed, and baked pumpkin pies between doing loads of laundry. My small studio soon smelled of cloves and warmed from the heat of the oven.

I put fresh sheets on my futon, put away the laundry, and settled down into a nice solo dinner. I was home, and happy, and grateful for the experience on the fire line, for the money I had earned, for people in my life who loved and supported me, and for having a roof over my head.

After dinner I sat down with a copy of Haruki Murakami's *Kafka on the Shore,* which I had picked up from a used bookstore in a tiny town I had passed through going from one fire to another. I couldn't quite focus, though, because I felt something I wasn't used to. It took me some time to identify it, and when I finally landed on it, I wanted to cry with relief.

I was content and savored the emotion, closing my eyes to let it flow through me.

My revelry was interrupted by the ringing of my house phone. I took the handset off the charger and answered it.

"Hello."

"Vivian. It's you mother."

All the newfound contentment dispersed in one fell swoop.

"Hi, Mom. What's up?"

"What's up? Vivian, you know how much I dislike that phrase. I—"

"What do you want, Mom? If you are just going to bust my ass, I am hanging up now."

"Oh fine. I am calling about Thanksgiving. I've left you several messages, but you haven't called me back. That's terribly rude. You—"

"Mom! Enough. I'm twenty-eight years old. Get off my ass." Silence fell between us and it felt wonderful. I had never been so direct with her about her constant disapproval, and it felt very empowering.

She drew in a long breath. "I am calling to see if you will be joining us for Thanksgiving. It's just going to be your brother and one of his recovery...friends."

"No. Thank you. I have other plans."

"Oh."

"I hope you have a great time. Happy Thanksgiving, Mom." With that I ended the call, smiled as I placed the phone back on its charger, and bundled back up in the blankets on the couch.

It took me a few minutes to regain the feeling of contentment, but it did return, and I delved back into *Kafka on the Shore* until I fell asleep.

*

The next day I poured heavy cream into a bowl, added some vanilla extract and sugar, and began whipping it with a whisk. It took quite some time to whip it by hand, but all the physical work on the fire line had improved my fitness and stamina tenfold, and soon enough I had fresh whipped cream to go with the pumpkin pies I had baked. I packaged it all up, got myself dressed in slacks, loafers, button-up shirt, bowtie, and blazer, and drove over to Audre's house.

I arrived a bit early so I could help her get ready. She gave me a kiss on the cheek and ushered me into the kitchen. Her Aunt Dot and sister, Josephine, were both busy cooking while her baby niece, Ruby, sat at the kitchen table pretending to mix things with a wooden spoon she had clasped in her chubby hand.

I rolled up my sleeves and got to work peeling sweet potatoes, or were they yams? Aunt Dot pulled an apron over my head and tied it behind my back for me.

"Thanks!"

I smiled as we all went about chopping, stirring, and peeling in the warmth of the kitchen. It was nice to be included as part of their family holiday, and I was happy to help with the prep work.

Aunt Dot spoke up after a while. "Vivian. Is this your first Thanksgiving with a Black family?"

I paused because that was not a question I had expected.

"Yes, ma'am. Well, I spent plenty of Thanksgivings deployed and was one of the only white people in the unit. But that's totally different than celebrating in a family home."

She nodded as she placed chopped yams or sweet potatoes or whatever they were in a buttered glass baking dish and sprinkled brown sugar over the top.

"Well, just so you know it'll probably be very different than what things are like with your family."

I paused, considering what she said. "I hope so."

And I truly did hope so. My family holidays were so sterile. Full of disapproval and tension. Everything ran on a tight schedule and there was no room for fun or casual conversation. Almost like a forced exercise, something that was required and expected. Manners had to be flawless, and don't even think about sitting on the couch in the parlor.

The Williams family felt real to me. Like the way a family should be. They welcomed each other, flaws and all, and celebrated each day as a blessing. I was grateful to be spending the day with them rather than my blood family.

Aunt Dot considered what I had said. "Well, Vivian, I want you to know that you are very welcome here."

I smiled at her and looked back down at the dish I was washing to hide the tears that were welling up in my eyes. And what she had said had proven to be correct. Thanksgiving with the Williams family was very different than anything I had experienced before, and I was indeed welcome. I went to bed that night, lying on my futon awash in that feeling again...contentment.

*

After I returned from grocery shopping, I enjoyed a bowl of vegetable and wild rice soup with a side of green salad and a mug of tea. I read a book and did my best to ignore the blinking light on the house phone, indicating that there was a voicemail waiting.

After I had cleared up my dishes and found a good place to stop in the book, I dialed the number to retrieve the voicemail and listened.

The message began with loud street noise. "Hey. Viv. It's your brother. I, uh...I got my license back and got my motorcycle out of impound. I wonder if you'd like to go on a ride with me soon? I know the weather is getting cold, but an afternoon ride to the foothills could be fun. Give me a call."

I replayed the message two more times, listening for the slightest hint of slur or sign that he had been drinking, but his voice was clear and steady. I considered his request and sighed. He was trying to mend fences and he had never made it this far out of rehab without a relapse, which I gave him credit for. I called him back and we scheduled a ride to Apple Hill the following Monday. I insisted that I lead the ride, and he agreed.

We met up at a gas station on Broadway and hopped on the highway. The wind chill on the bike was biting, but the afternoon promised to warm up to the mid-sixties, which would make for a pleasant ride back. I led the way up Highway 50 into the foothills and then snaked us through the beautiful back roads to Apple Hill. We enjoyed the gentle curves of the narrow roads, covered in orange and yellow leaves.

Each of the farms we stopped at were fairly deserted, some even closed after the weekend rush. We eventually found one that had a nice outdoor area to sit, with benches under propane heaters. I got us each a cup of hot apple cider and some apple fritters. We sat in silence, watching a van full of preschoolers disembark for a field trip. I didn't usually have sweets, so my bloodstream immediately began pulsing with the sugar spike. I got up and got us each a bottle of water, wanting to flush out my system.

After the excited children had filed off to go to the petting zoo things quieted down and Joey and I began to talk. Tentatively at first, grazing on easy subjects: weather, traffic, New Year's Eve plans. After another lull Joey looked right at me, which I realized he hadn't really done since we sat down. He ran his fingers around the rim of his paper cup and chewed his bottom lip for a moment.

"I need to tell you something about myself that I don't think you are aware of, since you're younger."

I raised my eyebrows, concerned about how he was pivoting the conversation and what may come from it.

"Okay. Go ahead."

"Do you remember our babysitter, Janet?"

"Yeah, barely. I was really little. All I remember is her yelling a lot. Why?"

"Well, she abused me and so did her husband."

"Her husband? Why would he have been around? I don't remember him."

"Be glad you don't remember him. Sometimes Mom would go away for the weekend, and Janet would stay at the house with us, and he would come too." He ran his hand roughly across his forehead, swiping his shaggy bangs off to the side. "Uh, this isn't something I talk about much, but...do you remember them making us go to church with them? Her husband was a pastor or something."

"I vaguely remember going to church with you and Janet."

"Well, one time I really didn't want to go and told them so. Janet started yelling at me, so I went and hid under my bed. Her husband yanked me out by my foot. It scared me so much I...peed my pants. Shit, this is really embarrassing to talk about."

I nodded and a cloud of sorrow overcame me. For the first time in my life, I felt sorry for Joey.

"Anyway, I hit my head on the bed frame as he pulled me out. And then they forced me to sit through church with wet pants. It was humiliating. And that's an example of a good day with them. Verbal abuse, hitting, withholding food and water, you name it."

"I know I was little, but I wasn't *that* young. Why don't I remember any of this? And...I am not asking because I don't believe you. I am asking because I truly don't have many memories of her."

"You were there, and the abuse happened to you too. But I got the brunt of it because I was older and a mouthy little shit. You were always the quiet, well-behaved one."

I looked down at the weathered tabletop, taking some time to absorb everything.

"Did Mom know?"

"Yeah. I told her. She said I was overreacting."

"Fucking Bernadette. Jeez, Joey, I had no idea about any of that. That's a lot. It makes me understand, a little. Do you remember us all going to family therapy? That was pretty advanced for the time, I think. I'm surprised Mom did that."

"Well, there were reasons."

"Do you know why after the first few months of family sessions the therapist started making me sit in the lobby while you and Mom went in together?"

"Uh..." He rubbed the back of his neck and looked up at the sky. "There were some new things to talk about that it was better you didn't hear or know about."

"Like what?"

"You sure you want to know more?"

I nodded and drank the last of my water.

"The year we were in family counseling, I was molested. That's why all of a sudden you had to start sitting in the lobby, cuz we had to talk about that."

Letting out a massive sigh, I looked at him, tears brimming in my eyes.

"Don't worry, Viv. It's been handled. He was caught and did some time in prison for it."

"Who was it?"

"Doesn't matter. Anyway, finally dealing with this stuff as an adult, and being able to talk about it has helped with my sobriety. Rather than drinking to try to numb it, I'm facing it head on. And that's what's important. Aside from going to AA meetings, I'm also in therapy to work through this stuff more. I understand now why I've been such a terrible human being, though none of what I have just told you excuses how I have treated you. I know I already apologized to you, but I want to say again how sorry I am."

He started to reach across the table to take my hand but let his hand drop into his lap instead. We watched cars come and go in the parking lot for a while. After he finished his water, I cleared my throat.

"Thank you for opening up to me today. I know how much it must have taken for you to do that, and I appreciate it. I hope you understand that it is still going to take some time for me to come around. Trust doesn't come easily for me, especially with you, and it's even harder when we are coming back from such a massive deficit. I'm not trying to be an asshole here, just speaking the truth. All of that to say, I'm glad we got together today." He nodded and smiled, his eyes crinkling at the corners.

We had a nice ride back into town as the sun hung low in the sky despite it still being early. When I peeled off at the Twenty-sixth Street exit, he waved as he continued on to his exit.

I took a hot shower to thaw out. I did my best to process all that I had learned about my brother's life and I got caught in a weird space where I felt bad for him, but also still held anger around how his treatment of me had such long-lasting impact that I had spent a lot of time trying to undo.

*

That evening I walked down the hall, Audre on my arm, to Ang's apartment for dinner and game night. It was a quasi-double date because Kate was also there. The four of us dug into some hearty lasagna and garlic bread. I prepared a salad with mixed greens, artichoke hearts, mushrooms, and other assorted veggies. Audre poured the wine and Kate put on a jazz CD that she liked. Conversation over dinner was easy and I took a moment, as I sat back from my plate, to consider if such a thing would have been possible for me even a year prior, and my answer was steadfastly no.

Polyamory had not been easy for me, but I had taken a lot of time to identify what had upset me about poly and worked on it. It all boiled down to some old, deeply ingrained insecurities. But with lots of therapy and exposure, I found myself totally happy and at peace while sharing dinner with my former primary turned lover, her partner, and my partner. I smiled down at my plate and Audre squeezed my hand.

"Would you like to share what's making you smile, babe?"

Kate and Ang looked at me expectantly. I drew in a deep breath and took a small sip of wine. "I uh...I was just thinking about how this sort of thing never would have been possible even a year ago. But I've unpacked a lot of crap and here we are. And I am grateful for all of you lovely people. I wouldn't be where I am if it weren't for each of you contributing in your own ways."

Kate and Audre smiled at me sweetly. Ang raised her eyebrows, and I knew she was about to do what she did best...kill the moment. I huffed and looked back down at my hand entwined in Audre's on her lap, waiting for it.

"Yeah. Well. You're right about those insecurities. I'm glad you feel like you've overcome them, but yeah, it was a rough go being in a primary relationship with you."

I kept my eyes down as my temper rose. Audre gave my hand a long gentle squeeze and she and Kate recrossed their legs under the table. I opened my mouth to speak, because I sure as hell was not about to allow Ang to talk to me like that, but Kate beat me to it.

"Ang. How is saying something like that helpful here? How is that supportive? Vivian was literally just thanking us...all of us...for having her back and helping her grow, and you pushed her down instead of lifting her up."

"I'm so sick of everything always being about Vivian. She is a vacuum of need. Every time I turn around, she is having some sort of catastrophe in her life. It's exhausting." She threw her napkin down on the table and took an enormous gulp of wine. That was when I realized she was well on her way to being drunk.

My stomach tightened and I tucked my head down between my shoulders as I shrank. One thing I had been trying to overcome was feeling like a burden by allowing myself to have needs, ask for help, and take up space. But it took one shitty comment from Ang to send me back to cowering in the corner. I knew I shouldn't let one person's opinion cut so deep, but it did. I had loved her. We had a deep and entwined history that kept me tethered to her somehow.

People were talking and I forced myself to refocus on the conversation. Kate was speaking. "...because that's what friends do. We support each other. Someday it could be me who needs help and I know without a doubt that Vivian would be there for me. I'm beginning to wonder if you would do the same."

"Oh, hey now, Kate. That's harsh. You know I'd help out." Ang took another swig of wine and Kate slid the glass away as soon as Ang put it down.

Ang's face reddened. "Give. That. Back." Kate didn't say anything but didn't return the glass. Audre cleared her throat.

"I think I'm going to take Vivian home. Thank you for the lovely dinner."

"Ohhh, yes. Of course. Go ahead and take delicate Vivian home and tuck her into bed with some warm milk and a lullaby. Pfft. This is exactly what I'm talking about. Everybody takes care of damaged Vivian."

"Angela Sorenson. You don't know the first thing about Vivian because you never could get your head out of your own ass long enough to truly get to know her when you had the chance."

Audre stood, still holding my hand. "Come on, Viv, let's go. Thank you, Kate, for a lovely time. You're welcome to come down the hall if you tire of Ang's bullshit tonight."

I stood, careful not to knock over her table like I had the last time I had argued with Ang, and spoke up.

"There is something to be said about the honesty that slips out of someone when they are drunk. It has taken my whole circle to prop me up over the years. And why? What have I done to reciprocate or deserve it? You all have no reason to stand by me. Don't take this as me playing the victim. Actually, don't answer those questions. Thank you, Kate." Kate stopped scowling at Ang long enough to give me a small smile.

All the way down the corridor I heard echoes of the argument that was unraveling inside Ang's apartment.

Once safely back in my studio I turned to Audre.

"God, what an asshole. I don't know why I am still involved with her. She has harmed me countless times, maybe this one was the final straw. Death by a thousand cuts and all that. It's so weird, though, because our first connection was her offering me help when I was having an anxiety attack in the parking garage. She cared once upon a time. But damn, that was some serious resentment boiling over, yeah?"

"Yes, I think that about sums it up," Audre said as she put water on to boil and pulled out two mugs for tea.

"But is she right? I don't expect you to answer, but she really has given me some stuff to think about. There—" I was interrupted by a knock on the door. Looking through the peep hole, I saw Kate, and opened the door immediately.

"Come on in, Kate," I said as I saw the tears running down her cheeks. "Audre, please add a third cup of tea."

I wrapped my arms around Kate, and she sobbed into my chest, her arms tight around my waist. We stood like that, in my narrow front hallway, until her sobs settled, and she released me.

"Come on in." I led her in by the hand and had her sit on the futon. She slid her feet out of her work clogs and crossed her legs. A blanket hung over the back of the couch and she covered her lap with it. I brought her a box of tissue and helped Audre with the mugs of tea, handing one to Kate as we sat on the couch next to her.

"Do you want to talk about it?" Audre asked gently, reaching across my lap to touch Kate's forearm briefly.

Kate blew her nose and took a sip of tea, nodding. "I broke up with Ang."

Audre and I both looked at her in shock. Kate and Ang had been in a solid relationship for quite some time.

"It's been coming for a while. Her drinking has been really bad since she got out of jail and got reinstated back at the sheriff's department. And she just never has been the same since being locked up. I have been very supportive and patient with her as she transitioned to being back at work and out of jail, but...this mean side of her. She never had it before. Granted, she's always been selfish, but never mean-spirited. But now...I just can't tolerate it anymore. What she said tonight was totally uncalled for. If she wants to push all her loved ones away, that's her business. I won't be a part of it anymore."

I put an arm around Kate, and she rested her head on my shoulder for a bit. Once we had all finished our tea, Kate sat up and looked around.

"Hey, wasn't this supposed to be dinner and game night? Come on, let's play a game."

"All I have is Skip-Bo." I motioned toward my sparsely appointed studio.

"Great! Let's play. Audre, you in?"

"Yep, let's do it."

I grabbed the deck of Skip-Bo cards, sat on the floor across the coffee table from them, and shuffled the cards while they chatted. Kate seemed to enjoy the distraction of conversation and cards and soon we were laughing as we played and shared stories. After a few rounds of cards, Kate's cell phone rang. It was the hospital. She was called back in to work. Despite it being her night off, she had to go in. She slipped on her clogs, gave us both big hugs and many thanks for the fun evening, and let herself out.

As Audre was cleaning up the cards, I slid up behind her and wrapped my arms around her waist. She leaned back into me and I kissed the base of her neck, whispering to her. "Thank you."

She nodded and I released her. We were carrying the mugs into the kitchen when I heard shouting on the street outside. They were voices I knew. Kate and Ang.

"Oh shit," I growled as I grabbed my cell phone and ran out of the door. I could hear that the voices were coming from Twenty-Fourth Street, so I hustled out of the side door and through the gate, skidding out onto the sidewalk. I booked it across the dark street toward the brightly lit light-rail station, following the voices. I reached for the stun gun on my waistband, but it wasn't there. As a sheriff's deputy Ang was always armed, even when off duty, usually with a small pistol in an ankle holster.

I slowed to a fast walk so I wouldn't startle Ang. Kate stood near the platform under the bright streetlight, waiting to catch a light-rail train to work. She held her bag closely with one hand and was holding the other one up toward Ang in a gesture I took to mean for Ang to back up.

Ang, at six feet three inches, towered over Kate and was leaning over her, shouting and pointing in her face. Kate was so petite that, despite her being exceptionally fit, she looked like a child cowering under Ang's massive form. No one else waited to catch a train at that late hour.

"...how dare you defend Viv! You know I'm right." She stumbled back a half step, swaying as she steadied herself. "I mean, come on! What about me? You're always running to her aid, making her soup, and bringing her tea. Pfft."

Kate continued to hold her hand up between them, as a barrier and a clear sign to Ang.

"Look. I do those things because I like Vivian. She is a good person, and she clearly has so little support in her life. And aside from that, I do those things because, in my world, that's what a good metamour does." She paused, taking a breath, and looked up the track briefly to see if the train was coming. "Ang. Look. Please just go upstairs and get some rest. We can talk more about this once you have had a chance to sober up."

Kate's eyes flicked in my direction and she spotted me waiting in the shadows. I was staying back because I didn't want to insert myself unless it became an emergency. This was technically a conversation between the two of them, and, while I was the topic, they were hashing out their personal business. I scanned Ang and saw the usual bulge of an ankle holster under her slacks. I looked to her hands and was relieved to see they were empty and there weren't any bulges around her waistband.

"Sober up? I'm fucking fine. You just don't like what I have to say cuz you know I'm right!"

The front porch light turned on at the house closest to the light-rail station. Someone cracked the front door open and hollered, "Shut up! Get outta here with your nonsense." The door immediately snapped shut. Ang turned sharply on her heel, ready to take that person on, but they were gone.

Kate took a step back, closer to the platform, as Ang turned to face her again. I could hear the faint sound of the light-rail alarm from the next station down the line, which was a few blocks away. Kate looked down the line nervously.

"Listen, Ang. I need to get to work. I've been called in."

"Oh! Nice! That's mighty convenient. You're off tonight, Kate."

"Yeah. But they are short-staffed, and I got called in. Jesus, Ang, how long were we together? You know I get called in all the time."

Ang roared. "Were? Just like that, huh? You're already talking about us in past tense? Wow! You are unbelievable, Kate." She wiped roughly at some tears. Her hands clenched into fists and I took a step toward them. Kate put her hand up between them again and Ang stepped up so Kate's hand was pressing into her abdomen. Kate took another step back.

I stepped forward, out of the darkness and into the light of the platform. Ang had her back to me and didn't know I was there. I was within ten paces of them because I didn't like the way Ang was escalating. She ran her hand over the back of her neck, still shouting about Kate using past tense. The train rattled and its headlight appeared as it got closer. I also caught the faint trill of a police siren a few blocks away.

Ang roared and swatted Kate's hand down.

Kate responded as I imagined she did with irate patients and families at the hospital. Her voice and face were calm and even. Rock steady. "Ang. Please. Enough. Please go upstairs and get some rest. I am getting on this train and going to work. We can talk tomorrow."

The train approached the street level platform, bell clanging and wheels clattering on the rails. Ang glanced at the train and lunged at Kate. I bolted toward them, sidestepping so I'd come at them from the side, closing the gap quickly. Audre screamed, police sirens wailed, and the train horn honked frantically as a burst of light exploded and my feet left the ground.

Chapter Eighteen

My body was incredibly cold to the point that my teeth clicked together from shivering. There was the sound of stern voices and sobbing. A bright light overhead blinded me. I was confused and dizzy, and pain bloomed all over my body.

I tried desperately to recall where I was and what had happened. I tried to sit up but a firm hand on my shoulder pushed me back down.

"Miss. Please stay still."

The bright light overhead was like daggers in my brain, so I tried to turn my head, but my neck wouldn't budge. I blinked rapidly and then closed my eyes against the light, drawing in a deep breath and forcing myself to focus. I checked in internally, scanning myself from head to toe for injury, making my way down until it was time to wiggle my fingers and toes. They complied and I sighed with relief. Aside from being concussed, I didn't detect any major injuries.

I opened my eyes.

"I'm fine," I blurted out to whoever was nearby. Someone leaned over me, blotting out the light. He wore a paramedic uniform. "Ma'am, please lay still. We will be transporting you to the hospital shortly, but there are others with more serious injuries we need to attend to first."

"No. Listen, sir. I'm fine." My tongue was too big for my mouth, and the words blended together. I reached up and discovered I couldn't move my neck because they had slapped a cervical collar on me.

"Off? Please? I'm fine."

He gently, but firmly, pushed my hand away from where I had been trying to unlatch the collar.

"Cervical collar is protocol for loss of consciousness and head injury."

I tried to sit up again and he placed a hand on my shoulder, keeping me down. I grew angry and was trying to gather my scrambled brain enough to figure out how to talk myself out of the situation when I caught a familiar scent on the breeze and Audre was at my side, leaning over me.

"Viv. Oh, thank goodness." She wiped tears from her cheek, her highly varnished dark-gray fingernails flashing in the light.

"What? What's ha-appening?"

She ran her hand up and down my arm, gently, comforting, and then took my hand in hers.

"There was an...accident. With the light-rail train."

Confused, brain foggy, I tried to sit up again. She patted my chest lovingly, insisting that I lay back down. The concrete underneath me was cold and my tooth-rattling shivers doubled. I reached up and pulled at the cervical collar again. She placed her warm hand over mine and took my hand away from my neck.

"Please do as the paramedic says. They are going to need to take you in and scan your head. You...bumped it hard."

I blinked away the hot tears of frustration that had formed. They spilled over and ran down into my ears. Frustrated because I was confused and because I couldn't get up and help.

I wanted to ask how Ang and Kate were doing, and what had happened, but forming that many words was too hard.

"Ang? Kate?"

Audre started to speak but was interrupted by people shuffling me on to a backboard, loading me onto a gurney, and strapping me down under a wonderfully warm blanket that smelled of bleach. They raised the gurney up to full height with a sickening quickness, like an elevator that goes up much too fast. I groaned. Dizzy. Spinning. The bright overhead light went away, and I saw the starry night sky. There was some shuffling around as people loaded up and doors shut. The inside of the ambulance was dimmed and quiet and warm. Audre's hand found mine under the blanket. We rode in silence to the hospital, no lights or sirens, which I considered a good sign. Neck still immobilized, I couldn't turn to look at Audre or the paramedic who was sitting in the jump seat near my head scribbling notes on a clipboard.

I highly disliked hospitals and the shivers came back despite the warm blanket. Soon enough, chill wind gusted in as the back doors opened up. There a lot of bumping around and conversation over me as the gurney was rolled into the emergency room. Audre was gone, no doubt being hustled off to the waiting room.

It was so bright that I closed my eyes tightly against it. Rattle. More talking across the gurney. Then I was moved from one gurney to another, which made everything spin so badly I thought I might puke. And finally, everything stopped except for the bright light.

I opened my eyes tentatively to see what was happening, still frustrated that I could not turn my head. I was on a gurney, pushed against a wall, parked in a hallway. I couldn't see if anyone else was around, but given the silence, I figured I was alone. Frowning, I stared at the corner where the wall and ceiling met, and then closed my eyes against the lights. The wall was the typical institutional beige white. I shivered some more under the blanket. I started to sit up but realized that I was strapped down across my chest, waist, and legs. I knew my brain was mixed up, but I had had enough. I mustered up some energy and cleared my throat.

"Hello?" I waited, listening. The was no response. I drew in a breath and said it louder. "Hello?" Listened. Nothing. I grew angry. "Hello! I need help! Hello!"

I heard shoes squeak on linoleum.

Somebody in scrubs stood at the foot of the gurney so I could see her.

"Yes?"

"I...uh. What's happen...?" Getting the words out was frighteningly difficult.

"You are in the emergency room. You've been in an accident. We are waiting for your turn to get your head scanned, but there are other more urgent folks ahead of you."

"Uh. 'Kay. Lay here? Wait?"

"Yes."

"Cold."

"I'll get you another blanket." She left and came back quickly with another one of those white hospital blankets. As she tucked it over my body it emanated so much wonderful warmth. The only thing I liked about hospitals was the heated blankets. I immediately stopped shivering and my eyes grew heavy. I started to drift under, and she touched my shoulder.

"Miss...Chastain, is it? You need to do your best not to fall asleep. You are concussed, at the very least, and until we know what the damage is, you need to stay awake."

I opened my eyes and looked at her. She nodded at me and then walked away, her voice drifting to me over her shoulder. "Just hang tight. We will get to you when we can."

Hmph. I couldn't go anywhere even if I wanted to. Strapped down and head and neck locked inside a damn cage. Sleep tried so hard to pull me under that despite the pain of the bright overhead lights, I forced my eyes to stay open. I stared into the fluorescent strip and ran through drills in my head to keep myself awake. I recited the Soldier's Creed in my head over and over again because it was the only thing that came to mind.

I am an American Soldier

I am a warrior and a member of a team.

I serve the people of the United States, and live the army values.

I will always place the mission first.

I will never accept defeat.

I will never quit.

I will never leave a fallen comrade.

I am disciplined, physically and mentally tough, trained and proficient in my warrior tasks and drills.

I always maintain my arms, my equipment and myself.

I am an expert and I am a professional.

I stand ready to deploy, engage, and destroy, the enemies of the United States of America in close combat.

I am a guardian of freedom and the American way of life.

I am an American soldier.

After a while, my brain tired of the exercise. I was curious how the creed was so ingrained in me, even after having been out of the army for six years. I wondered how Audre was doing and about Kate and Ang. Were they okay? Had I been forgotten, tucked away in a vacant hallway, away from the bustle of the ER?

Eventually a technician of some sort came and checked my wristband. *When did they put a wristband on me?* He asked me to state my name. I had a hard time getting it all out; my brain and mouth still seemed to be experiencing some sort of disconnect. He nodded and rolled me through a maze of hallways and eventually through double doors into his domain. I was placed on a narrow table and slid inside a machine. In less than a minute it was all over, and I was slid back onto the gurney, strapped back down with the blankets, and dumped back in the hallway. Nobody had said much to me. I was just another body to be dealt with.

In an effort to stay awake I ran through the Soldier's Creed some more. Eventually someone, a nurse maybe, came by and, after checking my wristband, removed the cervical collar, unbuckled me, and slowly raised the back of the gurney until I was sitting up. The world swayed and wobbled and spun. I clenched my teeth until it steadied. She gave me some ice water and told me the doctor would be by to talk to me.

More Soldier's Creed as I tried to clear my head and focus. I started reciting it slowly out loud, forcing my tongue and lips to say the words. One word at a time. I sipped on the wonderfully cool water while bundled up in the blankets. My head hurt and my body had started to ache. But I did my best to ignore it. The doctor did surface, checking my wristband and shining a pen light in my eyes without even introducing himself. I looked at the badge hanging from his scrubs and then at his haggard face. He was dead on his feet. I wondered how many hours he had worked.

"Miss Chastain. You are very, very lucky. You have a concussion and some bumps and bruises, but it looks like you are going to be okay. You will need to rest for a few days. It will get worse before it gets better. Due to the concussion, I want you to take a baby aspirin daily for the next month. Do you need a note to excuse you from work?"

"Uh, no. Thank you."

"Okay, head on down to the discharge counter to make payment and get your paperwork." He looked at me in such a way that I knew I had somehow dodged a terrible outcome and had gotten off lucky.

"Thank you, Doctor," I said, and he nodded before walking away, his sneakers squeaking on the linoleum.

I wandered around until I found someone who could show me where the discharge window was. I followed a yellow painted line on the floor through a maze of corridors. The yellow line dead-ended at the discharge area, which had no lobby and no chairs. It was just a window cut into the wall, and a blue line painted on the floor indicating where I should wait. An adult and child waited in front of me, the kid's arm in a fresh cast, the adult muttering *I told you not to do it* as the child whined from exhaustion. It was very late. In front of them was an elderly woman who sat on her walker seat speaking to the clerk at the window.

I swayed and stared at the wall, waiting for my turn. The sound of heels on linoleum echoed down the hallway, and I looked up to see Audre approaching. I swooned with gratitude and smiled. She put her arm around my waist, steadying me. She kissed my scarred temple and the scar on my cheekbone and spoke into my ear quietly about how much she loved me. I leaned my head on her shoulder and we shuffled together as the line moved forward. I wondered why they did not have chairs there. People were being discharged from the emergency room and would be in various states of health. Not having chairs seemed like a liability waiting to happen.

The discharge process was unpleasant because I did not have health insurance, which caused the clerk to produce a massive eye roll and another stack of forms. In the end I signed my life away and they said they would mail me the bill. Audre shuffled me outside and we caught a cab back to my place. She used her own key to let us in and shepherded me inside.

As I lowered myself slowly onto the couch, careful not to give myself more vertigo, I recognized that somehow, we had developed a pattern of me having a health issue and Audre helping me. I didn't like it because she had never needed me for anything, yet I seemed to always need her, and others, to help me. Perhaps Ang had been right.

I heard Audre in the kitchen making tea in the dark.

"Doesn't it get old?" I croaked through cracked lips and with a tongue that still didn't quite feel right.

"Hmm?" she asked as she came in with two mugs of steaming tea and sat next to me. She placed a small aspirin in my hand.

I cleared my throat, trying again. "Doesn't it get old?" I paused, collecting myself to speak more. "I mean, maybe Ang was right. Her delivery was terrible, but the message did hold some truth."

I stopped and listened to the fish tank burble for a moment. "A vacuum of need. Damaged. That's what she called me. It must be exhausting to have a partner like me. I am not looking for pity. Just stating facts."

Audre leaned back on the couch, blowing on her tea, and looked at me over the mug rim. The light-rail gate bell clanged, and I decided that if the train was up and running again nobody had died. I wasn't ready to ask yet though.

Audre lowered her mug and tucked her legs up under her. "Vivian, I recognize that you are injured and tired, so I'm going to let this lapse go. But I want you to really listen right now."

I sat up a bit and looked her straight in the eye.

"I wake up every day and consciously choose to have you in my life. The lens I see you through, my experiences with you, are not the same as Ang's. What she said was her own opinion. Not mine. I love you and stand by you because you are fierce, confident, capable, kind, and you take no shit. When you need help, I choose to give it freely. If you think back, all of the times that I've been here to help you recover...you never once asked for that help. I gave it freely because I saw the need and I *wanted* to help you. And I know Kate would say the same for the times she has stepped up. And, as Kate said earlier, I know without a doubt that if I needed you, you'd be there. I bet Jared and Bear would say the same. It just so happens that the last couple of years have been rough for you, and it's your turn to receive. When it's your turn to choose to give, I know you will."

She placed her hand on my leg and I absorbed what she had said. All the shadows of doubt that had been planted by Ang were chased away.

"Now take your aspirin so you don't have an aneurism, please."

I swallowed the aspirin with some tea, and through the window saw the faintest hint of dawn touch the sky.

"Jesus. That was a long night." I rubbed at my eyes and swum around in a dizzy spell for a moment. Sleep was trying so hard to take me down. "I would like to know what happened...how everybody is."

"And I will tell you, after you've gotten some rest."

"I thought I wasn't supposed to sleep. Head injury and all that." I fluttered my hand in the direction of my head.

"They said you can sleep now that you've taken an aspirin and the CT scan didn't show anything scary. So, sleep. I need to get home, but I will be back later with breakfast. Okay?" She stood and took the mug from my hand before covering me with a blanket. I slouched down into the couch.

"Okay," I mumbled as sleep grabbed me hard.

*

I woke to sun streaming in around the corners of the blinds. My head throbbed and spun. I sat up very slowly, trying to avoid more vertigo. I turned my head and looked at the fish tank.

"Ya'll, this has got to be my worst concussion ever." The fish flitted about, oblivious. *Hmph.*

I walked carefully to the bathroom, went pee, and started up the shower. Stripping down, I saw various new scrapes and bruises, some heading toward dark purple and black, scattered around my body. They were in stark contrast to my patchwork of old scars, which were mostly pink. I got into the shower daintily. The hot water hitting my skin was perfect. I washed my hair and body gently, careful not to press on any of the wounds. I discovered that I had hit my head on the back, just over the occipital protuberance, which was exceptionally tender and had a slight lump.

I dried off and got dressed in some insulated hiking pants that were super comfortable, plus a thermal top and thick socks. I turned on the wall heater, fed the fish, and looked out of the window at the light-rail station. One lone light-rail cop carried a clipboard and used a measuring wheel along the walkway where we had, I think, collided with the train. I noticed chalk marks and a large dark stain on the concrete.

I leaned against the windowsill on shaky legs and watched as a fire truck pulled up and hosed down the stain once the investigator had finished doing his thing. *Whose blood?*

There was a knock at the door and then the sound of a key in the lock. Audre let herself in. She gave me a big smile and we met in the little kitchen to serve up breakfast, which turned out to be a mountain of an omelet, bacon, hash browns, and fruit. It was packaged in plastic food containers, not takeout boxes from a restaurant, and was all still warm, the omelet steaming.

"This looks amazing. Who cooked us breakfast?"

"My Aunty Dot. She heard me come in late, so we chatted about what had happened, and when I woke up, she was cooking up a storm for us. She really likes you. A lot."

We sat and ate. Despite the nausea from the vertigo, I was hungrier than I thought, and had to force myself to slow down. Once we had finished, I sat back and looked at her. She was in work clothes: a tight gray pinstriped pencil skirt, flowy burgundy blouse, heels, and matching silver necklace and bracelets. Her makeup was flawless, she smelled amazing, and her hair was styled in finger curls.

"You look fantastic. Did you sleep at all?"

"I did. A little. I took the morning off to sleep and have breakfast with you. I'll head in to the office when we are finished."

"Thank you. I appreciate you."

"I am happy to do it. I *want* to be here. I wouldn't want to be anywhere else right now."

I smiled and braced myself. "Okay, you told your Aunt Dot what happened. Can you please tell me now? I don't remember anything after lunging toward Kate and Ang...and the train coming."

Audre drew in a breath and glanced down at her plate for a moment. Then she looked back at me, clasped her hands together, and spoke.

"When you ran off, I waited for a few minutes but then realized things were going bad when I could hear Ang's shouting on the street get louder. I called 9-1-1 and then came down. I didn't know about the side door, so I walked out the lobby door on *Q* Street and then came up behind you on Twenty-Fourth. Things were clearly in motion by the time I arrived because I saw you stepping closer to them and pausing. And then, it just...happened. The train was about to pull into the station when Ang grabbed Kate, and you jumped into action, running at them from the side. It looked to me like Ang was trying to bundle up Kate and step in front of the train. Like... a murder suicide. You spread your arms wide and scooped them both, hitting them like a linebacker, but Ang's momentum was also still going so you all three bounced off the side of the nose of the train. I mean...it would have been splat on the front of the train if you hadn't hit them from the angle you did."

She paused, shuddering. "The police literally pulled up as it was happening, so they got the paramedics there quickly. Several people on the train were injured because the driver had slammed on the emergency brake. Kate and Ang...they are both alive. Their injuries are...significant, and they both have long recoveries ahead, but from what I heard at the hospital last night, they will survive."

She stopped there and I took her hand, absorbing the news, relieved that they weren't dead, but also despairing for their injuries and how those injuries happened.

"This is going to go deeper than them recovering from their injuries, yeah? I mean, Ang is a sheriff's deputy and she, I think, tried to jump in front of a train with Kate in her arms."

"Yes. And the police officer who showed up saw the whole thing. So, thankfully, the onus of the whole witness situation isn't wholly mine to bear. I heard them talking while the paramedics were working, and it sounds like once Ang is stabilized, she will probably be arrested and charged. But...that's up to the district attorney, I think. Either way it's not looking good."

"This is all so...fucked up. She has never been the same since she went to jail. Spending months in Ad Seg, by herself, couldn't have helped. Something happened to her in there that changed her at the core. And all because of false accusations and charges that were dropped later. So unfair. The system she has spent her career upholding truly failed her. This isn't the Ang I used to know. This isn't the Ang that Kate and I originally fell in love with."

We both sat with our thoughts for a bit and then cleared the table and washed the dishes.

"Okay, Viv, I need to get to the office. Please just rest today. Doctor's orders, and mine too."

"I am so glad we had this time together this morning. Please tell Aunt Dot that I say thank you for the breakfast. It hit the spot. And I'll be sure to tell her at Sunday lunch too."

We hugged and I saw her to the door, her heels clicking down the corridor as she left. I did as I was told, spending most of the day on the couch because every movement brought on vertigo and throbbing in my head. I was grateful that my brain was clear enough to able to read, so I lost myself in *Cloud Atlas*.

Chapter Nineteen

The following day I felt well enough to make some phone calls. I started by calling Jared during his lunch break. He answered on the second ring.

"Viv! Hey! How are you?"

"Hey, bud. Is it okay if I bug you during your lunch break?

"You know the answer to that. As long as you don't mind the sound of me eating my sandwich while we talk. It's too cold lately to sit on my favorite bench by the water so I'm in my car...by the water. Heh."

"No worries. You chewing in my ear is the least offensive thing you have done around me." We chuckled at that.

"Are you intentionally dodging my question about how you are?"

"Nah. Things have been crazy. Ang got hammered and did something really out of character. Something very bad. Lots of people got hurt. She and Kate are in the hospital, and Ang will likely be arrested when she stabilizes. And during that I got the worst concussion I've ever had. So...I'd say it's not been a great week so far."

"Jesus. How can I help?"

"Tell me about you. Distract me."

"Uh. Well. You remember the guy living in the studio under my house?

"Yeah. Nuclear engineer out at the power plant, right? Kind of a creeper."

"Yep. Well. He mostly kept to himself, but things got weird. The water heater in his unit blew and was flooding his place so I had to go in there. He had Nazi flags and pictures of Hitler on his walls. The place looked like an Aryan German home in the 1940s. I couldn't look at it much while I was stopping the flood. But once I got the water turned off and had shop-vacced it up he started talking to me. We hadn't really ever spoken aside from generic greetings as we passed in the driveway. He started asking about my family origin and going on and on about how as a second generation Mexican-American I am impure, a pestilence. He pulled out neo-Nazi books and pamphlets to show me. Like...he was trying to convince me, to get me to agree that as a person of color I should be wiped out. He told me not to breed with a white woman. It was...bizarre. I did my best to remain neutral and calm until I could finish cleaning up and get the hell out of there. As soon as I left, I called the property management company who handles the rental unit downstairs and told them to boot him. He was on a month-to-month lease, so it isn't as hard as when I used to do yearlong leases." I heard him take a sip of his drink.

"Now it's my turn to say Jesus. Jesus, dude, wow. How did you not punch his teeth down his throat?"

"It was hard. But I knew that he wasn't worth going to prison for. He moved out and now I'm trying to rent the unit out again. I told the property manager to do a better job of vetting tenants this time. I may just fire them and start doing it myself again. Hey, wanna move back? The downstairs is all yours if you want to rent it."

I took a moment to consider his offer. A couple of years earlier he had asked me to move back into the upstairs with him, as a couple. I had rejected him and had to out myself as gay. That conversation had crushed him, and it had taken a long time to fix our friendship afterward.

"Um. I…"

"Oh. Hey. No, I don't mean it like last time. I worked through that and just am offering it to you as a friend. We had so much fun when we used to live together, so of course I want you to come back if you want."

"Thanks. It's a great offer. Despite that crazy stuff going on I actually am doing well up here. I have an amazing girlfriend who I don't want to leave behind. And I am starting EMT school next month. So…things are coming together. I'm…happy."

There. I had said it. I was happy. And for once, I meant it.

"Oh, Viv…that's great. I am happy for you!" The warmth in his voice damn near made me cry.

We bantered back and forth, catching up while he ate until it was time for him to go back to work. After we hung up, I dialed Bear's number.

"*Bueno bueno.*"

"Bear! It's Viv."

"Heyyyy, Viviiiiiiiiana. How are you, nice lady?"

We both laughed so hard. Bear always gave me amazing phone greetings. Once the laughter died down, we talked for a while. Bear had spent most of her adult life in therapy and fancied herself a bit of a therapist too. She was really interested in why I cut the road trip short, so we dissected that for a bit. Then she went on to update me on things in her life.

"I'm getting stir crazy down here. You know how I can get. Every time I come out of hibernation I gotta get a change of scenery."

"Yeah, that sounds about right. Oh, hey! I talked to Jared earlier and his downstairs unit is vacant. He's looking to rent it out. Month to month. And it's furnished. I bet he'd totally rent it to you."

"Huh. That's actually a great idea. I was thinking about closing up my house for the winter and venturing out. Making some art. Morro Bay would be a great place for that. I'll give him a call."

We said our goodbyes and I spent some time watching my fish before eating a late lunch, showering, and getting my head ready to go out into the world after a few days of laying low. My head still swum, but not as badly. I decided driving was a bad idea and pulled out the map of bus routes I kept tucked away with the phone book. I figured out the route and walked down to the bus stop, bundled up in a fleece jacket, gloves, beanie and scarf. It was exceptionally cold for Sacramento. Water sat frozen in the gutter even in the middle of the day. I rode the bus, hands tucked into my pockets and chin lowered into the scarf. I made a quick transfer and then got off at the hospital, which was a massive campus with buildings of concrete and glass. The main one had a helipad on the roof. I made my way to the main hospital building to check in.

"I am here to visit Katherine Castelucci." It was weird to say her full name, because to me she was simply Kate. The clerk tapped away at a keyboard and nodded. They wrote down a room number on a visitor badge before passing it to me. I stuck it to my jacket and got on an elevator that smelled like stale coffee. Once I got to her floor, I walked down a long corridor, similar to the one I had been parked in at the ER downstairs. I followed the signs to her room, passing by a nurse's station. Nobody looked up at me as they worked diligently on their charts. I found her door slightly ajar. There was a hand sanitizer container on the wall and a sign declaring that all visitors must use it. I peeled off my gloves, shoved them in my jacket pockets, and rubbed the liquid into my skin. Taking a deep breath, the smell of sanitizer strong, I knocked gently and entered. The curtain around the door was closed.

I stood between the door and curtain, not knowing what was on the other side.

"Kate?" I asked hesitantly.

"Come in." Her voice was so faint I almost missed it. I parted the curtain and found Kate in the bed closest to the door, another curtain drawn between her bed and the one by the window.

"Viv," she said, just a whisper, a tiny smile touching the corners of her mouth.

I entered the room and pulled a chair up to her bedside. Kate looked shrunken, like a small child tucked under the covers. She was a racing cyclist and had always had incredibly low body fat, her deeply tanned skin tight over her bones, veins popping at her temples, arms, hands, and feet. She had always exuded a glow of health. But as I sat looking at her, I noted that her skin had a sickly gray tinge, and her cheeks were sunken. The whites of her eyes were red with blood from broken vessels. I vaguely remembered it was called subconjunctival hemorrhage. It was eerie to see her brown eyes surrounded by bright red.

"Hey, Kate," I said, pushing out as much love and warmth as I had in me. It was my turn to sit at her bedside. She had been right that one day I would return the favor, and there we were.

A small plastic pitcher stood on the bedside tray. It was sweating and had a straw poking out the top.

"Water?" I asked and she gave a nod. I picked up the pitcher and placed the straw to her lips. She took a few tiny sips and then turned her face away from the straw.

"How are you doing, Viv?"

I grinned, recognizing that it was totally a Kate thing to ask about me when clearly it should have been the other way around.

"I'm...doing a bit better." I realized I had no idea what her condition was, and she probably didn't know anything about mine. After the train had hit us...or rather after we had hit the train, we had been cared for separately, transported separately, and had no contact. "I think I got off pretty lucky. Lot of deep contusions and a massive concussion." I reached up and touched the bump on the back of my head gingerly. "But I know nothing about what happened to you or Ang."

"Oh. You didn't go see her first?"

"Of course not. Not after what she did."

"What did she do? I don't remember anything other than us arguing on the train platform, and then waking up here. The police came to talk to me, but I don't remember anything, so they left. And the nurses clearly know but won't tell me."

I closed my eyes, not wanting to be the one to have to tell her. I looked into her deep-brown eyes and exhaled. "It's not good. Are you sure you want to know right now? Maybe let's wait until you are feeling a bit stronger."

"No. Tell me now. Don't placate me, Viv."

"Uh, so what I saw, and what Audre confirmed, is that as the light-rail train was pulling into the station Ang was angry and shouting. She bundled you up in her arms and stepped in front of the train. I came at you guys from the side to hopefully cut you off, but we ended up hitting the nose of the train and...I was knocked out for a while, so I don't know anything about what happened to you after that."

"Oh," she said quietly, her eyes immediately welling up. She looked to the ceiling as tears silently streamed down her cheeks. I pulled a rough, single-ply tissue from the box on the bedside tray and dabbed gently at her tears. Her lips worked as she tried to hold in a sob. I placed my hand gently on top of the blanket where her shoulder was. The blanket was pulled up to her chin, which left me not knowing how to comfort her.

I waited as she worked through the news, listening to the constant noise in the hallway, periodically wiping her tears and patting her shoulder. Eventually, she turned her bloody, sad eyes back to me.

"I am glad you were the one to tell me. And I am glad you were there. Otherwise, it sounds like I'd probably be dead instead of maimed."

"Maimed?" I paused. "Sorry. I don't know anything about the extent of your injuries. But given that you are in the ICU tells me it's serious."

She nodded, shedding more tears. She angled her chin toward the foot of the bed.

"They couldn't save my leg. It's gone." She paused, sniffing back some tears, her face shifting from sorrow to anger. "I am a nurse, for heck's sake. I am on my feet all day. I'm a competitive cyclist. My feet and legs are my life. This is...going to be a rough adjustment."

I had been so focused on her top half I hadn't looked at the rest of her, tucked away under the blanket. I slid my gaze down and saw that the blanket fell flat at the knee of her right leg. I sighed and rested my head in my hands and then took off my beanie and ran my hand through my hair, trying so hard to hold in... What...? There it was. Rage. If Ang had been in the same room, I would have gone for her throat without hesitation. But I knew I needed to contain it in that moment, for Kate.

"Goddammit. I had no idea. I'm so sorry." I wondered if I had acted a split-second sooner or hit them from a different angle if it would have made a difference in her losing her leg or not. My jaw clenched so hard my teeth ground loudly.

"I'm just about stable. I lost a lot of blood, and they were worried about infection. But after multiple surgeries, a few blood transfusions, and some antibiotics things are looking better. They've got me starting physical therapy and occupational therapy tomorrow."

"Wow, isn't it awfully soon for that?"

"Actually, it's pretty standard to start right away. They were able to close the incision and of course I will have drains for a while, but the sooner I get physical therapy going the better."

"Do you think you'll use a prosthetic?" I was worried that it may be too sore of a subject to ask about already, but I was genuinely curious. I had seen people lose limbs when I was deployed, but this was a wholly different situation.

"Oh yeah. For sure. I don't plan on giving up my job or cycling, so I'll need a prosthetic or two to make that stuff happen. I have an appointment for discussion about prosthetics in about two weeks. Of course, it'll take probably six to eight weeks for my wound to heal, but I'm ready to move forward."

I smiled at my friend. I had always known she was tough, but her resilience in the face of such a massive life change was commendable.

"When do you get out of here?"

"A couple of days before Christmas, barring any complications. I am trying for sooner, but it'll take some doing. I keep telling them that I am a damn nurse; I can change my own dressings, clean the wound, and empty out the drains. I think I need to prove myself with the physical therapy and that will hopefully seal the deal. They seem worried about whether or not my house is accessible enough."

"Well, you do have that flight of stairs up to your front door. But it's all one level once you get up there, right?"

"Yes. So, I will wow them with my agility with the crutches tomorrow and hopefully get discharged early."

Some color was returning to her cheeks, which I took as a positive sign.

"Do you want to sit up? Hungry?"

"Hmm. Yes to both. Funny, when you got here, I was in a bad place, but talking to you has perked me up."

I pushed the button to raise up the head of her bed and then I popped down to the cafeteria and got her some fruit, a muffin, and hot tea. She was thrilled with my offering and sipped her tea with joy as she nibbled on the food. After she finished, I pulled a Skip-Bo deck out of my pocket and cleared the bedside tray. We played several rounds, and she soundly beat my ass. During the final round, she started to fade, and her hands shook.

"I think I need to take a break." She pressed the button, lowering the bed down.

"Of course." I packed up the Skip-Bo cards and gathered the layers of warm clothing I had shed. "Hey, if they are worried about you being on your own after discharge, I am happy to come stay at your place with you for a bit to help out."

"Thank you, Viv, that would be amazing and will probably help my case."

"You want me to come back tomorrow?"

"Yes, please. You've been my only visitor and it really helped. You're the best." Her voice faded as she closed her eyes.

I stooped down and pressed my cheek to hers before heading out. I considered visiting Ang's room, but decided not to. I bundled back up before I rode the bus home, feeling good inside about having a role to play in helping my dear friend.

I checked my phone and saw texts from both Jared and Bear telling me that Bear would rent out Jared's downstairs unit for the winter. Jared also asked if I would consider coming down for New Year's Eve. I said I would and asked if I could bring Kate with me. Jared responded that he would love to have us both, and tactfully didn't ask about Ang.

*

The following weeks consisted of visiting Kate daily until the hospital agreed to release her, then staying with her at her home while she recovered. She had mastered the use of her crutches and relied on her sheer strength, stamina, and athleticism to stay out of the wheelchair as much as she could. I had plenty of talks with her about how using a mobility aid, be it crutches or a wheelchair, was nothing to be ashamed of. She assured me that it wasn't an issue of feeling ashamed, rather she was so used to being on her feet for work and she had every plan of returning to work, so she wanted to stay upright. We bickered a bit about that.

"Kate, you literally lost a leg to a train. You're allowed to sit down and recover."

Her response was to huff at me and crutch over to the sink and start washing dishes. And so it went. The two of us in her home going about the daily tasks of cleaning her wound site, changing the dressings, preparing meals, and me driving her around to appointments with prosthetic specialists, physical therapists, occupational therapists, chiropractor, and a masseur.

I had never seen anyone so hell bent on staying active and recovering as fully and quickly as possible. She sought a return to normal, while also adapting to her new body, with a fervor that was both worrisome and awe-inspiring.

She had occasional visits from her friends and coworkers, though no family came. She was an out of state transplant and both of her parents had passed away. Audre stopped by on her way home from work a few times, ready to give us both a break. She would snuggle down on the couch between us, and we would all talk about anything that came to mind, while eating Italian or Chinese or Persian food.

She would also bring us news about Ang since neither of us had been in contact with her. Audre informed us that Ang had been released from the hospital, her wounds not nearly as bad as Kate's, and was promptly arrested after discharge. All three of us gave multiple statements to investigators, though to me it was all a blur.

Kate and I went shopping at locally owned stores in Midtown to find holiday gifts for our loved ones. In an artist's co-op shop I found the perfect set of handmade matching bracelets, necklace, and earrings for Audre. They were silver with delicate floral patterns engraved in them. The necklace and earrings also had small bright purple stones, which I knew would perfectly match her favorite makeup and nail color, and compliment several of her outfits. As soon as I had purchased the items and had them gift wrapped, I was filled with excitement and couldn't wait to give them to her.

For Bear I found a custom-made wall clock made of motorcycle gears. And for Jared I unearthed some old vinyl records that I knew he didn't have yet. I looked forward to giving them the gifts on New Year's Eve.

I had a late Christmas Eve lunch with Kate and then headed out to join Audre and her family for Christmas Eve dinner. I brought poinsettias and chocolates for her mother, aunt, and sister, and arrived early enough to help cook and set the table. Audre had a full house, and I was welcomed warmly, as always. Children ran excitedly around the adults who stood talking and laughing. Her father walked in, stooped over and shuffling, a large serving platter in his hands. He wore a short-sleeve dress shirt, tie, and slacks, all which hung loosely on his withered body. I rushed to take the heavy dish from him, and he gave me a wink.

"Prime rib," he said with a spark in his eye, clearly proud of the job he had done cooking it.

With the arrival of Frederick and his prime rib, we all lined up and made our plates. The long kitchen table was full, so I ended up at a folding table at the end that was set up for the kids. Little Ruby and her cousins shoved handfuls of mashed potatoes in their mouths, though most of it ended up on their faces, clothes, and in their hair. Someone had cut the prime rib up into tiny little pieces for them. Sippy cups repeatedly got knocked to the floor and napkins were in high demand. The kids squawked with joy at their food and giggled at each other.

One young boy, maybe five years old, was much more reserved than the other kids. He ate slowly and carefully, trying not to get food on his clothes, and he kept his volume down. He wore a bowtie like me, and we had fun making faces at each other across the table. His skin was darker than the other children and his hair was shorn short and lined up nicely. He carried a level of seriousness that I connected with, because I had been the serious, reserved kid in my childhood too.

"Hey, young man. I'm Vivian, what's your name?" I extended a hand to him across the table, and he shook it, his hand small and warm.

"I'm Stokely." His voice was firm but low, and I struggled to hear him over the table noise.

"Stokely, you say?"

He nodded.

"I read about a man named Stokely Carmichael. Is that who you are named after?"

"Yes, ma'am." He nudged a piece of lettuce on his plate with a fork and heaved a sigh that I felt in my bones. Despite being so young, it seemed that Stokely carried a heavy weight on his shoulders. The only time he smiled during the meal was when dessert arrived, and he cast aside his worries long enough to enjoy some pie.

After everyone had finished up with dessert and dispersed into the living room and back porch, I stayed behind to help clean up and wash dishes. Audre stood at my side with a dish towel, drying and putting dishes away.

"You did great at the kids' table. Thank you for giving Stokely some attention. He often gets overlooked because he is quiet."

I scrubbed for a bit at some stubborn potato starch left behind on a pot.

"Thank you for including me in your family celebration again. It means a lot to me to be included. My family hasn't even bothered to contact me, but I am okay with that."

She ran her hand up and down my back as I continued to scrub at the pot, thinking about the evening.

The sound of kids squealing and laughter drifted in from the living room, and I realized that I was right where I wanted to be.

*

After the gathering wound down and the kids started falling asleep where they sat, I headed home to feed my fish. Entering the dark, cold studio after leaving Audre's warm, full home I was grateful to have both places in my life.

My upstairs neighbor began his pacing, the ceiling creaks telling me his exact route. It was late on Christmas Eve and I wondered what was bothering him. I sprinkled flakes into the fish tank and grabbed some clean clothes before locking up. As I made my way out to the corridor, I heard my house phone ringing through the door. I hesitated, wondering whether to answer it or not. I decided to, and hurriedly unlocked the door and hustled in to catch it before voicemail kicked in.

"Hello?"

"Viv." It was a man's voice, slightly hushed.

"Joey?"

"Yeah. Hey. Happy Christmas Eve."

"Happy Christmas Eve to you too. Kinda late, isn't it? What's up?"

I wondered if he was sober, if he was somewhere safe, and what he wanted.

He stifled a little cough. "Uh, so I'm at Mom's house and"—I heard him scratching at his beard stubble—"and I wanted to invite you to come spend Christmas Day with us. We are going to have lunch and do presents."

"I didn't buy you guys presents."

"Oh. Well. That's okay. We'd still like for you to join us."

I shifted my weight and adjusted the strap of the gym bag that was hanging from my shoulder.

"We. Or you? Last time I checked I was on Bernadette's shit list."

He chuckled. "Aren't we all? I asked her if she was okay with me inviting you and she said yes. So, would you, please? Things have been going well the last couple of months and I want to see you."

I considered what he said, still suspicious. "Have you relapsed since rehab, or are you still sober?"

"I knew you were going to ask me that. I'm still sober. I just got my ninety-day token."

"Congrats on that. Okay. I'll come by for lunch tomorrow. You know how Mom is, so should I bring something?"

"I'm handling the food and it's already covered. Just bring yourself. See you tomorrow. Thanks, Viv."

With that he hung up and I was left holding the dead phone to my ear, amazed. Joey, inviting me over. Joey, preparing the food for holiday lunch and asking for nothing but my presence. *Huh.* I wondered if maybe he wanted to see me in person so he could ask for money. But I resolved to be okay with getting up and walking out without a word, if my mother or Joey did anything I didn't like.

I put the phone back on its charger, grabbed an extra outfit, and drove to Kate's. I let myself in and found that she was in bed but had left a light on for me. I changed into some sweats and methodically brushed and flossed my teeth and then lay in bed waffling back and forth about Joey. I was tentatively hopeful that he was going to embrace his sobriety and truly become a contributing member of society.

*

Wind buffeted and bounced my truck as I drove across the causeway between Sacramento and Davis. The windshield wipers were on full speed, and I squinted through the road spray kicked up by the vehicles around me. My stomach ached and nausea was solidly in place. I drew in several deep breaths and checked myself. I knew I was anxious about spending time with Mom and Joey, and driving through a massive, windy rainstorm wasn't helping matters. I stayed in the slow lane and out of the way of the crazy drivers, hell bent on blasting along to their destination despite the road conditions.

My truck bogged down as I hit a huge puddle of standing water. It took a moment for me to steady out and center myself back in the lane. As soon as I did, I hit another huge puddle and again had to steady the truck. I slowed down to fifty-five, which was super slow for me, but the drive had become a survival situation. Rain pattered down on the roof and windshield so loudly that I switched off the Tom Petty CD I had been listening to.

The deep breathing helped cut back on the nausea a bit. I reminded myself that I had been in literally life or death situations in the military. If I could handle those, I could handle visiting my family. And yet, I found the anxiety to be a wholly different beast.

I took the exit and parked in the lot of a mall near my mother's house. The parking lot, normally bustling with college students, was empty due to the rain and holiday. Huge raindrops hammered the truck roof and I sat and breathed and worked through it. I asked myself what Alexia would have said to me in the moment. That thought helped guide me through an IFS exercise where I focused in on where in my body the anxiety was located and identified what age it was.

As was common for me, the anxiety was solidly located in my chest and was coming from my scared six-year-old self. So there I sat in my thundering truck talking to myself. Soothing the younger me inside who was scared to return to that house and be around the people who had abused and neglected her. I told her that she was loved and that I would keep her safe. And slowly, slowly she relaxed, and I was in control again.

I defrosted the window and drove on to my mother's house. The neighborhood was unchanged from my childhood. I parked my truck pointing toward the street that went to the freeway, for a fast getaway if needed. I took another deep breath, got out, and rushed across the street in the heavy rain. I walked up the steep driveway, past the crabapple tree a much younger Joey had hoisted my bike up into, resulting in a tussle that ended in him bloodying my nose.

At the big wooden front door with the brass knob, I hesitated, not knowing whether to just walk in or knock. I opted for ringing the doorbell. Through the glass panes on the door, I saw Joey approach with a smile. As he opened the door I was shocked by his appearance: freshly cut hair, clean shaven, and he was dressed in a button-up shirt and slacks rather than dirty, tattered clothes. Gone was the alcohol bloat, his face more angular and his belly flatter. But most striking was his glow.

As an adult Joey had always been red from working out in the sun, but sort of green around the gills from poor nutrition and...well, being a raging alcoholic. But that day he looked well-fed, happy, and healthy. Gone was the gaunt, sickly Joey. He spread his arms wide to me and as I stepped over the threshold of the house, I leaned into his hug, too, which surprised both of us.

He was much taller and broader than me, so his hug wrapped me up. In that moment we connected in a way we never had before. There had never been a well-intended hug between us as children, and as adults I had avoided contact with him as much as possible. For just a second, I forgot all the damage done, though I did sniff him, checking for the smell of beer and whiskey he usually bore, though he only smelled lightly of aftershave.

I stepped out of the hug when I heard Mom's heels approaching on the wood floors. She came around the corner dressed formally: high heels, glamorous flowing skirt, and blouse, accented with an understated necklace and earrings. Her hair flowed in a long, flawless wave, framing her face. I had a chuckle inside as I thought *Even her hair is afraid to disobey her.*

"Well, Vivian. It's been a long time." Her face fixed in a hard smile. "Will you please shut the door. You're letting cold air in."

"Good to see you, too, Mom. Thank you for inviting me," I said sarcastically.

"Oh, I didn't invite you. That was Joey's doing."

I spun on my heel and stepped through the door back out on to the cement porch, jumping down the three concrete steps as I had always done as a child. My long, angry strides ate up the front walkway and driveway. I paused, the heavy rain striking my waterproof tactical jacket, and waited for a slow-moving Prius to pass before I could cross the street. I heard loafers slapping on the wet concrete and then Joey was at my side, his hand gently encircling my upper arm. I had too many memories of him grabbing my upper arm much more roughly, and reflexively yanked myself from his grasp. He let his hand drop.

"Hey. Viv. Please come back inside." I turned to him; his eyebrows were scrunched up in desperation. "Please?"

"Joey. I am a grown-ass adult. I get to choose where I spend my time now, and I choose not to spend another second in there." I pointed harshly toward the house. "She's fucking toxic, and I don't need it. I have plenty of people who would welcome me with open arms today, or I could happily spend the day alone. Either way I have other options and I don't need her shit." Something inside released and flooded through me. The sensation brought a lightness that I didn't know I needed until I felt it.

"She swore she would be civil. I think maybe she just isn't even aware of how she is—"

"Don't you dare apologize for her. You two have been in some sort of fucked-up enabling relationship your entire life, and I want no part of it."

He pressed his lips together, squinting as the rain pelted our cheeks and soaked his clothes. I looked toward the house and saw her through the glass panes on the front door, her expression tight.

"Yeah. I'm sorry. You're right. I shouldn't defend her behavior. Where are you going?"

"Home...probably. Certainly not staying here."

I checked to make sure there were no cars coming and then stepped into the street. Joey grabbed my upper arm. I yanked out of his grasp and turned to him.

I growled at him, speaking in clear, clipped words. "Do not put your fucking hands on me, ever, without my consent. Do you understand?"

He clasped his hands behind his back, his brow furrowing. "Yes. Sorry. I understand."

I continued across the street, pulling the truck key from my pocket.

"Hey, Viv. Can I go with you?"

I stopped, key halfway in the lock, considering his request.

"Why?" I asked over my shoulder, shouting to be heard over the rain.

"I just..." He ran his hand over the back of his neck. "I want a relationship with you. I want to be a real brother to you. And I know I have a long way to go to prove myself. The only way I can see is for us to spend time together."

A car passed between us, windshield wipers clapping, the driver taking a long look at us, his expression asking if I was okay. I gave him a half smile and a wave, and he drove on.

"Come on then," I said and climbed into my truck. I fired it up and turned the heater on full blast. I watched through the rain spattered window as he ran inside and came back a few minutes later wearing his jacket and carrying a grocery bag. He got into the passenger seat and blew out a huge breath as he placed the bag on the floorboard.

"Wow, I'm soaked. That heater feels good." He cupped his hands in front of the heater vent and groaned in appreciation. I looked toward the house and saw the silhouette of our mother in the window. After a moment she walked away.

"What happened in there? And what's in the bag?"

"I told her that if she wasn't capable of welcoming you into her home that you and I would spend Christmas together somewhere else. And in the bag is lunch."

I snorted. "You packed up the lunch you prepared and just left? Oh man. I am sure Bernadette is having a conniption fit in there."

"I also told her to go to an Al-Anon meeting today. She actually said she would."

"And what about you?"

"I went to an AA meeting this morning and am due to secretary at another one tonight. The holidays are rough for us, so they run meetings all day."

"You're the secretary for your AA group?"

"Yeah. I help chair the meetings and stuff. I also get invited a lot to go to other AA groups and speak."

I realized that I had been gripping the wheel tightly. I forced myself to release it and sit back.

"Wow, Joey, that's really great." I turned my head and looked into his muddy-brown eyes. His expression was open, his smile tentative. We both took a moment to absorb it.

I considered this was possibly the first time I had ever praised my brother, and it looked like he had the same realization.

I buckled my seat belt and turned off the parking brake with a *thunk*. He rubbed his hands together in front of the vent.

"Where're we headed?" he asked, looking out of the window. The cab of the truck had started to fill with the smells of roasted chicken, garlic, and other warm, tasty things.

"Do you have a car here?"

"No, I caught a ride from Sac with one of my housemates."

"Is there enough food for three?"

"Yeah."

"Okay, buckle up. I have a dear friend in Midtown who is alone today. We are going to visit her."

"Cool. Does she have a dryer? Cuz I'm soaked to the bone."

"Yep, she does. Now buckle up."

"I don't wear seat belts."

"Two things. One: former drunkard you didn't wear seat belts because you didn't care if you lived or died. New sober you should give a shit. Two: you're in my truck and we are not going anywhere until you buckle up."

He grabbed the strap, pulling it across his body. The buckle clicked with a snap. I looked over my shoulder, making sure the road was clear, and pulled from the curb. Watching our mother's house grow smaller in the rearview mirror brought on a sense of accomplishment.

*

The drive back across the causeway was less treacherous. There were fewer people on the road and the rain and wind had lessened to something slightly more reasonable. Far down below, in the wildlife preserve, I saw hundreds of white and black birds floating in the water.

"Oh man. Mom is probably so pissed," he said. His throat sounded tight. Was he scared?

"Yeah, probably so. But guess what, that's her issue, not ours. We have no control over how she reacts to us and our choices. I chose to not put up with her bullshit and left. You chose to join me."

Midtown was exceptionally quiet, and we were one of the only cars on the road. I pulled into Kate's driveway and looked up at the house. Kate adored her home and took great pride in owning it. She kept her yard neat and tidy, the house was well maintained and looked freshly painted. As was typical of homes in Midtown, she had a covered porch out front, with potted plants and some nice chairs tastefully arranged.

"Whose house is this?" he asked as he followed my gaze.

"My friend Kate. She had a terrible accident a couple of months ago, which included losing a leg. I have been staying here with her since she was discharged, helping her out around the house, driving her to appointments and moral support. She doesn't have any family out here, which is why she is on her own today."

"She lost a leg? Like...how?"

"It's not my place to tell you. But I will say it was bad and traumatic...and please don't ask her or stare. Okay?"

"Yeah. Okay." He grabbed the bag and we climbed up the front steps. I opened the door a little and popped my head in, looking for Kate. She was sitting at her desk writing in her journal. She looked up and smiled.

"Viv. Come on in, silly."

"I have my brother with me, just wanted to let you know before we come trundling in and crashing your peaceful day."

She raised her eyebrows at me. Kate knew all about my how terrible my brother had been, and my recent struggles with what to do about his recovery and wanting to be in my life.

"Come in, come in." She motioned with her hand, and I opened the door wider so we could enter. The house was wonderfully warm. Joey wiped his shoes on the mat and stepped in shyly, clutching the paper grocery bag. I had never seen him act like that. He had always been overconfident and took up a lot of space, so that was a new thing to see. I shut the door behind us and hung up our jackets on the coat rack. Joey's dress shirt clung to his skin, so wet it was nearly see-through. His slacks were also soaked and clung to his legs.

"Oh hun," she said when she saw him. She stood up and grabbed a crutch. "What are you, about six foot and maybe one ninety?"

"Wow. Yeah."

"My ex was a bit taller than you. She kept some clothes here, come on to the back room and let's get you into something warm and dry."

He shed his waterlogged loafers, handed me the bag, and followed her to the back of the house. She had become so skilled at getting around with one crutch, it was impressive. Her natural athleticism shone even while she recovered and adapted to her new life.

I took the food into the kitchen and started microwaving the things that needed to be heated back up, and then piled three plates high with mashed potatoes, chicken, and salad. I put the homemade rolls in a basket in the center of the table along with the butter dish. I went to the stereo and put on a Norah Jones CD that Kate liked. I heard the dryer door slamming shut and then the sound of clothes tumbling. The two of them came out and grinned at the sight of the food.

"Come on, you guys, sit down." I motioned them over.

"Ohhh, this is lovely. Wow," Kate purred as she sat down and leaned her crutch against the table. "I thought you were spending the day at your mother's." She was clearly trying to keep her face and tone neutral in front of Joey.

"Uh well. She pulled her usual crap and I decided I didn't want to put up with it and left. And...Joey came with me and brought the lunch he made."

"Oh. Well..." She looked at each of us, always the nurse, gauging if we were okay. We both smiled back at her in return, and she nodded. "You made all of this, Joey? This looks and smells amazing."

"Yes. I am training to be a chef. I need to learn a new trade. Construction was good money but that is part of my old life. I'm getting a fresh start."

"Wow, Joe. I had no idea. I mean...how would I have, but yeah...I think that's awesome." I smiled at him as I said it and felt another brick fall loose from the wall inside me. "Well, shall we dig in and try out your food?"

"Please do."

We ate and it was fantastic. The chicken was succulent and perfectly seasoned, the green salad was full of goodies and dressed with his own Dijon vinaigrette, the garlic mashed potatoes melted in my mouth. I tried one of his rolls and found that it contained rosemary and had sea salt on top.

"Joey. Dude. This is so good." I truly was impressed. Kate nodded emphatically and she forked a pile of salad into her mouth with gusto.

He gave a humble smile and took a sip of water. Humble. My brother. I never thought I'd see the day when that happened.

We all went back for seconds and ate, while listening to Norah Jones croon and swoon over the pattering rain. As I finished up my second plate I leaned back and looked at Kate and Joey. That was when it registered what he was wearing. I had been so into the food I hadn't noticed that he was dressed in Ang's old sweats and long-sleeved T-shirt. All items I recognized and had seen on Ang many times. Joey was three inches shorter than her but filled the clothes out well.

"Well, it's lucky that Ang wore men's clothes and left some behind, eh?" As soon as her name rolled off my tongue, I wished I could retract it. I didn't want to poison the day with her presence.

"Yeah." He looked down at the clothes he was wearing. "I was always shocked at how tall she is. And man, her shoulders are broad too."

Kate and I exchanged a sad look and I decided it was time to change the subject before he asked where Ang was.

"Hey! I think I saw some pie in the bag. Who is up for pie?"

Both raised their hands excitedly, like kids being asked who wanted cupcakes. I carried the dishes into the kitchen and plated up generous servings of pecan pie, each with a dollop of fresh whipped cream. They both ooh-ed as I placed the plates in front of them.

The Norah Jones CD had ended so I put on a Van Morrison album in honor of Jared. I realized that I missed him and was looking forward to spending New Year's at his house. I sat back down at the table and enjoyed every bite of the decadence that was Joey's pecan pie.

While Joey cleared the dessert dishes, I stayed behind at the table with Kate, and we looked at each other when we heard the sink turn on and Joey humming while washing the dishes. Kate raised her eyebrows at me. She leaned forward and whispered, "Wow. He has come a long way."

"That's for sure. He is a totally different person. These are very welcome changes."

After he finished cleaning up, the three of us spent the rest of the afternoon and evening playing card games, listening to music, and talking. There was plenty of laughter and I slowly let the sky-high walls I had built to protect myself from Joey lower.

At the end of the evening, I drove Joey home through empty, rain-slicked streets and returned to bundle up in Kate's guest bed, where I slept soundly.

Chapter Twenty

The next few days Kate and I went about our routine: medical appointments, physical therapy, puttering around the house, grocery shopping, and shared meals. At the end of the week, I packed up travel bags for both of us, and a third bag for all her medical supplies. As I lined them up by the front door with her lightweight, folding wheelchair, she turned from her desk.

"Leave the chair here."

I met her gaze, making sure there wasn't any weakness in my expression. "If we go somewhere that has a lot of walking, you may need it."

Kate, normally warm and open, spoke in a voice tight with frustration. "Leave it. I'll just use my crutch." She turned back to the book she had been reading.

I walked over to her and sat on the arm of the couch next to her, placing my hand gently on her shoulder. "Kate. You are one of my best friends, and I love you very much. I want to remind you that you are a nurse, and you know what the right choice is here. When one of your patients is ashamed of or resistant to using their mobility aid, I know damn well you have a whole speech prepared for them about there being no shame in using tools to help you get around and have some independence."

She nodded, not looking up from her book, her thumb rubbing at the page as she thought. With a sigh she turned to me.

"Yeah. You're right. And I will still tell them those things when I go back to work. But it's different when it's...me. I have been a fiercely independent woman and an athlete my entire life. I know you understand that because you are the same way. Using my body to its fullest potential every day has been my goal. And pushing my body to its limits is how I relieve stress. Running, competitive cycling, racing, skiing, all of it keeps me sane. And...using a wheelchair feels like I'm admitting defeat."

She shifted her eyes down to the floor and I squeezed her shoulder, allowing her truth some space. Ani DiFranco crooned quietly in the background. Kate's cat, Hammy, slunk out from under the couch. He had long, calico fur and wore a blue collar with a bell on it. His appearances were so rare we both watched as he sniffed at our bags, investigated a stray Post-it note on the floor, and then settled on the windowsill to look out at the street. Kate and I raised our shoulders at each other and returned to the conversation.

"Using a tool to help you isn't defeat, Kate. I say adapting and overcoming is a victory to be proud of."

She swiped at her bangs, smoothing them back up into her ponytail, and chewed on a cuticle as she considered what I had said. Finally, she nodded and picked her book back up. I patted her shoulder and went into the kitchen to pack up snacks and lunch for the road trip. I also made sure Hammy's automatic food and water dispensers were topped off so he would be fed and watered while we were away. There was a knock at the door, followed by Kate hollering, "I'll get it!" I heard the thump of her crutch across the wood floor and the door opening. I peered around the corner.

Kate grinned. "Audre! I am so glad you are joining us for our trip. Come on in, come on in. Ooh, it's chilly out there." They hugged warmly and Audre came in carrying her own travel bag. I joined them in the living room, giving Audre a long hug and taking her jacket.

The three of us took our places on the couch, Audre settled comfortably between us. She spotted Hammy on the windowsill, his eyes closed.

"Wait, you have a cat?"

Kate chuckled. "Yes, that's Hammy. He's an asshole, so be careful if you try to pet him. He doesn't come out around humans very often. He has graced us with his aloof presence." We all watched him for a moment and then Audre spoke up again.

"Viv, you're sure Jared is okay with me coming too? I don't want to crash his party."

"I talked to him yesterday. He's thrilled that you are joining us. He likes you a lot and is excited that you are coming. I have to warn you, though, that the futon in the guest room is kinda small and uncomfortable. So, we will have fun sharing that!"

"Oh, so just like staying over at your house then?"

Kate let out a guffaw. "Oh, burn, Viv. Good one, Audre."

I laughed and waved her off. "Yeah, yeah, yeah. I know my futon 'bed' is terrible."

"You know they make better futon mattresses nowadays?"

"Hmm, yeah, I suppose they do. Maybe once I get picked up by a fire department and start making a salary, I will invest in one. Yeah?"

"Yes. Please do." She flung an arm around my shoulders so she could pull me in and kiss the scar on my temple.

Smiling, I checked my watch. "All right, you two, I think we better hit the road now that the sun is up. We've got a solid five hours in the car ahead of us. Kate, since you're officially the road trip DJ, don't forget to bring the CDs you picked out. And Audre, you're the official navigator. Did you bring maps, just in case?"

"Yep, sure did. Though I know you've done this drive countless times and that we are in good hands with you."

I nodded. "We are going to take Kate's wagon since we have three bodies plus all of this gear." I motioned toward our row of stuff by the front door. "I'll go pack up the car, so handle whatever last-minute stuff you need to."

I grabbed Kate's keys off the hook by the door and shouldered my duffel bag and then hoisted up her wheelchair. I made my way carefully down the front steps, the wood creaking under my weight, as I looked out for ice. I opened the rear hatch of her Subaru and placed the wheelchair in first, pushing it up snugly against the side so it wouldn't be damaged. Then I wedged my duffel bag in next to it so the chair to brace it. The cold was biting at my fingertips, so I hustled back in for Audre and Kate's bags. I managed to carry them all in one trip, filling up the back of the wagon with it all.

Back inside, I used the restroom and grabbed the snack bag and ice chest. Kate and Audre waited by the door for me.

"Ready, guys?" I asked, sweating under my jacket.

"Yes," they said in unison.

"All right, load up!" I said in my best voice left over from being Sergeant Chastain. I shut off lights, made sure the windows were all locked, closed the curtains, and looked at Hammy on my way out.

"Guard the house," I told him. He skittered under the couch, angry that I had closed the curtain, and cut off his view of the street. I locked up the front door and passed the ice chest and snack bag to Kate in the back seat. She was sitting sideways, her back against the door, the stump of her leg on the seat, propped on a small pillow.

I got in, finding that the leather seat was cold against my back and thighs, and there was ice on the windshield.

"Sorry, guys, I would have warmed the car up while loading it, but we all know it's not wise to leave a car running unattended in Midtown." They both nodded in agreement and rubbed their hands together as we waited for the engine to warm up and the defroster to melt the ice on the windshield. Soon enough we were on the road, the cabin toasty warm, and Kate's CD rotation in full effect.

The freeway south was mostly empty except for big rigs and the occasional RV or family car trundling along loaded down just like ours. The newly risen sun shone brightly on my side of the car, drying the wet road. Steam rose from the damp farm fields and orchards.

We shared stories of family road trips from when we were kids, most of which contained disasters that were laughable all those years later but were probably pretty terrible to our parents at the time. Carsick siblings, wallets left behind at gas stations, flat tires in the middle of nowhere, bickering children fighting in the back seat. All the usual things.

We stopped at the rest area just north of Patterson and got out to stretch our legs and use the restroom. It was still quite cold, so we did not linger. We passed mile after mile of open farmland, orchards, and dairies (which smelled to high heaven). I relied on the friendly chatter and music to keep myself from getting hypnotized by the long, straight road.

The topic of Ang came up briefly and a tense silence fell over the car for a while. At Kettleman City I turned west, and the scenery improved. The road narrowed and we climbed up and down some foothills, the open land spotted with farms and occasional homesteads. We got stuck behind slow-moving trucks a few times, and the conversation started back up.

Kate did a great job of passing out snacks and reminding us to drink water, which I was hesitant to do since public toilets were few and far between on that route. Though we did stop at the last rest stop between us and Morro Bay, which was in Shandon. Once again, we got out and stretched our legs a bit, used the toilets, and sat on a bench in the sunshine. The temperature was finally above fifty degrees, which was still awfully cold for a bunch of California girls, but we enjoyed the break from the car.

The lull that had fallen over us at the mention of Ang fell away and we chatted happily in the sunshine while eating sandwiches and peeling oranges. A squirrel approached bravely and sniffed around, looking for scraps. We watched as cars came and went, some releasing gaggles of little children who ran around in the grass squealing and enjoying their freedom. Eventually we cleaned up the remnants of our meal, used the bathroom again, and climbed back into the car with groans. All three of us were very active people, so sitting in the car for hours on end was a large ask.

"Come on, y'all. We can do it. Only like an hour and a half left." I ducked as Kate threw a wadded-up tissue at me in mock disgust. Then she passed forward the next CD. Tom Petty and the Heartbreakers' *Wildflowers*.

"That'll do. Thanks, Kate." I slid in the CD and pulled back out onto the highway. Traffic had increased, but was still manageable, and we rolled on. Soon enough we found ourselves at the junction of Highway 41 and Highway 1, and the Pacific Ocean silenced us until I was pulling into Jared's driveway, and shutting off the engine with a satisfied sigh. We climbed out and stretched, groaning. I heard the door upstairs open, and the *click-clack* of Baxter's nails racing down the wooden staircase.

"Baxter!" I shouted joyfully as he hurled himself headlong into my legs. I squatted down, both of my knees popping, and tousled his long golden fur. I wrapped my arms around him while he wiggled and panted and danced, a ball of excitement. I stood back up, my knees popping again, keeping my hand on his head, giving him lots of pets and praise.

"Wow, now that's a warm welcome," Kate said with a giggle. She steadied herself with her crutch and Baxter sniffed her shoes, legs, and hands curiously. He was gentle and didn't bowl her over. He went for her crotch, but I told him no and he redirected himself. He did the same thing to Audre and then ran to Jared as he came down the last two steps.

"Hey, guys! So glad you all could make it."

"You look great, buddy!" I said and meant it. His hair was freshly cut in his usual high and tight. He had shaved and he had clearly kept up with his running and workouts: but beside all of that, he just looked happy and relaxed.

"Thanks."

He made his way to each of us, giving hugs and asking how the drive was, all while Baxter followed along trying to be part of the conversation. "Here, let me help carry your stuff up."

I opened the rear hatch and handed over some bags, while shouldering the others. We left the wheelchair in the car and climbed up the wooden steps that had carried me to Jared's home in happiness and in turmoil. Kate did a damn good job of leveraging herself up the steps using the railing, her crutch, and a fair amount of muttering. Baxter rushed past us all, bumping our legs, and then waiting on the balcony up top, panting.

"Welcome!" Jared opened the front door and bowed, motioning us inward.

His house was warm and smelled like aftershave, bleach, and wood smoke. We unloaded Kate's bag in Jared's bedroom, and mine and Audre's in the guest room. I pulled Jared's Cal hat out from my bag and tucked it behind my back as I walked back out to the living room.

"I'm not sleeping out here on the couch?" Kate asked, pointing to the large sofa.

"Definitely not. I'm sleeping out here. You get my room. Though I will need to pop in now and then for clothes and the shower."

"Oh wow, thanks, Jared. Such a gentleman."

His cheeks colored briefly. To spare him from himself I whipped his hat out, bowed down, and handed it to him. "Thank you for once again loaning me your hat. I have returned it as promised."

He took it from me with a grin. "I never had a doubt you'd bring it back...again."

Tired from the drive, I flopped down into the rocking chair and everyone else sat down on the couch across from me.

"Hey, where's Bear?" I asked. I realized I hadn't seen her car or bike downstairs.

"Oh, she is probably out at the antiques mall looking for treasures. She has been on the search for items for some big art project she is working on."

"It's good to be back. Thanks for having all of us."

"You know me, Viv. I like to be surrounded by good people. And I consider each of you"—he looked at us in turn—"to be good people."

Baxter's tail thumped on the floor where he lay at Jared's feet. "You, too, Baxter." At the sound of his name, Baxter's ears perked up and the thumping increased. I smiled, recognizing how far we had come over the last few years. Our friendship had been through a lot.

I heard a *putt-putt-putter* from the street and stood to look out of the large picture window. I saw Bear pull up in her Beetle Bug and park next to Kate's Subaru in the driveway.

"Bear's home!" I announced and went out onto the front balcony. "*Buenos días*, nice lady," I said as I watched her climb out of the car.

"Ohhhh, Viviana! You have arrived, my friend." She stretched her arms out the way an opera singer does. "I am coming for you!" She lumbered her way up the staircase. "Oof, stairs. You know me and stairs," she said with a deep laugh as she wrapped me up in a bear hug, slapping my back and rocking me side to side. As we stepped out of the hug, she removed her sunglasses and hung them over the collar of her long-sleeved, Incredible Hulk T-shirt.

"Good drive?"

"Oh yeah, smooth. Glad to be out of the car, though. Hey, let's go on inside. I know everybody else is looking forward to seeing you too. I can't hog you all to myself, even though I want to."

We went inside and everyone started to get up from the couch.

"Sit. Sit. Sit." Bear motioned with her hand for them to stay seated. She walked around to the front of the couch and slapped Jared on the shoulder. "I seen you already today, sucka." She bent down and hugged Kate. "Kate. The one-legged wonder! You're going to be even more unstoppable now." She shifted down to Audre and stooped down to give her a hug. "Ohh, Audre girl, looking as good as ever. If this fool"—she aimed her thumb at me—"ever gets boring, come find me. Kidding. Good to see you all."

She pulled up one of the kitchen chairs and joined the circle.

*

The next morning, on the last day of the year, Jared and I went on a run. I took Baxter because I owed him one from my last visit. As I was putting on Baxter's collar and leash, I saw Kate watching from her spot at the dining room table in front of the picture window. She had been playing cards with Audre and Bear but had put her cards down and looked at me, her lips pinched into a thin line.

Baxter nearly tap danced, he was so excited for the run. I handed the leash to Jared and walked over to Kate. I squatted down next to her and gave her a big hug.

"Hey, Kate. I will do some wind sprints in your honor, 'kay? And next time we come you'll have your prosthetic leg, and you can get back to running circles around me." I wiped one stray tear that had run down her cheek.

"Yeah," she said and patted my hand. "Now get out there before Baxter blows a fuse."

He was bouncing around, whining. We giggled and Jared opened the door, Baxter pulling at his leash out to the stairs. I kissed Audre on my way out.

"What! No love for me, Vivi?" Bear exclaimed in mock terror. I blew her a kiss and she smiled, catching the kiss and holding it to her heart before turning back to the card game.

Jared and I ran down the hill and across Highway 1 to the beach, heading toward our usual route to Morro Rock. I jogged down to the wet sand, which was more solidly packed, and we got into step. Baxter wanted off the leash, but Morro Rock Beach doesn't allow dogs, so we were risking it even bringing him down there on a leash.

Jared and I had run countless miles together: in the sands of the central coast, on the red dirt trails of the Carolinas, and around whatever version of hell we had been deployed to at the time. We knew each other's pacing and could read the other's needs without a word. We got into a comfortable stride and fell into our usual silence. It was an icy cold morning with bright-blue skies. My bare legs, hands, face, and ears burned with the cold, but my torso warmed up quickly as we got into the heart of the run. The chilled air made my eyes water until I had tears streaming down my face. I swiped at them a few times with the sleeve of my fleece pullover.

We made it to Morro Rock and ran up and around the rock to the parking area at the end of the road. All three of us panted heavily and we walked in circles until our breathing and heart rates slowed a bit. Baxter, despite the run, was still full of energy and whined at the birds nesting up high on the rock.

"Down," Jared commanded, and Baxter lay down with a whine and huff.

We watched seagulls circle fishermen who were cleaning their catches, throwing the guts and scales back out into the ocean. It was reminiscent of so many other times that Jared and I had stood in that same spot to take our usual midrun break, and I knew what was coming next.

"Where'd you go this time?" Jared asked. I turned to him, noting that he had grown some stubble overnight, and his shirt was sweat soaked in the usual spots: down the back, underarms, and around the neck. His muscular barrel chest stretched the limits of his shirt with each breath.

I considered his question as the sweat on my own shirt grew cold, giving me a chill.

"I...didn't."

He tilted his head, looking at me in wonderment.

"You didn't?"

"Nope. Weird, right?"

"Not weird. Good...no...great. That's great!" He smiled, dimples and chipped tooth showing, and his hazel eyes shimmering.

"Yeah, I suppose you're right." I rubbed my hands together, trying to warm them up.

"Hey, it's super fucking cold out here. Let's head back before we cool down too much and start cramping."

I nodded and Baxter popped up. "Good boy, Baxter," I said as we began trotting back down the road toward the beach. We stopped at the top of the small dune and watched some surfers trying to ride the rough little waves that rolled in. I couldn't even imagine trying to surf with how cold the water and air were, but that's a Californian for you. We got to the hard-packed wet sand and headed back.

I relaxed my brain, waiting for a memory to hit me, but none came, and I arrived back at Jared's house unscathed. We cooled down and stretched out in the driveway. He placed a hand on the back of Kate's car, steadying himself as he stretched out his quad, when he tilted his head at me.

"Anything?"

"Nope. Nothing."

"Maybe all that therapy and stuff is helping you."

"Yeah. Maybe." As I said it, I wished I could pull the words back, afraid I had just jinxed myself.

I looked up and saw Kate, Audre, and Bear in the window waving at us.

"Looks like we better get up there," I said with a smile.

*

We spent the rest of the day inside, playing board games, listening to the records that I had given Jared for Christmas, and eating. Jared built a fire in the fireplace and kept it stoked up all day. Baxter took up a position in front of the hearth, sprawled out, his belly facing the warmth of the fire. The run had worn him out and he was a happy pup.

We all dispersed and took naps in the afternoon. Audre snuggled up under my chin, our bodies entwined. Her breathing slowed and I marveled at the feel of her body pressed against mine. I wondered briefly how Ang was faring in jail but reminded myself that I had seen her do something terrible to someone she loved, and knew she was forever changed. The Ang I had loved was no more.

I kissed the top of Audre's head and drifted off. I slept well; the bad things in me were docile and let me be. When I woke up the room was dark, and I was alone. I looked at the digital clock on the desk and saw that it was after nine at night. The sound of cooking and cheerful chatter seeped under the door. I got up, tugged on my fleece pullover, and rubbed my eyes as I walked out into the bright living room. Over the counter I saw Jared and Bear in the kitchen cooking. Audre and Kate sat on opposite ends of the couch reading. They both looked up from their books and smiled at me. I went back into the room and grabbed my copy of *Cloud Atlas* and then sat in between them. Audre had a blanket over her lap, and she spread half of it across my legs.

Soon the smell of Bear's beef stew and Jared's jalapeño cornbread filled the room, which roused us out of our books. The three of us set the table and poured drinks for everybody while Jared and Bear served up the food. We all looked at our bowls in anticipation. Baxter sat next to Jared at the head of the table, tail thumping. Jared held his glass of beer aloft.

"I'd like to make a toast," he said with a grin that crinkled the lines at the corners of his eyes and showed off his chipped front tooth.

We all raised our glasses.

"I am so grateful to have each and every one of you here, in my home, to celebrate the New Year. The last few years have been rocky...but also a time of growth. I think we are all coming out the other side of it a little tattered, but better for it. Thank you all for gracing me with your presence. I love you."

"Hear, hear," said Audre. She clinked her glass with mine, and we made the rounds clinking glasses and sipping our drinks.

"All right, enough with the sentimental stuff. Let's eat," Bear exclaimed, holding her spoon up like a weapon, eyes twinkling, and then digging in. I could taste all the elements of her dish: red wine, beef stock, celery, carrots, potato, onion. And Jared's cornbread was as good as ever, with the kick of jalapeño and caramelized cheddar cheese melted on top. The chatter died down as we ate.

Afterward we took turns washing the dishes and packing up thermoses of hot chocolate, coffee, and hot cider. Audre and I, after taking out the wheelchair, loaded up the back of the Subaru with bundles of kindling and firewood. Bear, Audre, and Kate squeezed into the back seat and we piled blankets and sleeping bags on their laps. Jared sat up front with the thermoses and some snacks and I fired up the engine. We had all bundled up in layers of thermal underwear, sweaters, jackets, beanies, scarves, and gloves.

"Everybody have a seat belt on?" I called back into the back seat.

"Damn, Viv, you're such a mom," Bear quipped.

"Don't make me come back there, dummy."

"Yeah, yeah," she said, and I heard the click of her seat belt.

As I backed out of the driveway, I saw the silhouette of Baxter in the upstairs window.

"Aw, poor baby wants to come with us on our adventure," Audre crooned.

"Yeah, I wish we could take him, but no dogs allowed at Morro Strand," said Jared. The drive was short, and we piled out into the semi-darkness. The moon wasn't quite full yet, but it did cast enough light for us to unload the car by. Audre and Bear carried the blankets, sleeping bags, and food and drinks. Jared and I made a couple of trips down with loads of kindling and firewood while Kate waited at the car.

"You ready, Kate?" Jared asked her as we approached the car.

"I'm not thrilled about being carried like a baby," she said, eyeing the silver sand beyond the parking lot.

"Not like a baby. More like a fallen soldier who we refuse to leave behind. A hero."

"Hmph. Okay. But don't you dare do the fireman's carry on me, cuz that'll make me puke."

"Okay, piggyback?" Jared asked, holding out a hand to her.

She nodded, handed me her crutch, and took Jared's hand. He squatted down and she climbed on. Jared used his exceptionally strong quads and core to stand up. Kate held on and I walked beside them into the sand.

We found Audre and Bear spreading out the blankets and sleeping bags in a semicircle, facing the ocean. Jared placed Kate down gently on a blanket and the two of us got busy clearing sand and setting up the firewood. I scrunched up a bunch of old newspaper and shoved it underneath to help the kindling catch. Jared dumped a bit of lighter fluid over the whole thing and produced a lighter. We huddled together, trying to block the wind as he flicked the lighter and set the newspaper alight. The first attempt blew out immediately. We smooshed together even closer and cupped our hands around the newspaper and he tried again. The second attempt caught and with the help of the lighter fluid the kindling also started to burn. We remained where we were until the logs began to catch and we felt confident the wind wouldn't blow it out.

I squeezed into a two-person sleeping bag with Audre, and Jared huddled under a pile of blankets between Bear and Kate. Kate asked everyone what they wanted to drink, and filled cups, which we passed down the line. I had a nice steaming mug of apple cider and Audre had coffee.

We sat looking at the surface of the ocean and sand made silver by the moonlight, and the countless stars overhead. We were far enough away from the light pollution of the larger cities that the universe spread out endlessly overhead.

I leaned against Audre and took a sip of the cider, sweet and tart on my tongue. I looked around at the faces of my dearest friends and knew I was exactly where I belonged. It had been a challenging year between losing my job and my relationship with Ang, but I had developed a deep love for Audre and her family, had grown closer to Jared, Kate, and Bear, was embarking on a new career, and had even started to develop a healthy relationship with my brother.

An alarm beeped on my watch.

"Okay guys, one minute until midnight," I announced, breaking everyone's silent contemplation.

I watched the seconds tick down on the green Indiglo face of my watch.

"Okay, guys, here we go!" We all raised our mugs and began the countdown in unison.

"Ten, nine, eight, seven, six, five, four, three, two, one. *Happy New Year!*" we shouted at the ocean and laughed. Someone father down the beach set off a couple of fireworks. I turned and took Audre's face in my hand.

"Happy New Year, babe." We had a long, lingering kiss and her lips formed a smile against mine. We broke off the kiss and leaned our foreheads together for a moment. I looked up and, much to my surprise I saw

Jared and Kate kissing. Bear saw it, too, and we silently mouthed *whattttt* to each other. Bear let out one of her boisterous cackles that were so contagious we all joined in. The fire cracked and shot sparks up into the sky.

Acknowledgements

As Vivian's journey continues, I have relied on my amazing circle to keep the story consistent and flowing. I'll start by giving thanks to my steadfast and brutally honest beta reader and mentor, Pat Henshaw. Thanks to Shelia "Licherish" Scott and Nicki "Hugger" Hill for showing up and supporting me. I'd also like to thank my fellow writers from the Queer Sacramento Authors Collective, and the Bay Area Queer Writers Association; your advice, humor, and cheerleading skills revive me.

Of course, I give many thanks to my editor, Elizabeth Coldwell, for her thoughtful and thorough handling of my manuscripts, as well as all the staff at NineStar Press who have made the publication of this book possible.

On a more personal note, I'd like to thank my family, friends, wife, and son for providing me with support even when my writing is not their cup of tea. To my big brother, Doug, I just want to say how proud I am of you.

And finally, I'd like to thank the East Bay Regional Parks District for being such good stewards of our public lands and of course, Briones Regional Park, which has challenged me, inspired me, and comforted me even as my health has declined.

About Liz Faraim

Liz has a full plate between balancing a day job, parenting, writing, and finding some semblance of a social life. In past lives she has been a soldier, a bartender, a shoe salesperson, an assistant museum curator, and even a driving instructor. She focuses her writing on strong, queer, female leads who don't back down.

Liz transplanted to California from New York over thirty years ago. She now lives in the East Bay Area of California and enjoys exploring nature with her wife and son.

Email
liz.faraim@gmail.com

Facebook
www.facebook.com/liz.faraim.9

Twitter
@FaraimLiz

Website
www.lizfaraim.com

Other NineStar books by this author

Vivian Chastain series

Canopy

Stitches and Sepsis

Also from NineStar Press

The Illhenny Murders by Winnie Frolik

District Nurse Mary Grey saves the life of young architect, Anthony West, when he is involved a car wreck, only for West to tell her it was no accident. Someone tried to kill him. Mary is skeptical at first, but when West dies, she's determined to investigate the matter. More blood is spilled, and Mary becomes embroiled in a tangled web of intrigue and murder as she joins forces with exiled Jewish German detective Franz Shaefer. And on top of everything else, Mary finds herself dangerously attracted to Anthony's beautiful and unattainable sister Harriet.

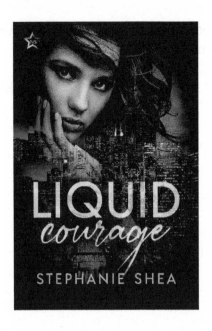

Liquid Courage by Stephanie Shea

Alexandria Van Kirk has always been a slave to her romantic nature. When a night of liquid courage lands her in bed with one of her best friends, Alex is confronted by a host of feelings that terrify her. Feelings about her friend and, unexpectedly, a barista from her favorite café.

It's a tug of war between heart and body. Desire against all her daydreams of someone to share silence, sunsets, and coffee with.

But Alex's past is also about to catch up with her. Tortured memories and the girl they're all about. It's like fighting the pull of a whirlwind. A surefire losing battle. But embracing a newfound romance amid the return of an old flame is a precarious balance, one not even Alex herself is sure she can manage.

How the hell does she choose between the girl she loves and the one she could never confess loving to begin with?

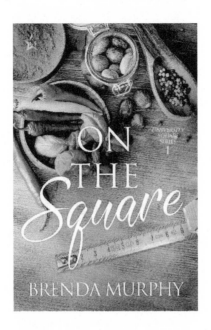

On the Square by Brenda Murphy

Dropped from her television show after a very public split with her cheating ex, celebrity chef Mai Li wants nothing more than to reopen her parents' shuttered restaurant and make a fresh start in her former hometown. So what if twenty years of neglect has left the building in need of a major renovation?

Seduced by Mai's charm and determination, hard-edged contractor Dale Miller agrees to take on her renovation project.

After a spring storm causes significant damage to the building and renovation costs exceed Mai's budget, Dale offers her a deal, but is it a price Mai is willing to pay?

Connect with NineStar Press

www.ninestarpress.com

www.facebook.com/ninestarpress

www.facebook.com/groups/NineStarNiche

www.twitter.com/ninestarpress

www.instagram.com/ninestarpress

Made in the USA
Las Vegas, NV
02 August 2021

27427374R00198